THE LOVECHILD

THE LOVECHILD

ASHEA GOLDSON

URBAN CHRISTIAN

www.urbanchristianonline.net

Urban Books
1199 Straight Path
West Babylon, NY 11704

ISBN- 13: 978-1-60162-966-1
ISBN- 10: 1-60162-966-4

First Printing August 2008
Printed in the United States of America

10 9 8 7 6 5 4 3 2 1

This is a work of fiction. Any references or similarities to actual events, real people, living, or dead, or to real locales are intended to give the novel a sense of reality. Any similarity in other names, characters, places, and incidents is entirely coincidental.

Distributed by Kensington Publishing Corp.
Submit Wholesale Orders to:
Kensington Publishing Corp.
C/O Penguin Group (USA) Inc.
Attention: Order Processing
405 Murray Hill Parkway
East Rutherford, NJ 07073-2316
Phone: 1-800-526-0275
Fax: 1-800-227-9604

Dedication

To my Pastors Creflo and Taffi Dollar of World Changers
Church Int'l, for instilling in me an irrevocable love for
the Word of God and for constantly motivating me
by example.

Acknowledgments

To my Heavenly Father, for giving me salvation, strength and joy. For also giving me the words and the means to give birth to this book. May it bring glory to your name.

To my loving family, Donovan, Anais, & Safiya, for understanding the times when I needed to lock myself upstairs and write, for taking up the slack around the house, for proofreading my rough drafts, for being my cheering section throughout this process, and for helping to make home a refuge.

To Mom, for helping to instill in me the love of books from an early age. Your love, encouragement and prayers carried me through the rough days.

To Dad, for making me feel special to be your first born.

To Grandma Ruthell, who always believed in me, even when I was a little girl putting stories and pictures together.

To Tamicka McCloud, my business partner and close friend, who adds laughter to my daily itinerary. To the McCloud household: Darryl, Lashydra, Emmanuel, Hannah, and of course, Faith, I love you all.

To my WCCI church family: Thank you, Minister Carol, because without your guidance and prayers, my own vision might still be clouded. Thank you, Sister Angela

Holder, for always making me and my family feel welcome. Thank you, Sister Jennifer Beane, for picking up the ball and running with it without complaint. Thank you, Brother Victor and Sister Icilda Hogan, Brother Horace and Sister Yvonne Holmes, Brother Phillip Rich and the WCCI Community Groups, for exemplifying excellence in ministry.

To Cousin Thelma Davis, for consistent promotion in New York City. For this and for all the little things you did for me when I was growing up, I am so grateful.

To Bernadette Page, Hope Raymond, Sherri Holmes-Knight, Joy Garett and Alfonso Jackson, for remaining true friends over the years (despite the distance).

To the Christian fiction writers who have come before me: Jacquelin Thomas, Victoria Christopher Murray, Kendra Norman-Bellamy, Stephanie Perry Moore, Patricia Haley, Tia McCollors, Sherri Lewis and countless others, thank you for staying true to the vision—to lift up the name of Jesus.

To my writer-sisters from the ABCFW's Critique Group: Sherri Lewis, Tia McCollors, Dee Stewart, Veronica Johnson, Vanessa Madden, Rhonda McNain, Sharrun Rhone, Lamonica Smith, Trina Charles, and Shawneda Marks, for holding me accountable to the craft, and for always doing so with love and integrity. What gifted ladies you are.

To the American Christian Fiction Writers and the ACFW Southeast Regional Chapter–Visions in Print and to Kendra Norman-Bellamy, our VIP group organizer, for being a valuable resource for information and inspiration.

To my editor, Joylynn, thanks for being undoubtedly instrumental in making my dreams come true.

To my literary agent, Sha Shana Crichton of Crichton and Associates, thank you for working out all the legal details and for ultimately believing in me as a writer.

To Tanya McKnight, my sister in Christ, for always being an example of honesty and integrity, even under uncomfortable circumstances. Thanks for your encouraging words and prayers. And to Helen, thanks for following closely in your mom's footsteps.

To Leon Anderson, for upgrading my computer. Thanks for making me technologically up-to-date. And to your children, Brandon, Breanna, and Aaron, for just making me smile.

To Robbie Brock, church sister and event planner, for adding your wisdom and magic to my book release party plans.

To my Anointed Minds' students, for invigorating me daily with both your humor and your innocence.

To my readers, thank you so much for buying this book. May it be all you hoped it would be. To anyone I may not have mentioned who may have helped in any way, whether in words or in deeds, I thank you.

THE LOVECHILD

Chapter One
Makaeli

Destiny is a funny thing. In seven days, it changed my life in a way I didn't think was even possible in a lifetime.

As I walked into La Villa De Meriole, one of the most popular cafés in Venice and my personal favorite, I had the feeling that something was about to go terribly wrong. Although I walked through the familiar room, out the back door to my usual patio table and saw my usual waitress, the flurry in my stomach told me that something was different about today.

I sat down and loosened my scarf to get comfortable. As my waitress delivered a meal to the next table, my eyes met hers and I nodded. There was no need to look at a menu because I had eaten here so many times before, I practically had it memorized. I knew I wanted shrimp scampi, and all I had to do was lean over and whisper it to her. She smiled graciously and walked away.

I checked my watch and quickly realized that it was already twelve o'clock. Antonio, my tall, dark-haired photographer, hadn't arrived yet. Anxious to settle in, I scooted up close to the table and placed my snakeskin purse in his seat. I rubbed my hands together over and over again, but I couldn't pinpoint the reason for my anxiety.

Everything seemed to be normal except for the knot that tightened in my stomach. Despite the cool weather, I was already perspiring around my eyebrows and neck. I peeked inside my coat to check my underarms. Surprisingly, my silk blouse was still dry. Still, I just didn't feel right.

I leaned forward and began to drum my fingernails on the tabletop. Then my cell phone rang. I snatched up the phone after the first ring barely ended.

"*Ciao*."

"*Ciao*, Makaeli. I'm sorry, but I'm not going to be able to make it for lunch," Antonio said.

"Oh?"

"I'm stuck over here at the studio. The models were late and these gentlemen want this shoot done by this afternoon." Antonio sounded flustered. "I'm sorry."

"No problem. I thought we'd finalize the details for the show, but I understand." I took a deep breath and swallowed my spit.

"I'll make it up to you, I promise." Antonio never made promises he couldn't keep, but it didn't matter. I wasn't going to let him off the hook so easily.

"Don't make promises. It's all right. You don't owe me anything," I said.

"But I was looking forward to having lunch with you."

"I'll be heading back to my office right after I have a few bites anyway." A little lie never hurt anyone.

"Again, I'm sorry."

"And I'm sorry too, but unfortunately, I've got to go." I was ready to pounce on him, to make him really sorry for what he had done. My jaw tightened because I was hot, but I had to play it cool.

"You're upset with me?"

"No, I'm just very busy." I tried not to sound like I had an attitude, but as upset as I was, he probably heard my lips poking out over the phone.

"Right. I'll talk to you later then."

"Maybe." I ended the call and turned off my cell. No more interruptions.

Determined to disguise my disappointment even from myself, I reached into my Italian leather briefcase, took out my sketchpad and attempted to focus on my upcoming fashion show. No more thoughts of Antonio.

Instead, I tried to run through the designs in my mind one at a time, visualizing each silhouette, each pose and each turn. Then I tried to sketch what I imagined. Daydreaming about fashion didn't compare to the innocent flirtation I expected from Antonio, but it was certainly better than looking at his empty chair and feeling deserted.

I didn't really mind eating by myself though. Back in Jersey, dining alone used to go with the territory at least three or four nights out of a week. It usually gave me time to think, to plan and to create. In fact, some of my best designs came to me when I was eating or sleeping, and most of them came when I was alone. Alone, except of course for God, who inspired my ideas. Such an awesome God, and yet I continued to fall short.

The winter breeze caressed my face and legs, the only body parts, besides my hands, that were somewhat exposed. When I reached down to adjust my skirt underneath my leather coat, my mocha-colored stockings caught my eye. They were two shades darker than my skin, and I closed my eyes, straining to remember when I started the habit of hiding myself.

When I opened them, I realized that if hiding myself was my mission, then hiding by the water was my sanctuary. From the little stone table, I saw the boats pulling into the canal. One by one the *traghettos,* being the cheapest and fastest rowboats, boarded passengers, tourists and natives alike. I watched the people huddle together, separated only by their own anxieties. The fresh water repeatedly splashed against the sides of the wooden vessels as they were paddled downstream.

The ethereal scenery always provided the calm I needed for designing, and as a result, I usually flowed, without interruption, in my element. But today was so different, so strange, I gave in and put my work away.

"*Ecco, signora.*" The short, heavy-chested waitress smiled as she set down my plate. Her hair was a thick, unruly wave of blackness that commanded its own attention.

"Thank you. I mean, *grazie.*" I dug my fork into the shrimp scampi like I had not eaten in days.

She set my cappuccino next to my plate. "I haven't seen you in here since the holidays. Did you go home?"

"No, I didn't." My eyes avoided hers.

"Couldn't get away?" She stood over me, not moving. Her body was an intrusive mass, blocking my view of the water.

"More like I didn't want to get away," I offered. "My family and I don't always get along. Letters and postcards do just fine. At Christmas, it's FedEx that brings the love to the U.S." I smiled, but cut it short when she didn't smile back.

"I'm sure it's not the same as having you there in person, *signora*. What did your *madre* say?"

What in the world was she thinking? She didn't usually probe like this. In fact, we hardly had more than a two-sentence conversation in the few months that she had been working there.

"My mother didn't say anything." I dropped my head because I hadn't talked to Mama in years.

"The crowds are getting thick. Aren't you going to *Carnevale* today?" She stuck her hands into the pockets of her beige uniform.

She must have picked up on my discomfort because she dropped the previous subject. Needless to say, I was relieved.

"I usually don't." I forced a smile.

"But it's tradition."

"It's evocative, but I don't like the eerie masks."

"You're not one of those religious fanatics, are you?" She squinted her chestnut brown eyes at me.

"No, *signora,* but I do have my beliefs." *Even if I don't always practice them.*

I reached down to fondle the cross pendant that hung between my breasts. It had been so long since I had practiced anything spiritual. Too long. I'd have to change that one day soon. I'd have to make my way back into the church, any church at this point, as long as God could forgive me. Again.

Her big brown eyes finally met mine.

My fork went slowly to my mouth. "I've always loved Italian food."

"*Signora,* you no look like you 'love' no food." She squeezed my arm, smiled and then walked away.

Although she insulted me, I brushed her comment aside and grinned. Whenever I was at the studio, surrounded by beautiful models, I never felt "too" thin. I shook my head at the audacity she had displayed today.

Just as I was about to take another bite, a dark-haired, olive-toned waiter approached my table, holding a sheet of notepaper in his hand. "*Buon giorno, Signora* Hunt."

"*Buon giorno, signor.*" I wiped my mouth with the cloth napkin.

"I'm so sorry to disturb you, but there is an important call for you in the office," he said.

"A call? *Grazie, signor.*"

Since Nina, my personal assistant, was the only person besides Antonio who knew I was here, I wondered what had gone wrong at the office. I followed the waiter inside the café, squeezing through tables and chairs until we arrived at a tiny shell of a room. It was furnished only with a desk that was cluttered with papers, two chairs and a file cabinet. He gestured for me to come in.

"S*ignora.*" He led me to a telephone on the wall and handed me the receiver. "Line one."

"*Grazie.*" My Italian wasn't as refined as that of the natives, but I could certainly hold my own.

"*Buon giorno.*" I fidgeted with the phone cord.

"Makaeli, is that you, girl?"

"Oh, Lisa. Hi. I didn't realize—"

"I tried to reach you on your cell, but it seems to be off. I called your office, and your assistant said you could be reached at this number." Lisa's voice was low. "You've got to come home."

"Why? What's going on? Is it Mama?" My heart began to beat faster than it ever had.

"No. It's Raquel. She overdosed and she might die," Lisa said.

"What happened?" It wasn't that I was fishing for details, but I needed a moment to process the information.

"Raquel is in the ICU. I found her passed out in her room. She was just—just come home, please, as soon as you can."

"You know I haven't been home in a long time."

"Six years to be exact, but who's counting? That's even more of a reason for you to get yourself home." It was typical that Lisa was demanding.

"I can't just up and leave. I'm sure you can handle things without me," I said.

"Handle things without you?"

"My schedule is just impossible." I started the usual cat and mouse games, hoping she wouldn't catch me and eat me alive.

"Look, Mama wants everybody home now, including you. It has been long enough. And don't tell me about your 'impossible' schedule. You're the boss. Make it possible."

"Okay, okay. I'll see if I can get an evening flight." I hated when she used her authority like that.

"No, see if you can get a *now* flight. There's no time." Her voice didn't waver.

Same old domineering Lisa. I closed my eyes at the thought that even though years had passed, nothing had changed. I raised my hand to my forehead. The stress of going home brought on an instant headache. My heart began to beat faster and I felt the beads of perspiration forming at my temples.

"Okay, I'll call you when everything is in order." I sighed and leaned against the wall to steady myself.

"I'll see you when you get here." Lisa rendered me powerless, ending the conversation as abruptly as she started it.

I walked out of the tiny office a little dazed.

"Is everything all right, *signora?*" the waitress asked.

"No, I've got an emergency situation to deal with." I peeled out the euros from my wallet and practically threw them at her before I headed out the front door. "*Grazie.*"

Without even buttoning my coat, I grabbed my briefcase and ran quickly down the *riva,* headed for my villa-styled apartment in South Marco Square. It wasn't easy running in Anna Molinari stilettos, but I knew I had to do this fast or I might change my mind about going.

Although this moment had been a dream of mine a million times before, and although Raquel's destruction had once been my only ambition, now that it had actually happened, I couldn't even savor it. Mrs. Pearl's voice kept popping into my head. *"Forgive."*

Good old Mrs. Pearl, my former mentor, was always big on God and forgiveness . . . but what about the unforgivable?

Inside my apartment, I threw off my coat and changed into a denim pantsuit. I called Nina to make all the necessary travel arrangements. Then I went to my closet and started throwing things around in search of my Gucci overnight bag. When I finally found it underneath a pile of shoes, I filled it with a few basic essentials. Then almost as an afterthought, I remembered to pack a black dress, just in case. Finally, I went to my velvet jewelry box and took out the note.

I wasn't sure if it was the right time, but I had to bring it in case an opportunity arose. I squeezed the paper in my hands and held it against my chest for a few minutes before stuffing it into my purse.

Feeling quite satisfied with the progress made so far, I called Antonio. Not wanting me to go to the airport alone, he decided to end his session early and meet me at the Santa Lucia Railway Station.

I hung up the phone, waited for the driver, and before long, I was at the train station.

Seeing Antonio across the platform, my heart leaped at the sight of his deeply chiseled features and silky black hair. As he approached, I raised my gaze to take in his six foot two frame. How did I ever turn him down? His dark eyes scanned my body and shivers went through me. It was amazing how he still had that effect on me.

Antonio was no ordinary man; not one a woman would just pass over or throw away. He was a worthwhile "brother"—except he wasn't a "brother" at all. Figure that out. How did I go and get myself involved with an Italian-American man as if I didn't have enough racial drama in my family already? But I guess love knew no reason.

Not that I was sure I was in love or anything, but he definitely thought he was in love with me. He proposed, was rejected and still hung around even after all of my refusals. Don't get me wrong; it's not that I didn't care about him, or that I didn't have moments when I regretted my choice, but it's just that he wasn't ready for my kind of mess. A sister had too many issues. Besides, my family would kill me if they knew I was even trying to date a white man. I knew it would never work.

"We've got important things to discuss when you get back." Antonio took my hand and gently rubbed my ring finger.

"You mean *if* I get back. I'm going into a war zone, remember?"

"It can't be that bad." He squeezed my hand and it soothed me.

"Probably worse. I haven't seen any of these people in six years."

"These people, as you call them, are your family. You'll be okay."

"I'm glad you're sure, but I'm not."

"You can handle it. You're strong." Antonio directed his lips toward mine, but I turned my cheek to him. I couldn't deny the physical attraction between us, but I could tame it as much as possible.

"I just hope my demons aren't stronger." Laughter sneaked from my mouth, but my insides were disintegrating.

"Remember, *Dio è amore.*"

"You're right. God is love." But, with the way I'd ignored God in the past few years, I was ashamed to even claim that.

Being the gentleman that he was, Antonio offered to ride the Eurostar train with me. We rode for two and a half hours with stops in Verona, Padova, Vicenza and Mestre. It was a quiet ride because as I contemplated the challenge ahead, I was in no mood for talking. I was glad Antonio was considerate enough to understand.

Finally, we reached the Aeroporto Malpensa in Milan. Antonio held my hand with just the right amount of pressure and stayed just close enough not to alarm my better judgment. When he leaned forward to kiss me goodbye, I backed away. Temptation. The mind was willing but the flesh was weak.

"I love you." He touched my ring finger again and then pointed to his heart.

"I'll call you," I said.

Marriage. The thought of him being tied to me was scary because my desirability and worthiness seemed so far fetched.

Every morning, when I looked in the mirror to get ready for work, I'd paint myself with a darker shade of foundation to hide that other part of me. I wasn't even secure yet with myself, so what in the world would I do with a husband? A white one, at that?

Even though I knew most people called me beautiful, I didn't buy into that. Beauty was more than the sum total of smooth skin and well-formed body parts. A person should have something on the inside to qualify as being beautiful. And I was hollow; not because I was a horrible person and not because I wanted to be, but because of what was stolen from me.

Antonio quoted The Lord's Prayer before the plane boarded its passengers. Even though I appreciated his religious upbringing, I remembered when I had a real relationship with God.

After I was seated, he waved to me and then walked

away. I watched his broad shoulders as he eased down the walkway and disappeared into the crowd.

Through the glass, I admired *la serenissima,* the most serene, the beautiful Italy that offered me everything. Silently, I said goodbye to the Golden Triangle, the shopping district where the fashion houses of Giorgio Armani, Roberto Cavalli and Versace produced their exclusive labels. I knew in my heart that one day, when my business reached the next level, I would bring my own high fashion boutique to this area too. It was one of my favorite places in the world. I blinked away a tear, feeling that moving across the sea was undoubtedly the best decision I ever made.

Adulthood wasn't all I expected it to be, but it sure was better than that nightmare I called my childhood. Not once since I came to Italy did I endure ridicule for the white blood that ran through my veins, as if I didn't bleed and hurt like every other person of color. But I was on my way home to Jersey, away from the beauty to a place of cruelty and chaos.

I took out the crumpled note from my purse and smoothed its brown edges, proud that I had enough courage to bring it with me. For years this note had haunted me. *Maybe now is the time.* There were so many secrets and so much sorrow back in New Jersey that my expectations for this trip were nothing nice.

I was seated in an aisle seat next to a burly middle-aged man.

"How are you?" He loosened his tie and extended his hand.

"I'm fine, thanks." I started to fumble around in my purse, securing the note in my wallet.

This was going to be a long flight. I had hoped he wouldn't start small talk this early. I motioned for the flight attendant to come over.

"Excuse me. Are we still landing in New York on time?"
I asked.

"We should be only a few minutes off schedule, *signora*.
We always anticipate minor delays." She looked like a Barbie doll in her perfect-fitting uniform and long blond
hair.

"*Grazie*," I said.

As turbulence shook the plane, restlessness overshadowed me. As I looked out of the window at the clouds and
then at the swaying wing, my shrimp began to rise in my
throat. I leaned forward just in case my stomach betrayed
me, but it didn't. A can of ginger ale settled my nausea.

I reached down to pick up my Armani handbag and
patted it to assure myself of its contents. The note I carried was the only clue to my family history, so I couldn't
misplace it.

Looking through the window provided a little too
much excitement, so I decided to study the man sitting
beside me instead. He had a sharp mustache, a bald head
and was wearing a loose-fitting linen suit. He was reading
the newspaper, so I couldn't see his eyes.

First, I wondered how many skeletons were in his closet.
Mistrust was a bad habit of mine. Then I quickly decided
not to assume the worst of people and turned my glare
away from him.

"Are you from the States?" He looked over and gave me
a toothy grin.

"Yes, as a matter of fact, I am. Are you?" I was grateful
that he spoke fluent English.

"Yes. I was in Italy on business. What about you?"

"I'm visiting my family in New Jersey, but I live here, actually," I replied.

"Really? What made you relocate to Italy?"

"Well, I received a scholarship to Domus Academy a few
years back."

"Domus Academy?"

"It's a post graduate school of design in Milan. I had just finished my degree at Fashion Institute of Technology in New York City."

"Yes, I know of F.I.T. I'm a native New Yorker."

"Oh, well, I'm originally from New Jersey. Anyway, have you ever heard of Designs by Makaeli?"

"That does sound familiar, but I must admit, fashion is not my customer base." He didn't look impressed or interested.

"Well, Makaeli, that's me." I kept my smile broad, but I decided to leave him alone.

The rest of the eight and a half hour ride was peaceful. Sketching kept me occupied as usual. It kept me dreaming and functioning; trying to hide my pain far from my heart. Lisa's words about the overdose wouldn't leave my mind. She said they weren't sure Raquel would live, and I wasn't sure if a monster like that deserved to live anyway.

I opened my eyes wide, careful not to sleep, not wanting to dream. *Not now.*

Chapter Two

Lisa

"I'll see you here," I commanded before I clicked off the cordless phone.

I fell back onto my paisley comforter, still holding the receiver. It felt like a gun in my hand. All the power I held and had always held, excited me. I had forced Makaeli to come home. She'd come for Mama if for no one else.

From my window, I glimpsed ice on the trees, on the grass and on the concrete outside. The temperature was dropping, so I snuggled into my king-sized bed and pretended Phil was there. I wrapped my arms around his pillow and smelled his Calvin Klein cologne on the sheets. Even though it had been a while since we shared the same bed at the same time, his scent lingered from his occasional off-hour naps. I turned over under the covers and started to stare at the phone. Phil would be happy I talked to Makaeli, I thought.

I rarely talked to her at all. We had a routine of five-minute birthday calls and quarterly picture postcards, which were supposed to hold us together. A failure is what

I'd call my relationship with my youngest sister, Makaeli. The mixed one. And I mean mixed up in every sense of the word. She'd been doing her own thing, operating in her own world and paying the rest of the family and society little or no attention since I could remember.

Sometimes I rationalized that it was just the trauma of losing her mother while she was so young. Not that Mama was dead, but she certainly was gone—gone in body, mind and every part that mattered. *Biochemical imbalances, genetic factors* and *inappropriate emotional responses* were the words they used to describe Mama, but I said it was all garbage. They didn't know anything about Mama—the real Mama, not the shell of a woman she was now.

Other times, I didn't know what to think about my estranged sister.

My cell phone vibrated in my pocket. I took my time answering it because I knew it was Phil. I had so much to say to him lately, and yet my mouth couldn't form the words.

"Lisa."

"Hello, Phil." I made my voice lighthearted.

"I'm on a break for a little while. I just came out of the ER. I just wanted to check on Raquel's condition." Phil spoke in his most professional voice, as if I were not his wife, as if we hardly knew each other.

"It's the same." I swallowed my hurt and pretended I didn't notice his ambivalence.

"Are you going back to the hospital?" For a moment he sounded concerned.

"Of course. I just came home to take a quick nap and then freshen up."

"Have you heard from your brother yet?"

"Not a word from Matt yet. I left several messages." I held the phone close to my ear, wanting to drink in his presence.

"What about Makaeli?" Phil was abrupt.

"I just spoke with her. She should be on her way shortly, I guess."

"Really?" Phil breathed heavily into the phone. "I'm surprised she agreed to come back."

"What do you mean by that? This is a family crisis. She had to come," I said.

"Not when it's her family that ran her away in the first place." His words made the hairs on my neck stand at attention.

Now I was seething. "We did no such thing, Phillip Jackson. How can you say that?" It was a good thing he couldn't see me rolling my eyes. "It's not my fault she's a master of avoidance."

"What?"

"She must've gotten that from her dad's side of the family, the white side." I knew how he felt about the subject, but I didn't hold back. I never did.

"You're so impossible."

"Don't get me wrong. You know I don't hate white people, but I just think we've endured too much and come too far to mix with them." I thought of my own father, a proud black man. "I don't know what Mama was thinking ever marrying that white man." I hit my fist against the wall.

"I didn't call to get into one of your racist political debates."

"What did you call for?" I calmed myself down again, careful not to **drive him** any further away than he already was.

"I told you time and time again that Makaeli was hurting, but you ignored me, Lisa."

"Ignored you? I thought you were a surgeon, not a psychiatrist." Fire rose up in me instantly.

"What difference does it make? You wouldn't listen anyway."

"Oh, I won't listen, huh?" I was bent out of shape in a dozen different places by now.

"You never have. I told you long ago to be honest with her, to stop torturing the girl by not acknowledging her pain." Phillip's voice was louder than I expected it to be.

"Torturing her?" I couldn't believe he said that.

"That's what I said." Phil's voice remained stern.

"I raised her. What pain?"

"The pain of losing both her parents, for starters."

"That was a long time ago," I said.

"That doesn't mean she isn't hurt."

"I didn't say that."

"You've got to level with her soon."

"Look, this is neither the time nor the place for this conversation."

"You're right. It's not." He hung up the phone so gently that the click was barely noticeable.

I couldn't believe he hung up on me. The dial tone was deafening, a reminder of what was dead in me.

Back in the bathroom, I pulled down my silky stockings and prepared to fill the cup. I had no trouble going, not with all the Pepsi I drank the night before.

Not another baby, not now. Our marriage and my state of mind can't take any more pressure.

I dipped the strip into my urine sample and waited for what seemed like a lifetime. Faded blue, faded like the love in my marriage, faded like forty-eight years of yesterday's promises, faded like my childhood dreams. Faded. I watched and waited as the strip became my destiny.

Chapter Three
Makaeli

When I got off the plane, the first thing I saw was that the ground was covered with a grayish snow. The second thing I noticed was that all the signs were in English. Since I had only one piece of carry-on luggage, I didn't have to do the whole baggage claim thing and I was glad, because that was my least favorite part of traveling. When I got to the exit, a hired driver was waiting to take me to the Marriott in New Brunswick. It was already nine o'clock Friday evening.

The five star hotel was everything I expected it to be, complete with valet parking, an elegant lobby, a health spa and in-house dining. I probably would have enjoyed its luxurious accommodations if I had been visiting under more pleasant circumstances. Unfortunately, after checking in, the only thing I wanted to do was to get a few hours of sleep.

So I threw off my clothes and climbed into the queen-sized bed. Unable to fall asleep at first, I tossed and turned until I covered my head with the blanket. This secure feeling was what I needed to finally fall asleep.

Awakened by my own nightmares, I woke up trembling and was in no way ready to face my fears, but my choices were few. So I showered, got dressed and reapplied my makeup. Same dark foundation. It was a habit of mine I needed to stop, but I wasn't sure when I would be secure enough. Then I bundled myself up in my coat and put my earmuffs over my ears because I hated hats.

I picked up the hotel phone to call Lisa, to let her know I was here, but suddenly, I changed my mind. I didn't want to talk to her again until we were face to face, so I placed the phone back in its cradle. Then I called the driver and went downstairs to meet him in front of the building.

Ten minutes later, he arrived and we headed to Newark Medical Center.

"Are you going to be in town for long, Ms. Hunt?" The driver looked back at me and smiled.

"Not if I can help it." I didn't want to be here at all.

As we drove away from the hotel and through frost-covered familiar neighborhoods, I became even more tense. We got closer to our destination. I unzipped my purse and looked at the brittle note again. Carefully, I slipped it back into my wallet. *Soon.*

When we arrived at the hospital, the driver opened the door for me and I hesitated before stepping out of the car. He politely offered his hand, so I let him assist me across the slippery sidewalk to the front door. I told him I wouldn't need his services for the remainder of the trip before I walked through the main entrance.

Since I had never visited Newark Medical Center before, I stopped at the information desk. A gentleman who looked to be about my age, who wore a low haircut and a thin mustache stood there dressed in a medical uniform and wearing a name badge. I didn't bother reading what it said. After all, he looked capable enough. After I asked what room my sister was in, he looked at the computer and told me. Then he pointed straight ahead.

I walked in the direction I was told. My feet felt like they were locked in cement, with each step I took bringing me closer to that which I did not understand. When I reached the other side of the building, a gray-haired nurse escorted me into the intensive care unit. I followed her through a long corridor to a small room. She immediately began to adjust the fluids. The substances dripped with no life at all. They ran through the intravenous tubes, looking like little snakes of poison. Drip. Drop.

What a distressing task to be a life liquid, keeping alive this woman who deserved death. The heart monitor beeped, and its lack of activity indicated to me that she had very little life left. I stood still, not knowing what to do or say.

"You said this is your sister, didn't you?" Strangely enough, the nurse had a heavy Southern accent, as if she had just come up from Mississippi.

"Yes, I did." I didn't look at the nurse's face because I didn't want her to see my eyes.

"Her condition is very unstable." She shook her head and then touched my shoulder gently.

"Unstable? What do you mean exactly?" I wanted to know everything.

"Her heart is very weak, as you can see from this machine right here." The nurse pointed to the heart monitor.

"Maybe I should go then." I nervously stepped back away from the bed.

"Oh no. Stay for a little while and talk to her. I'm sure she'll be glad to know you're here."

"How do you know she'll know I'm here?"

"Sometimes our patients come out of comas and actually remember things that they heard, and sometimes a comatose patient's condition will make a turn for the better after a particular visitor shows up."

"Oh." I spoke quietly, as if I were trying to fade into the background, to disappear.

"We believe talking helps. It also helps the families."

"I've heard about that."

"Talk to her, but say soothing things. Try not to upset her. Just remember she's very weak." The nurse walked to the other side of Raquel's bed.

Problem was, I didn't have anything soothing to say.

The Raquel Lenore Cambell that lay in the hospital bed was not the sister I remembered. Sixteen years my senior, she looked totally helpless and surrendered to her current physical state. Her face was dry and cracked. Even though her lids were closed, her eyes looked haunting, like two bulbs of onions that had been sitting in the sun too long. It repulsed me. I could see the peaks on the heart monitor become slower, then weaker—too weak, I imagine. The tick-tock came from the hall clock, almost bursting my eardrums. And yet I felt nothing.

"Are you all right, dear?" The nurse looked back at me before she left the room.

Good old Southern hospitality. "I'm fine, thanks." But I wasn't fine.

I cupped my face in my hands, holding back the long, light tresses that were my curse. Seas were crossed to make it back to New Jersey in time, but in time for what? There was a gnawing sensation inside my stomach. Emptiness. I didn't feel love or sadness for my dying sister. I didn't feel anything.

Instead, I had an awkward, unfamiliar wound, unlike the pain of being trampled under the foot of my own sister, or unlike the pain of being repeatedly thrown against a wall until I almost lost consciousness. It wasn't like any of those things, and so it was hard for me to understand it, hard for me to feel it.

My head and heart were filled with nightmares, and what once felt like raw pain was now a battle scar. I earned it, and I was destined to see it through.

Chapter Four

Lisa

The moment I walked in, I made my usual observations. As a physician, I was used to making plenty of those. The hospital cafeteria, with its mint green formica tables and chairs, was alive with medical personnel and patients scrambling to gain sustenance in the midst of life-altering illnesses and circumstances. Something inside me wanted to pity this poor crowd, but I had too many problems of my own. Big ones.

An obviously homeless woman sat in a chair near the door clutching her greasy paper shopping bags. Her long strands of gray hair framed her small, brown, wrinkled face. A teenage mother with platinum blond hair and bright sea green eyes sat at a table feeding a crying infant as another young child played at her feet. I could hear the sound of coughing and wheezing nearby. There seemed to be an unidentifiable odor invading my nostrils as well.

As I looked around, I realized that in all my years in medicine, I never worked in a hospital like this, a haven for the low-income community and the uninsured. I had never been classified in that category either and for that, I was grateful.

Despite my present surroundings, I welcomed the opportunity to be away from Raquel's depressing room, to clear my aching head. While I was eating and reflecting on my dilemma, my friend, Lashawn Coleman, walked over.

"Hi, Lisa. I've got a few minutes left on my break, so I decided to grab some coffee." Lashawn gave me a quick pat on the back and sat down at the table.

"Hi. This is the first time I've eaten since breakfast yesterday." I held up the remaining crust of my bagel.

"Were you here all night?"

"Yes. Can't you tell?" I pointed to my wrinkled appearance.

"How is she?"

"Still just holding on." I looked down at the paper plate and cup in front of me and started to clean up my mess.

"Unstable?" Lashawn grabbed my hands to stop me.

"Very," I said.

"How are you holding up?"

"That's just it: I feel like I'm holding everything up."

Lashawn Coleman, my closest friend, was a staff physician here for the past five years now. She was, in my opinion, one of the best pediatricians around, known for the extra attention and care she gave her miniature patients. The limited conditions under which she worked didn't bother her at all. She never complained. In fact, she thrived on it. And I loved her for being the martyr I wasn't willing to be.

We talked easily about Raquel's condition until I dropped the news on her.

"Guess what I did yesterday?" I didn't expect her to know what she was getting herself into, but seeing her sit on the edge of her seat in suspense made it worth the wait.

"Aside from hanging out in the ICU, I have no idea." Lashawn looked up at me as she sipped her coffee.

"I took a home pregnancy test." I looked directly into her eyes and waited for a response.

"A pregnancy test?"

"Yes, a pregnancy test." I could hardly wait another minute.

"You're pregnant?"

"Of course." I slammed my hand down on the table in mock misery. "What other excuse would I have to look this pitiful?"

"At your age?" She covered her mouth as if I said a dirty word.

I gave her the same look I had been giving her since medical school: *You know I wouldn't play about something like this.*

"Girl, there's a lot on your plate right now." Lashawn pushed her braids out of her face as she shook her head.

"You're right about that. Just look at me."

"I'm looking, but I'm not believing." Lashawn put her hands on her broad hips.

"Well, believe it. I didn't believe it either at first," I said.

"What changed your mind?"

"My doctor confirmed it."

"So, it's definite?"

"Definitely. I'm forty-eight years old and I'm definitely pregnant."

"Oh my goodness." The way she raised her freshly arched eyebrows above her almond eyes spoke volumes in seconds.

"I should be pre-menopausal, not pregnant."

"But you look good, though."

"Yeah, right. Then on top of me being over the hill, things are just too shaky at home," I said.

"I know."

"No, you don't know. I mean, I have one child in grad school, one in his senior year of college and one in high school, for goodness' sake. What in the world am I going to do with a baby?"

"I know things aren't perfect, but a new baby is kind of exciting."

"How can I think about birth and life when my marriage is dying?"

"Don't worry. It may be a challenge at your age, but Phil loves you," Lashawn said.

"It's funny how I used to live for that, but now I'm not so sure."

"What do you mean?"

"Things are so bad between us. We've been sleeping in different rooms for the past two months. It started out with him not wanting to disturb me when he came in late, and gradually it became easier and easier to avoid each other."

"Now, that's a sticky situation."

"I'm sure Johnathan has noticed, but he hasn't said anything. I'm kind of glad because I don't even know what I would say to him if he did. Phil just politely makes the bed in the guestroom and goes off to work like everything is fine." I let out a big sigh. "Then to top it all off, we've been at each other's throats over this Makaeli thing."

"Really?" Lashawn looked surprised.

"He blames me for this rift in our relationship."

"Oh. Well, they used to be pretty close. But why would he blame you?"

"It's a long story. You know Makaeli and I have never seen eye to eye on anything, and Phil has always kind of been in the middle." I wanted to, but I couldn't tell her everything.

"Maybe this visit from her is just what you two need."

"Maybe." *Not likely when she hears what I have to say.*

"Everything will work out."

"I hope you're right."

"I'm always right." Lashawn smiled and tears came to my eyes. "But please don't cry."

"No, I'm fine."

"You don't look fine."

"You're always the voice of reason. Thanks." This crying on a whim wasn't like me. I was stronger than that.

"I've got to get back to my rounds, but I'll call you tonight." Lashawn put her hand on my shoulder.

"Okay."

"About eight o'clock?"

"That's good."

"Keep your head up." Lashawn pushed back the copper-colored weave from her face and hugged me.

"I will." *If only it was that easy.* "I'm heading back to Raquel's room."

We waved to each other before she made her exit.

Lashawn always managed to make me feel better. She was one of those people who, despite whatever catastrophe was going on around her, and there had been many in the time that I'd known her, would never let anything keep her down. Like when her divorce from her first husband, Tim, became final. She was angry for a couple of weeks, but by the end of the month, she was planning an engagement party for him and his fiancée. Now, that's where I drew the line of understanding. I didn't see her kind of optimism every day. And I wasn't sure I even wanted to.

I tossed my empty plate and cup into the trash can, left the cafeteria and began the long trek down the hall. Before I turned the corner, the head nurse rushed toward me. She squinted her eyes to look apologetic and she extended her hand. *Why was her face so solemn?*

"Dr. Jackson, I'm sorry," she said.

My heart developed a new rhythm. *Please, Lord, if you exist, don't let it be Raquel. Please don't let it be too late.*

My heart plummeted to my stomach. A million *what ifs* and a zillion *I should haves* rolled through my mind.

I should have told her. I should have told her.

Chapter Five

Makaeli

Since the moment of my arrival, all I had done was walk around Raquel's tomblike hospital room like a prisoner who had been sentenced to it. I looked at my watch and saw that it was ten-thirty. I knew that Lisa was waiting for my call, but I needed more time to prepare myself before I saw her. I needed more time to toughen up. Fifteen minutes wasn't nearly enough time.

I looked at Raquel's emaciated body covered with only a thin cotton sheet. Then I forced my eyes to look at her face. Despite the stillness I saw before me, I remembered the past, her contorted expressions, discolored lips and bulging red eyes. I stepped back from her bedside as the memories came flooding forward. The bitterness. The beatings. The words. Hateful words.

I wanted to say something, but my words wouldn't come out. Besides, who would even hear them? I had been silent for so long, but now I was ready to put a voice to the anger bubbling over inside of me.

I balled my hands up into fists, feeling like I'd go off in there if I didn't have someone to talk to, someone who would understand. My teeth chattered and my knees buckled. Putting my hands over my ears was my desperate attempt to drown out the confusion. Needing a quiet place, a refuge from all the noise in my head, I turned toward the door. For a minute, I hoped I wasn't losing it like Mama.

My stomach felt like it was turned inside out, so I left Raquel's room and quietly closed the door behind me. I stood with my back against the wall, breathing hard, perspiring hard, and then I unbuttoned the top of my coat. I felt the coldness of the cross pendant dangling against my chest. I touched it, and as my eyes filled up with tears, I wondered why Jesus would make such a sacrifice for me. Suddenly I knew I needed God's presence; something I hadn't felt in quite some time.

As the head nurse approached me, I stopped her.

"Excuse me, ma'am. Do you know where I can find a— I mean a minister or—?"

"We have a chapel downstairs if you want someone to pray with you or something."

"A chapel. Yes, that's fine. Downstairs, you say?"

"Just take the elevator down to the first floor, then make a right and go down the first corridor. You'll see a sign," she said.

"Thanks."

"You're welcome."

Riding the elevator down didn't help my stomach condition, nor did it settle my anxiety. After following the nurse's instructions precisely, I finally reached the chapel. I hesitated before going in, wondering what I might be getting myself into; however, once I went inside, my fears disappeared. It looked just like a real church, with wooden pews and an altar. There were a few artificial plants, but there were no windows. I couldn't help feeling suffocated by the stuffiness in the small room. *Is God really here?*

As I was about to sit down on the front row, a tall, bearded white man with eyes as blue as a Caribbean sea came over to me. He was wearing a beige polo shirt and matching Dockers.

"Hello, my sister. My name is Reverend Cowan. I'm the chaplain here." He shook my hand and then sat down.

"Hi." I looked at him carefully, trying to decide if I could trust him, if I could trust anyone.

"And your name is?"

"I'm Makaeli," I said in a quiet voice.

"Nice to meet you, Makaeli. Can I pray with you about something?"

"No, thanks. It's nothing." I bowed my head, wishing I could say all that was in my heart.

"Are you sure? Maybe I can help." He had a soft, soothing voice, one that reminded me of my brother-in-law, Phil.

"My sister is in the ICU." Since he looked genuine enough, I decided to give him the basics.

"I see. We get a lot of visitors like you, I'm afraid."

"She probably won't make it." I bit my lower lip.

"I'm sorry."

I'm not. "It doesn't really matter anyway."

"Of course it matters. The way you feel always matters to God."

"I didn't mean it like that. It's just—never mind." I wrapped a strand of my hair around my finger with my head still bowed.

"Whatever it is that's bothering you, you can heal."

"Maybe." I wasn't so sure.

"Do you want to talk about it?"

"No." But I did, and the tears were coming down again.

"Sometimes it helps to talk about it with someone." He reached into his shirt pocket and handed me a few tissues.

"I've talked about it before and it hasn't helped." I took two and dried my face.

It was true. Back in the day, talking was all I did, and those words never helped. I talked to my brother, Matt. I talked to my friend, Mrs. Pearl. And I cried out to God, but no one could help me. I had to fight my own battle, and that's what I did—fight.

"But have you tried talking to God, Himself? He is the right one to lay it on. He wants to help you."

"I don't think He can anymore. I'm just—" I bowed my head and ran my fingers through my hair.

"Depressed?"

"No, disgusted." I lifted my head up, but I didn't make eye contact.

"And don't you want to be healed, my sister?" His voice was so gentle that it was almost a whisper.

"I don't know. I don't think I'd know how to live without—"

"Without pain?"

"Yeah."

"I don't believe you don't want to be helped. You're here, aren't you?"

"Maybe I just wandered in," I lied. I knew I wanted to be there, but I wasn't sure why.

"I don't believe that and neither do you."

"What are you trying to say?"

"I'm just saying that you knew where to come to find help."

"Help?"

"I believe God led you here." He looked up to the ceiling and then brought his eyes back down again.

"I don't think He led me here."

"Why not?"

"Because He's probably not too happy with me right now." I touched my eyelids with my fingers to stop the tears from falling. Becoming unraveled was not my intention.

"God loves you, regardless."

"I know that but . . ."

"Then why blame God?"

"Oh no, I don't blame Him. I just don't think He can help someone like me."

"Then you obviously don't know my omniscient, omnipotent God."

"I used to, but . . ." I used the tissue to wipe my nose and then I pushed my hair out of my face.

"Things didn't change fast enough."

"How did you know that?"

"The Holy Spirit told me. You can't put a time limit on God just because things didn't happen fast enough."

"I'm not timing God. I'm just saying . . ."

Where was the Holy Spirit when I needed him? Now I was stuck in this deep conversation with a stranger and I brought it all on myself. The last thing I needed was a sermon. *I shouldn't have come here.*

"God is bigger than our schedules and our expectations. Don't give up on Him. I promise He won't give up on you." His words reminded me of Mrs. Pearl.

"Thanks, Reverend Cowan, was it?"

"Yes."

"I've got to go." I fixed my purse on my shoulder, stood up and walked toward the door.

"Are you going back to see your sister now?"

"Yes, I am."

"Good. I expect to see you again."

"Maybe." I wanted to trust him, to dump all my emotional baggage on him, but I couldn't. This innocent man didn't deserve my wrath, so I decided to hold it in a little longer and wait.

When I left the room, I rounded the corner, went into

the elevator and back upstairs to the ICU waiting area. I couldn't go back into her room yet. Tired of watching a half-dead Raquel in her hospital bed, I decided to stretch my body across a striped armchair. It offered little comfort, despite its practical design. I pulled off my Armani pumps to rub my sore feet, knowing I should've brought my sneakers.

When I looked up, I saw my oldest sister, Lisa, coming down the hall and I stood up to greet her. Dr. Lisa Cambell-Jackson, the rock of the Cambell-Hunt family.

She was nineteen and a half years older than me, and she walked down the hall in her shiny two-inch pumps with perfect posture. She had gained a few pounds since I had seen her last, but she wore it well. Her hair looked like she had just stepped out of a salon, and she wore copper-rimmed glasses. She was smart, attractive and dignified, but what I admired about her most was her sense of responsibility; the way she picked up the ball when Mama became ill. As far as I know, she never looked back. At least she never let me knew about it if she did.

"Oh, I'm so glad you came." Lisa gave me a quick hug. Then she held me at arm's length and smoothed back my straight hair. I wasn't sure if she was aware that she was frowning, but she was obviously focused in on my blondish-brown hue. The last time she saw me, it was jet black.

"You don't dye your hair black anymore?" Lisa held me away from her, staring at my light hair, my light face and my light eyes.

"No, I've been wearing it natural for years."

"Well, I guess it goes with your complexion." Lisa let go of me and smiled as if she suddenly remembered I was her sister instead of an ugly stranger. "I'm just glad it's you the nurse came to tell me about and not what I thought she came to tell me."

"What do you mean?"

"It's just that I'm a little paranoid, and when I saw her coming toward me a minute ago, saying she was sorry, I thought that Raquel had . . ."

"Oh."

"As it turns out, she just wanted to let me know that you were here with Raquel. She was apologizing because she thought I had already left the building, but I overreacted."

"Oh, that doesn't sound like you." I sat back down and she sat next to me.

"I haven't been like me since this happened." Lisa turned her body toward me. "Anyway, I can't believe you're really here."

"Believe it. I'm here for you and for Mama." *And to avoid the whispers behind my back if I didn't come.*

"And for Raquel too, of course." Lisa stood straight up.

"Not really. Raquel never cared if I lived or died my whole life," I said.

"That's not true." Lisa put on her deepest big-sister voice.

"It's no lie. Anyway, what exactly happened to her? You didn't really explain over the phone."

"Overdose, probably on purpose." Lisa crouched back down into the armchair next to me.

"On purpose? Why kill yourself when you've got so much hatred to spread around?" I swallowed hard, waiting for resolution and restitution.

"Shhh. I know you and Raquel have never really gotten along, but—"

"Now, that's an understatement," I said.

I once hoped Raquel would be shot in a drive-by while visiting one of those dangerous areas she liked to frequent, or that she would fall down an elevator shaft while visiting one of her crackhead pals in the projects. But overdosing and silently lapsing into a coma sounded a little like cowardess to me.

Where was the big, bad Raquel whose bloodshot eyes I wanted for years to scratch out? Where was that big bully who twisted my wrists until they were scarred? Why was that big, bad Raquel hiding behind the cowardess of an overdose?

"Raquel came in acting very suspicious yesterday morning. She was agitated and paranoid. She said someone was following her," Lisa said.

"Okay." I tried to sound concerned, but I was sure my voice didn't measure up.

"Then she said she had a headache and went to her room. Next thing I know, I heard her vomiting in the bathroom. By the time I got upstairs, she had passed out in her room." Lisa sat very still and kept her voice very even-toned.

"What makes you think she did it on purpose?"

"They found five hundred milligrams of cocaine in her system along with enough alcohol to put a horse to sleep." Lisa put her hands on her small hips. "She must've been trying to kill herself."

"I see." I didn't blink.

"She had a heart attack, so she's in a lot of danger."

"Okay," I said in my most humble voice. I wanted to react with gladness, to jump up, to throw my hands in the air and shout, "Hallelujah!" but I kept myself calm. I kept myself respectful.

"Raquel hasn't been herself in a while." Lisa moved her lips, but kept her face still and without expression.

For a minute, Lisa looked like Mama; with her short, black waves softly framing her dark brown, oval eyes and caramel face. In fact, they all looked like Mama; my sisters Lisa and Raquel, and my brother, Matt. Everyone except me. My only resemblance to them was that I was tall and slim. My life was marked by split ethnicity and despite my best efforts, this part of me couldn't be hidden. It kept abandoning my wishes and floating to the surface.

"How was she different?"

"She was just so irritable and withdrawn," Lisa said.

"That's nothing new." I shrugged.

"No, but she was seeing this guy for a couple of weeks and then they broke up a few days ago. She had been drinking and smoking her life away ever since."

"Still nothing new." I was unmoved by her sob story.

"She stopped partying, stopped talking, and she stopped hanging out with that pitiful crowd of hers."

"Wow, now that's new," I said.

"I tried to get her back into rehab," Lisa continued.

"For the fifth time, right?"

She ignored my question. "She wouldn't listen. You know how pig-headed she is."

"Among other things, yeah."

I didn't see worry on Lisa's soft caramel face, but I knew it was there. She carried so many of the family's burdens that letting her suffer further seemed a little unfair.

"Lisa, don't worry. Everything will be okay," I said.

"You really are all grown up now." Lisa looked me up and down and then picked a piece of lint off my sweater.

She always made me nervous when she did that because there was usually criticism following closely behind. Surprisingly, she didn't make a comment.

"I never got a chance to thank you before I went away to college." I put my face cautiously close to hers.

"Thank me?" Lisa squinted her eyes.

"For taking care of me when Mama went away. For you and Phil moving in, taking over and loving me when no one else would." She wasn't the sister I hated.

"What do you mean, when no one else would? Mama never stopped loving you, and loves you still," Lisa said.

"I didn't mean to imply that, but you know what I mean," I said.

"She's just not herself anymore since . . ." Lisa couldn't go on.

I thought I could almost see a tear welling up in her eyes, but she must have pushed it back inside. She would never show weakness. Not even if it meant holding up more than she could bear.

"I know, I know—since her breakdown. I'm not trying to judge her. I'm just saying that being back here in the States has made me remember your sacrifices." I used to have such admiration for her. I wasn't sure how much of it was left, but I knew I still owed her something more than basic gratitude.

"Seems like sacrifices come naturally to me, but life isn't easy. You've got to do what you've got to do to survive," Lisa said.

"That's for sure." I knew about survival.

She leaned forward to give me one of those once-in-a-lifetime hugs, and neither of us rushed to let go. I smelled the scent of White Diamonds on her neck. When we separated, she stared at my face until I looked away. If I could have erased my apricot skin and replaced it with at least a mocha almond, I would have.

"You've come a long way, Lovechild." Lisa fixed the silk collar of her gray blouse.

"Oh, please don't tease me with that awful middle name." I thought about the note in my purse.

"Mama loved that name, Lovechild. She was a die-hard romantic," Lisa said. "Makaeli Lovechild Hunt."

"So I've heard . . ." I pretended to play a violin. "I wonder if my dad ever liked that name."

"Don't worry about that. We're all better off without him." Lisa threw her hand up in front of my face as if I were speaking to her hand.

My eyelids closed and my eyes rolled underneath them, remembering that it used to be just like this. *Never mention your father. Don't even think about loving him.*

Perspiration was thick on me now. "Will she live?" I asked Lisa in the lowest voice I could manage.

"They don't know. Her heart was already so weak from all the drugs she used to do, and then with the heart attack, I—They just don't know if she'll survive this." Her voice was so faint that it seemed almost imaginary. She gestured to me and went into Raquel's room. I followed her in.

Raquel's fragile body was still connected to all the machines of life, the best that medical technology could provide. But none of the metals and plastics could truly make our lives any better.

There stood one sister, and there lay the other. Lisa held Raquel's hands, and the sight of them made me gasp. Her hands made me remember how helpless I used to be, screaming and waiting for Lisa to come home, wishing Raquel wasn't a part of my family. A single tear fell onto my cheek, but I wiped it away with one hand because I was determined not to be sad anymore. I was determined not to let her wretchedness destroy me. She was the one who deserved to be destroyed, and I had vowed long ago to make sure that it happened. *God, help me.*

Chapter Six

Lisa

After a few minutes, Makaeli and I decided to take a restroom break. We walked arm in arm down the hallway, even though I'm not sure it was comfortable for either of us. It had been so long since we had done anything like sisters. She bounced with her youthfulness, while I had to force my body to keep going.

Then I pushed open the door to the ladies' room, anxious to relieve my bladder. I left her standing by the sink and went into one of the stalls to use it. The pressure from this pregnancy was already on.

When I came out of the stall and walked up behind her, I saw her reading something, but she hurried to stuff it back into her purse. She was acting stranger than I felt. I turned on the faucet to wash my hands while Makaeli rummaged through her purse. I wondered if she was hiding something, but with all that was going on, I hardly had time to care.

A pregnant young woman with reddish brown dreadlocks walked into the restroom, wearing a fashionable maternity blouse, stretch jeans and black Timberland boots. She was tall with an average build, and she looked like she was in her last trimester. Although I wouldn't be caught dead in an outfit like she was wearing, I was fascinated with the way she moved with such ease. She glided back and forth on the tiles as gracefully as if she were a dancer. She stood in front of the mirror, lotioning her hands and applying her lip gloss.

While drying my hands, I watched her as if I were watching my future unfold, until she caught me staring. Then I quickly turned away and walked toward the door. She frowned and walked past me, letting the door slam behind her.

"Are you okay?" Makaeli looked at the door and then at me.

"I'm fine," I said.

"The way you were staring at that pregnant lady, I know you're glad you're way past all of that, huh?"

"Yes, I am." *If she only knew.*

"After all, a woman your age has already done it all, and now you can relax a little, right?" Makaeli playfully tugged at my sleeve.

"Right." I looked at her like she was crazy for wrinkling my blouse, then I straightened the material of my sleeve. She should have known I don't play like that.

I couldn't believe I was in this predicament. All the complications and implications. I was still trying to register the fact that I was going to have another baby fifteen years after my last one, and that I, the always-in-control one, was totally out of control.

We walked back into Raquel's room for the remaining minutes of our visit. I was determined to be a fortress, a pillar of emotional strength, no matter how weak I was. As a physician, I recognized that Raquel's veins looked worn and useless from years of drug needles, and when I touched her skin, it felt cold and slimy.

There was nothing good about this situation, this waiting to see if the coma would pass. Never did like waiting. I was Dr. Lisa Cambell-Jackson, always a doer, like the generations of Cambells who came before me.

In fact, that was one of the reasons I decided to become a doctor. I chose neonatal medicine because I wanted the power of sustaining new life. I never wanted any baby to have to suffer and die, not if I had the chance to save him or her. So saving babies had become my mission at work, and I was completely professional, if not somewhat detached.

"I just don't know what to say. I'm very serious about the work I do in the neonatal unit. I monitor, diagnose, advise and prescribe." I counted these duties on my fingers.

"I know." Makaeli looked at me and sighed.

"Yet here I can do nothing." I turned away from Raquel's body and balled my hands into fists. I felt my blood pressure rising.

"You mean you feel helpless." Makaeli put her hands on mine and squeezed them gently.

"Like you can't imagine."

"I can imagine being helpless." Makaeli walked away from me, looking down.

"I'm used to solving problems, not waiting. But ever since Raquel fell out, I can do nothing. Nothing."

"I know what you mean."

"Then you know that *nothing* isn't a word I work well with," I said. "I'm a doctor, for goodness' sake."

"I know. You're a distinguished professional." Makaeli said the words slowly, almost mechanically.

"What's that supposed to mean? Are you mocking me?" I put my hands on my hips.

"I'm not mocking you, but you talk as though you're God or something."

"I used to think being a doctor was close enough to being God, but after practicing medicine for over fifteen years, I don't anymore." I pointed up to the ceiling.

"Good." Makaeli turned back to Raquel.

"It's just that I don't like this hospital. It's crawling with amateurs. I can see that it's not like the hospital I work at."

"Different places are different." Makaeli never looked back at me.

"Difference I can tolerate, but incompetence is unacceptable." I put my hand on Makaeli's shoulder and spun her around. "A few minutes ago I wanted to snatch the chart from those bumbling nurses and make a few decisions myself."

"Well, that seems a little harsh, don't you think?"

"Harsh situations call for harsh measures," I said. "I wanted to take over, not because I have nothing else to do, but because I don't want their neglect to kill my sister."

"But you can't." Makaeli's words were cold.

"No, I can't. All I can do hour after hour is watch her laying there, looking like the life has been sucked out of her, looking like she has been through hell," I said. "In a sense, we all have."

"You've got that right," Makaeli said.

When I held Raquel's hand, the adrenaline rushed through my veins. Her body seemed to flinch, but it may have been my mind playing tricks on me. I wanted so much for her to move and for her to be all right, but I, with all my professionalism and knowledge, couldn't make her all right. It was a reality I wasn't at all ready for.

"Is Matt coming?" Makaeli asked, facing me.

"He said he would. He should be here by now." I looked at my watch.

"It will be good to see him after so long." Makaeli smiled for the first time since we had been together.

"It sure will." I nodded.

The things we experienced and the bond we shared was undeniable. We were a family who was broken, but a family, nonetheless. Even as I waited, I wondered how I could patch this mess called our family back together to vaguely resemble what used to be.

I took a quick glance at Raquel's chart and shook my head.

"It looks like chicken scratch, but what does it say?" Makaeli came and stood right beside me.

"Basically, her heart is in bad shape." I stared at the chart for a minute longer and then put it down.

"Oh." Makaeli's smile was gone. All that was left were those thin, pouting lips.

"That's enough bad news for me. I'm done." I walked toward the window and fixed the curtains so that they were neat.

Makaeli looked over my shoulder and stared at me with those catlike gray eyes. She looked as if she was judging me, always judging me. Even when she was a child, I stood corrected by those piercing eyes. If she only knew the truth.

"Have you been here the whole time?" she asked me.

"Pretty much the whole time." I turned to face the clock on the wall.

"Oh." Makaeli's voice sounded sad, but I wasn't convinced the sadness was because of Raquel's condition.

"I'm very tired," I said.

"I'm sure you are."

"I just didn't feel right leaving when she has been on

the edge like this." Guilt was what made me explain. Guilt was the force that drove me minute by minute.

"She's lucky to have you." Makaeli walked away from me.

"She's lucky to have all of us," I said.

"If you say so."

Makaeli walked back and forth in little semi-circles, which wore down my nerves. Her constant presence and cynicism reminded me of what I hid from her. My mind tried hard, but it couldn't shut out regret. *Maybe if I had told her . . . if I had only told her.*

Chapter Seven

Makaeli

Pushing the front door open, I walked outside as the wind whipped my hair in all directions. I didn't want to seem anti-social or less than compassionate, but I had to get out of there. I told Lisa I was going to the water fountain, and then I detoured to the elevators and snuck past her roaming eyes. Too uptight to look behind me, I kept on walking.

Before I knew it, I was standing in front of a wide, rust-colored building, Greater Love Christian Academy. There were children lined up in front of the steps and a school bus parked on the street. I assumed they were going on a field trip, and I smiled because they looked so happy. I wondered what it was like to attend a school where the focus was on God. I wondered if it would have made a difference in my life.

Although I was cold without my coat, it was as if I were hypnotized by the students as they carefully boarded the bus in their monogrammed blazers, ties and dress slacks.

One little boy looked up at me and said, "Lady, are you lost or something?"

"No, I'm okay. Thanks." I snapped out of it, but felt a little silly standing there.

He gave me a curious look before he climbed aboard, and I stepped aside so I wouldn't be in the way.

I noticed that the children were all colors, shapes and sizes, but they were all beautiful. And I wished someone had thought I was beautiful when I was their age. Maybe a kind word, other than "At least your hair isn't nappy."

I sighed like I had been sighing for years, and then I turned on my heels to go back into the hospital. When I got back, Lisa asked me where I had been. I told her I was wandering, but I didn't say where.

Raquel was still unconscious, and I felt like my consciousness was slipping away too. My eyes watered. My pulse raced. Yet Lisa was the picture of calm.

The overwhelming gloominess of the room slowly but surely got to me. It wasn't what I saw that was depressing, but rather what I didn't see. No flowers, no real colors, no laughter, barely any life at all. Just the monotonous drone of man made machines and the soft, squishy sound of nurses' sterile white shoes.

A tall nurse stood in the doorway. She reminded me of a ghost with her pasty white skin and white hair. She pointed to the overhead clock with one hand and held the door open with the other.

"All right, people, your time is up. It's time to move out," she said.

"Let's step out so the nurse can do her vitals." Lisa took me by the arm.

"Where is the bedside manner these days?" My voice was no more than a whisper, but Lisa nodded her head. I stood up, threw my leather coat across my shoulder, grabbed my purse and proceeded to the door. A crooked smile did the trick for the nurse, even though I was tempted to scowl instead.

Lisa followed, pulling her sleek blazer down over her narrow frame and shaking out the flared legs of her slacks before leaving the room. As we walked into the waiting area, we saw our brother, Matt, sitting in one of the armchairs.

He stood up wearing a Roca Wear jogging suit, revealing a small tattoo on his neck and two small gold earrings in his left ear.

"Matt, you're here." I jumped into his arms.

"Hey there, girl." He hugged me and then kissed my forehead gently. In an instant, I became a kid again.

"Hi." He reached for Lisa's hand.

"Matt, it's so good to see you, bro, but what happened to your hair? You mean to tell me you couldn't just get a haircut and a shave?" Lisa brushed her hand against his raggedy beard.

"It's good to see you too, Lisa," Matt said.

"Don't pay her any attention. You look good," I complimented.

"That's easy for you to say. You've always liked that 'carefree' look," Lisa said.

"I just believe in freedom of expression." I laughed.

Lisa touched the earrings in his ear and shook her head. "Freedom of expression? Is that what you call all of this?"

"What? You've got a problem with me, big sister?" Matt smiled, revealing a gold tooth.

"Not at all. You're a grown man. If you want to represent yourself like that, it's your business." Lisa gave him a quick hug and then backed away.

"I'm glad you're here," I said to Matt.

"So am I. I didn't know if you'd be able to come." Lisa gave him one of her closed-lip smiles.

"I had to come," Matt replied.

Matt was the type of individual who took loyalty very seriously. I wondered if he was always that way or if it was just a part of the jailhouse code he picked up from his time in Rykers. In any case, by the time I was fourteen and a half and met him for the first time, he proved himself to be trustworthy beyond reason. No matter where I went or what I did, he never snitched. When I complained about Lisa or Raquel, he empathized with me. In fact, he was my best friend up until fate took him away from me again three years later.

I thought about the three of us standing in the waiting area. We must have looked like the perfect family, but I knew it was all a lie.

Life was so much better for me in Italy during the past six years. No family, no drama, no hassle. *Relocating is everything.*

Relocating certainly looked like it worked for Matt, too. I was glad he was able to find love with his wife, Carmen, after spending so many years in jail for attempted murder. Even though he was a little rough around the edges, he didn't seem capable of such violence. Despite what he had done, I thought he deserved some happiness.

"Hey, Matt, I heard you're going to be a father in a couple of weeks," I said.

"That's right." A huge grin covered Matt's face.

"Wow, your first baby." A smile spread across my face at the possibility of having my first niece. A baby girl who I could design dresses for would set it off, especially since I had no relationship with Lisa's sons, Phil Jr., Andrew, or Johnathan. My joy became bigger with the vision of the outfits I planned to make.

"I'd be more excited if he and the baby lived on the East Coast, but I don't suppose you'd consider moving back," Lisa said to Matt.

"Never!" Matt shook his head and hands.

"Right. You love California, don't you?" I smiled my biggest fake smile.

"Yeah, I do. I know I'm going to get my big break soon. But never mind me. Are you all right? You don't look so good," he said to me.

"I'm fine, just a little stressed out about this Raquel thing." I paced back and forth.

"Hey, I hear that." Matt sighed.

"That's understandable under the circumstances." Lisa had been coming to my defense since childhood.

"I'll get us all some coffee and I'll be right back. Why don't you sit down?" Matt signaled me to sit.

"Thanks." I sat on a soft blue sofa and rested my head in my hands.

"Don't worry. All of this pain will soon be over one way or another." Lisa ran her hands through her hair.

I looked up and for the first time in my life, I saw fear evident in Lisa's dark eyes. She said it would soon be over, but I didn't know how it would end. This kind of aimless ache was rooted; it would never be over.

Through the glass window, I reassessed Raquel, Mama's child, and tried to love her for Mama's sake. I wondered if she was ever lovable and innocent. Surely she must have started out that way. A moment of natural compassion made me wonder what happened to make her so bitter. I thought that maybe during this trip I would find out.

Matt returned with the coffee and put the three cups on the little table.

"Hey, when was the last time you saw Mama?" Matt pulled on the strap of Lisa's leather tote.

"Yesterday. Unfortunately, I had to tell her about Raquel," Lisa said.

"And you, Makaeli?" Matt scratched his chin.

"Oh, uh, I don't know. It's been at least six years for

me." I folded my legs and started biting my nails. "I never liked to see her like that. It's too weird."

Guilt fell over me and I couldn't think of anything else to say.

"Don't worry. We'll all go to see Mama later on." Lisa looked over at me with her eyebrows raised.

I unfolded my legs and sat up straight. "That's fine. Of course we'll go to see her."

"It will be good to see her. I know what you mean, though, Makaeli. Mama is real different than she was back in the day." Matt stood to put his hand in his pockets.

"I wish I knew her when she was normal," I said.

"Makaeli, don't be so—" Lisa put her hands on her hips and threw her head to the side.

"What? Honest?" I knew it was getting hot now.

"No, hateful," Lisa said.

"It's true, though, isn't it? I'm sorry if I can't pretend that we're this happy family." Contempt spilled over from my heart onto my tongue.

"I didn't ever say we were," Lisa said.

"No, you didn't, but you never talked about the problems either," I said. "Like the mother I didn't have and the father I know nothing about."

"What do you mean we never talked? I was only trying to—" Lisa said.

"I know, I know. But you can't protect me forever." My eyes locked with hers.

"Hey, ladies, I think we need to chill out a little." Matt stretched his long, muscular arms around both of our shoulders.

"I'm not angry, Matt. I just want to keep it real without everybody else getting an attitude," I assured him.

"Makaeli Lovechild Hunt!" Lisa began looking around. *Reputation is everything.*

"Lisa, you and Phil did your best, but there were still

days when I needed to know what pushed our mother over the edge. And why I couldn't even say my father's name in the house. Still can't mention him without a fight," I said.

"Oh, come on. Nobody stopped you from—" Lisa said.

"Really? Then why was I told so casually that my father had a heart attack, died and I was never allowed to attend a funeral, see a grave or anything?" I didn't even blink.

"You were too young." Lisa's eye began to twitch.

"At eight years old? Okay, then why did I have to endure those double-edged remarks coming out of the sides of your mouths whenever you thought I couldn't hear you? As if my father was a nobody."

"No one ever said that. Oliver Hunt was a prominent attorney," Lisa said.

"Prominent?" My mouth dropped open. "I've never heard you give him any respect."

"That's a lie," Lisa said.

"It's true; yet it was as if there was this sacred memorial to your father, the late great Douglass Matthew Cambell, military hero, civil rights activist and father of the year."

Lisa sucked her teeth. "You're exaggerating."

"I wish I were. Since your father was so perfect, who could compete with that? How could my father compete with being black?" I was fuming.

"Oh, come on. I was eighteen and a half years old when Mama brought that man into our lives. There is more to it than that."

"Is there? Then tell me what else there is. Let's keep it real." I trembled from years of frustration.

Lisa and Matt looked at each other briefly then turned back to face me. No doubt they were surprised by my wrath.

"We're sorry you're taking it like this, but peace out. We didn't mean no harm, baby girl," Matt said.

My mind went back to the note, that carefully preserved piece of history that, in and of itself, was a mystery. *What does it really mean?*

"Look, I'm all grown up now," I said.

"We've always tried—" Lisa began.

"I know you've tried to protect me, but it didn't work." The words had grown from years of suppression, and I couldn't wait to shoot them from my mouth. *Ammunition.*

Lisa wiped a tear from her eye, grabbed me and squeezed like Aunt Lucy did when Uncle Mark passed away. Her intensity seemed out of place, and I fought myself not to push away from her.

At that moment, Phil walked in and she let me go. She went to embrace him, but he held her slightly away from him.

"What's wrong, Lisa?" Phil's eyebrows were raised as he looked over his glasses.

"It's nothing, Phil. Makaeli and I just got into it, that's all." Lisa immediately regained her composure. No one would accept her falling apart. She was the one who usually held things together.

Phil hugged me, and I was ashamed of my outburst. He was a peaceful man, and the last thing I wanted to do was to make him feel awkward. His only fault was working too much. Even through his thick lenses, I could still see his disappointment.

"We're a family," Phil said.

"I know that. I didn't mean to sound like we aren't." I put on my apologetic look. "I just want everyone to stop hushing me like a kid."

"I understand. It's good to see you." Phil reached over to squeeze my hand. "I've always been sure of one thing: that Lisa is the backbone of this family." Phil's eyes narrowed.

"No one is attacking Lisa." I clapped lightly. "In fact, I applaud her efforts."

Phil still looked young in his khakis and button-down shirt. I could see that he hadn't gained much weight in all these years. The small patches of gray were the only hint of his age that I noticed. I was proud of him for working out and taking care of himself. He was four years older than Lisa, but he had always taken an active approach to his health with frequent jogging, weight lifting and a fat free diet.

"Hi, Matt. I'm sorry I didn't speak to you right away, man. I guess I got caught up in the moment." Phil patted Matt on the back.

"I know. This Raquel thing has us all tripping," Matt said.

Unable to suppress my emotions, I slipped into Phil's arms in search of a childhood safety I once knew there. He hugged me back and when the tears came, he didn't even seem to mind. He grabbed Matt's and Lisa's hands and pulled us into what became a group hug.

"No matter what, we're family." Phil swallowed hard as if there were a lump in his throat.

"True," Matt said.

For a minute, it seemed as if we were perfect, lacking nothing; yet we stood in our individual shoes, knowing that if we walked a mile in anyone else's, it would still be filled with pain. Despite my attempts to bask in the present, my mind kept going back to the note. Prepared to visit Mama, I knew the day would certainly get more difficult.

Chapter Eight

Lisa

When Phil said goodbye, I followed him around the corner to the elevator.

Two nurses, probably in their mid-twenties, passed by in their tight little skirts, talking. One of them wore her hair in long corkscrew twists and the other wore hers in short, thick curls. They were very cute. Instantly, I hated them both for their youthful energy and for the possibilities ahead of them. With my failing marriage and all the physical and emotional changes my unexpected pregnancy would bring, my possibilities were over.

Phil turned his attention toward me. "You take it easy today."

"I will, and thanks for coming." I was drawn to his compassionate nature. He used to be like this all of the time, but not anymore.

"No problem. I meant what I said. We're a family." He put his fist up to my chin.

"Speaking of family, I need to talk to you about something soon. How does your schedule look for later on today or tomorrow?" I was glad to sense some warmth, even if only for a few minutes.

"Right now it looks doable. Are you okay?" He pulled out a small planner and studied it in a very matter-of-fact way.

"I'm fine. It's two o'clock and we're about to go see Mama."

"Be careful. I know how those visits upset you." He put the planner back into his pocket and took off his glasses.

"Right." I didn't know how to respond to that. It was embarrassing to have a family with a history as shaky as mine had.

"And Lisa," Phil said as he grabbed my hand.

"Yes?" His touch was almost more than I could bear. Two months of longing for intimacy had brought me to this point, where not even the slightest brush against the skin was taken for granted. I wondered if it meant something to him too.

"Look out for Makaeli. You've got the opportunity to turn things around." His words chilled the moment.

"I'll try." After digging for the words, my mouth felt dry. *Stop hounding me.*

"I appreciate that." He squeezed my hand and then let it go.

He was already in the elevator when I called his name.

"Phillip?"

"Yes?"

"I love you." I let it loose in one breath and hoped it would find solace.

"I'll see you later." He didn't commit to anything, but he smiled as the doors closed.

Wrong time for everything, especially truth.

I ducked into the restroom before anyone else could see me. Cool water on my face usually did the trick, but I was feeling exceptionally nauseated and dizzy. I went into the stall and leaned over the toilet, waiting to see what would come up.

Only tears came, but I managed to choke back the sobbing. After using nearly half of the toilet paper left on the roll to dry my eyes, I leaned up against the door of the stall. I knew I had to come out sooner or later, but I was in no hurry. I had nothing to come out to. So I stayed in a little longer, whimpering slightly and mumbling to myself. I must have sounded like Mama during one of her relapses, but for the first time, I didn't care. *Pull yourself together, Lisa.* Then I began to do something mysterious, something I had not done for most of my adult life. I prayed.

I leaned my back against the door and put my hands together. "Lord, I've been hearing about you here and there my whole life, and if you're really out there, then please help me. Not that I expect an answer, but I do need one. I always thought this religious stuff was for losers and old people who had no life, but now I'm beginning to wonder."

When I was done, I neatened my clothes and hair before leaving the stall.

As soon as I came out, I saw Lashawn looking in the mirror and applying her makeup.

"Hey, girl, was that you in there talking to yourself?" Lashawn said.

"Actually, I was praying." I washed my hands at the sink.

"Praying? I knew you were down, but I never knew you prayed," she said.

"I didn't used to, but I'm desperate." I signaled for Lashawn to come over to the wall farthest away from the door. I couldn't chance anyone overhearing my business.

"Desperate?" Lashawn raised her eyebrows at me.

"Yeah, desperate. I've got absolutely nothing to lose."

"That's true. I just never—"

I took a deep breath. "Years ago, Makaeli worked for

this older lady named Mrs. Pearl, a really nice lady, and to make a long story short, her spirituality seemed to rub off on Makaeli."

"Spirituality?"

"I mean Makaeli picked up on whatever Mrs. Pearl had. This lady practically lived at the church, and she started taking Makaeli with her all the time."

"I know the type."

"At first I disapproved, but Makaeli was so hard to deal with back then, I just gave up." I leaned up against the wall. "Next thing we knew, Makaeli was calling on the Lord all the time during those last months before her high school graduation."

"Really? I don't remember that."

"You were living in Michigan at the time."

"Oh." Lashawn leaned against a sink and began drumming her fingers on it.

"I thought Makaeli was going to end up like my Aunt Lucy."

"Good old Aunt Lucy. Now, I remember her."

"Please, don't remind me. Now, she was a mess, an embarrassment to Mama's side of the family, always hollering and falling out with the Holy Ghost."

"Just like my grandmother." Lashawn chuckled.

"But Makaeli turned out to be different in a good way. Her attitude changed and—"

"So what does that have to do with your sudden change of heart?" Lashawn stood up straight, grabbed both of my arms and looked me straight in the eyes.

"Maybe it's not so sudden. I mean, I always knew there had to be a creator of the universe."

"Right." Lashawn let go of me and put her hand to her forehead.

"A part of me wanted to get involved back then and confront them about this God they were talking about."

"So why didn't you?"

"Because I felt like a fool, so I didn't." I leaned in close to Lashawn. "I just stood back and watched my sister smiling and changing before my eyes."

"Don't worry about all that church stuff. It's just a bunch of happy songs and happy words. Phoniness, really. Those people aren't any better off than we are."

"That's what I used to think too. I made up my mind that as long as I wasn't hurting anyone, I'd be okay."

"But you don't feel that way anymore?" Lashawn's pupils grew large.

"Well, now I know I did hurt a few people, so I guess I was wrong. Not on purpose, but I did hurt people just the same. So, like I said before, I'm beginning to wonder. *Who do I call on when there is no one else to call on?*"

"And you thought you'd try prayer?" Lashawn shook her head and started walking toward the door.

"Shouldn't I at this point?"

"Sure, why not? There is nothing wrong with that, honey. My grandmother always told me to pray."

"Really? You never told me that."

"It never came up. Look, I'll talk to you later. I've got to run." Lashawn ran out of the ladies' room like she was on fire. It was obvious how she felt about the God stuff.

I took another minute to compose myself and to fix my makeup before I left the restroom. As soon as I opened the door, I felt a finger on my shoulder that made me jump. There was Matt.

"Don't ever do that," I said.

"Sorry." Matt backed away a little.

I followed him down the hallway, back to the waiting area. "Where is Makaeli?"

"Water fountain," Matt said.

"Good." I sighed.

"What's so good about it? We've got to handle our business."

"I know that, but I'm ready to go." I belted my coat and walked forward.

"Are we going to tell her tonight? I say we get it over with." Matt's voice was barely above a whisper.

"I don't know, Matt. She'll probably never forgive me." I tried to imitate his volume, but it was difficult to keep my emotion contained.

"I think you're tripping." Matt zipped his jacket.

"I'm not."

A pretty red-haired nurse passed by and smiled at Matt. He smiled back.

"We've got to tell her," Matt said.

"Now you're riding me, Matt, and I'm the one who usually does the riding."

"We've got to tell her now."

"Then you tell her." I raised my voice in frustration. My hands rested on my hips and as we turned, we looked into Makaeli's face.

"Tell me what?" Makaeli leaned over the two of us, waiting for an answer.

Chapter Nine
Makaeli

L isa and Matt managed to avoid my question. It was obvious they had something they wanted to say to me, but I figured it was more of what I didn't want to hear, so I decided to play their game for a while. I'd confront them again when the time was right.

I threw my coat over my shoulder and followed my siblings out of the building.

At Saint Ann's Psychiatric Hospital, the smell of rubber and sanitized plastics was almost too much for me to take in. The room was institutionally cool and sterile, with boring pastel walls and gray tiled floors. The windows were all barred and the doors were all latched. A guard stood in a booth in the lobby. Security was everything at Saint Ann's. The silence hurt my conscience.

For years I believed Mama's mental health was ruined by my late birth. But Lisa, being a woman of extreme reason, assured me that my theory was preposterous. Then I wondered if the divorce inadvertently caused Mama's problems or if the illness itself drove my father away. Although it was clear that my family circle believed it was all my father's fault, I didn't know which was the truth. They were all rumors I caught in the wind from one-sided telephone conversations, through closed doors and from glasses against walls.

Before Lisa sat down by the window, she straightened her collar and her hair. Then she crossed her legs in typical "Lisa style," holding Mama's bouquet of flowers in front of her. Matt and I plopped down across from her and waited for Mama to be brought in.

A chocolate brown nurse with deep dimples dragged herself in, wearing a tight-fitting uniform and long black braids. She was carrying a tray. She spoke briefly to two male patients who were playing checkers and then she disappeared through a steel door. It seemed like an eternity before Mama was wheeled in. A dark-haired medical assistant accompanied her. She rolled Mama into the room and then quietly walked away.

There sat Tanya Cambell–Hunt, once a stunning woman, according to her pictures. She used to have smooth caramel skin, deep oval eyes and wild, wavy black hair. Now she was a woman whose suffering took all dignity from her. A crust of tears were dried around her eyes and there were lines, looking like drawn ones, by her once dainty mouth. A smile should have been there, but it wasn't. Instead, she was swollen and discolored, probably from the anti-psychotic medication.

Lisa broke the awkward silence.

"Hi, Mama. We brought your favorite flowers." Lisa extended a bouquet of fresh white roses.

Mama wheeled herself over to the visitors' couch where Matt and I were sitting. Lisa and Matt pulled Mama's unwilling body close to theirs, with the roses still in her lap. Her arms were still limp around theirs. I stood hesitantly and brushed my lips gently across Mama's cheek. The blank look in her eye chilled me. Suddenly, it was as if she had been awakened from a dream. She grabbed Lisa by the hand and kissed it.

"It's so good to see you, Lisa." Mama didn't let go of Lisa's hand.

Matt and I shot each other a glance.

"Mama, we're all glad to see you too." Lisa managed to pull her hand away from Mama.

"I know. I'm glad to see everyone. Matthew, is that you, boy?" Mama asked.

"Yes, it's me, all the way from Los Angeles, California," Matt said.

"California? That's why you haven't been here to see me." Mama's eyes didn't stray from Matt.

"Mama, Matt is married now, remember? He lives in California with his wife, Carmen, and they have a baby on the way." Lisa helped to fill in the blanks.

"Married, yes, I remember. Such a shame you moved out. You used to take such good care of the girls." Mama looked sad.

"He did, Mama, but that was a long time ago. We're all grown up now and don't need protecting anymore. Besides, you'll be having another grandchild soon. Won't that be nice?" Lisa said.

"Yes, that would be very nice." Mama looked down at her lap.

"Makaeli is here too, Mama, all the way from Venice. How do you like that?" Lisa paved the way.

Mama turned to me and looked me up and down. Then she smiled.

"Lovechild? I like that very much. Come and give me a hug, my children." Mama's smile began to fade.

We moved in carefully to hug her and already I felt drained.

"Where is Raquel? Is she dead?" Mama had a faraway look in her eye.

"No, Mama, she's not dead. She's still in ICU, and the doctors are taking good care of her," Lisa said.

"Those doctors aren't taking good care of her. Lisa, you're a doctor. You should be there with her." Mama's eyes narrowed.

"Well, I've been with her since yesterday." There was an obvious disappointment in Lisa's eyes.

"No, I mean you should be her doctor. You've got all your medical degrees and I've got all those medical school bills to prove it. You should be practicing medicine." Mama spoke with authority.

"I stopped working full time, Mama, so I could raise my boys and have more time with my family, remember? And I don't even work in the same hospital Raquel is in." Lisa looked down.

"Seems like you should've had your sister in the same hospital you work at. Are you ashamed of her?" Mama sat up straight in her chair and looked directly at Lisa.

"Mama, you know I work in the neonatal unit with the new babies. And Raquel had no insurance, so she couldn't have stayed at Mercy." Lisa didn't look directly at Mama anymore, probably fearing the consequences.

"Well, what kind of name is that for a hospital if they won't act accordingly and help people? You doctors and your so-called health care system. I don't care for it, you know. So what if she didn't have insurance? Does that make her less human?" The lawyer in Mama was stirred up now.

Poor dogged-out Lisa. I almost felt sorry for her, until I remembered how she bossed and manipulated everyone else.

"I'm sorry, Mama, but it's not my system." Lisa seemed as humble as she could possibly be. It was only Mama who could take down the formidable Lisa Jackson a couple of notches and come out without a scratch.

"Enough of this foolishness. Makaeli Lovechild, now, where have you been? Don't you care about me anymore?" Mama's look was piercing.

"Oh, Mama, of course I do." I reached out to touch her hand. Mama moved hers before our fingers could make contact.

"Makaeli has been a designer in Italy, and doing quite well for a few years now, Mama. You knew that, didn't you?" Lisa looked relieved to have escaped the previous subject.

"No, I didn't know that." Mama's eyes were still and dark.

"You've just forgotten, that's all. And Matt here has been singing at all the hot spots in L.A., really making a name for himself," Lisa added.

"Rapping really, Mama," Matt said.

"Rapping? Don't tell me you're fooling with that mess." Mama turned her eyes to Matt.

"But that's what I do, Mama." Matt looked down at the floor.

"That's what you do for a living? When did you get out of jail, boy?" Mama sat up straight in her chair.

"I've been out a long time now." Matt straightened his posture before he answered, looking a little embarrassed.

"Good, because I cried for you when you were in jail. Being locked down is a bad thing. I'm locked down now." There was the sound of tears in Mama's voice before we actually saw any.

"Oh, Mama, don't say that," Lisa said.

My feet felt like they were frozen and stuck to the floor. Not a single word came from my mouth.

"I'll say what I want. Makaeli has her designs and Matt has his rapping. Raquel has her drug addiction, but what do you have that's all yours, Lisa?" Mama raised her finger at Lisa.

"I'm a happy homemaker, so I guess I can say I have a happy home." Lisa looked around the room as if she needed our support.

"Lies! You're a doctor. Don't let anyone take that away from you. You should be practicing medicine." Mama's voice was firm.

"But it's my choice, and right now I choose to practice medicine on a part-time basis. I'll get back in full swing when Johnathan graduates from—" Lisa's explanation sounded desperate.

She didn't owe anyone an explanation. Least of all Mama.

"Graduates? It's not like the boy is still in diapers. I raised all of you and still worked full-time the whole time. Every day until . . ." Mama put her hand up to her forehead.

"I'm sorry. I didn't mean to upset you. Phillip takes good care of us." Lisa started fussing with Mama's armrest.

"Takes care of you? Take care of yourself. Phillip is a fine doctor, but so are you. Don't you ever forget it." Mama squeezed Lisa's hand. It seemed like forever before she let it go. The sweat trickled down Lisa's brow. That was the way it was. You never knew what would set Mama off.

"If only Raquel had gotten on her feet." Mama shook her head.

"Yes, she had just gotten a job as a waitress at a little place downtown," Lisa said.

"A club, no doubt. A job, with her record? Are the people who hired her blind or fools?" Mama raised her eyebrows as she often did when she was frustrated.

"An older gentleman decided to give her a second chance." Embarrassment colored Lisa's face. I tried to look away, but she caught a glimpse of me staring at her.

"Second chance? Ha. He was probably going to use her," Mama said. "Probably would've had her dancing on top of tables."

"Maybe things would have worked out for her," Lisa said.

"Worked out? That drug thing has worked her into a hole she shouldn't be in. I've been in a hole and there is no life there," Mama said.

"You're right," Matt said.

"Mmmm. Makaeli, you'll be out of school soon, won't you, dear?" Mama motioned for me to come closer.

I kneeled down in front of her with my hands at my sides and I felt her fuzzy slippers against my knuckles.

"No, I'm already out of school. I work now." The right answer was unclear, not because she was fragile, but because she was so unpredictable. She had been this way for so long that I couldn't remember when she had been different.

The diagnosis of schizoaffective disorder, along with post traumatic stress disorder, was a devastating event in all our lives. The hallucinations, the delusions, the overwhelming sadness and psychomotor disturbances. Who knew if she'd ever recover.

"When you graduate, don't let them drag you down, baby. You keep on moving, you hear?" She grabbed both of my arms and held them tight.

"Okay." I didn't know what else to say. She was drifting.

"When you stop moving, you lose ground and get old. You lose everything around you, including yourself. I always wanted my own law practice, but—" Mama held me and leaned back in her wheelchair.

"I know, Mama, your health." My arms loosened her grip as I raised them.

"No, my health had nothing to do with it. I gave up. I stopped moving." Mama began to moan softly.

"Okay. Calm down now." Lisa jumped in as if it were her job to be family lifeguard.

"I'm tired now. I want to rest." Mama began to rub her arms and legs. As she lifted her gown slightly, scars that she had put on herself from constant rubbing became visible. There were separate scars from the straps. This reminded me that she was still contained and that she would still have to be.

Mama ran her hand over her mildly pruned face. She looked aggravated, the way she squinted her eyes. When she did this, it made her look like a dark Asian. It was funny how an expression could change her whole appearance at times.

"All right then, bye, Mama. We'll come again soon." Lisa stood and leaned over to give her a hug. Mama used Lisa's arm to pull herself forward and to balance herself. Lisa called over one of the nurses for assistance, and we waved as she prepared to be rolled away.

"I don't like the bars on the windows. When can I go home?" Mama grabbed Lisa's sleeve and looked into her eyes for an answer. So much pressure rested on the oldest.

"Soon, Mama, soon," Lisa said.

Lies, all lies. The words sounded like crystal in my ears. When the lies were first told to me, I believed them. Mama would be coming home soon, very soon, they said.

By fourteen, I stopped pretending she would one day meet me at the bus stop, put her arms around me, or take me out shopping like the other moms did. I knew then that if she had already missed so many rough years before, nothing would give her the courage to come back now. If she hadn't missed her sweet little girl, I doubted that she missed the tall, awkward stranger I had become.

But at twenty-nine years old, the truth had been painted gray.

Matt and I rushed to hug Mama as if we were cued. Then we stood back and watched as she and the nurse disappeared through the double doors.

When we left Saint Ann's, each of us walked silently down to the parking lot level two and rode away. The potholes underneath Lisa's new BMW confirmed that this was really New Jersey. Like it or not, I was home.

Chapter Ten

Lisa

Since the moment we left the building, there wasn't much talking going on. It sounded just like the old days. Perpetual silence. A stranger would probably think we didn't even know each other, and in a sense, we didn't. I didn't know what to say to those two weirdos: Matt with the earring and tattoo, and Makaeli, flaunting her high yellow color like it was some kind of badge. Then there were the worn out jeans and unacceptable hair. I was almost ashamed to be seen with them, but I knew I had to deal with it.

As we rolled out onto the highway, we each sank back into the leather seats of my car to contemplate our dilemma. I turned the radio dial to the oldies station and put the volume on low. It was just loud enough to drown out my thoughts and keep me entertained on the bumpy road home. Home, where all of our lives were built, intertwined and where they slowly deteriorated.

I watched the streetlights change color again and again, bringing us farther away from this busy part of the city. People walked back and forth on the pavement, some carrying shopping bags or briefcases and some empty-handed, hastily going about their daily business. Cars zoomed past us with their frustrated owners honking their horns and swerving in and out of lanes. Impatiently and deliberately, they went on their way, these strangers who mocked slowness. What was the hurry? I wondered. I was in no rush at all. Maybe youth had a reason to hurry. I didn't remember.

"I'm going to pull into this Amoco." I began to search for an empty parking space.

"I didn't know you needed gas," Makaeli said.

"No, I don't. I just want to grab something to drink and maybe a little snack." I hopped out of the car, already feeling a little dizzy.

Inside the convenience store, the restroom was small but sufficient. I looked at my tired face in the fingerprint-smudged mirror and pulled back the bloated skin of my cheeks. The pathetic pregnancy look had started already. There were two stalls and one was occupied, so I pushed the door to the other one. I quickly latched it with one hand and unbuttoned my pants with the other. My bladder couldn't hold out any longer. I felt foolish going through this inconvenience at my age. I should've stayed on the pill.

When I came out of the restroom, a sharp craving for Doritos commanded me to the chip section. Before I found what I was looking for, however, my stomach began to rumble and nausea set in. So I headed back to the restroom instead. *Get yourself together, Lisa.*

Matt was standing at the snack counter buying gum and cigarettes. Unfortunately, walking by him quickly didn't facilitate the escape I hoped for. He tugged at my coat and my eyes caught his.

"Are we going to tell her tonight?" He fumbled with his thin mustache.

"I don't know, Matt. I don't know if I can. And this is not the place to discuss this. She almost caught us talking the last time, remember?" He was out of his mind to antagonize me like this.

"Never mind that. I say we tell her tonight when we get home."

"Look, I don't know if I'm up to it tonight." I put one hand over my eyebrows.

"Up to it?"

"Matt, just get out of my face, please," I said.

"What's wrong with you?"

"Nothing is wrong with me. Just get out of my way, please." I tried to grab hold of Matt, but I stumbled and missed his arm. I didn't know what was happening, but my body started to shake uncontrollably.

"Lisa."

"Matt, I can't—" I felt my body dropping down as I grasped air. Then I felt myself hit the floor.

"Lisa!" Matt's voice was the last thing I heard before the room went black.

Chapter Eleven

Makaeli

Sitting in the back seat with my forehead pressed against the window, I wondered what was taking Matt and Lisa so long.

I looked out the window and saw two boys building a snowman. They reminded me of what Lisa's boys used to look like when they were young. *I probably wouldn't even recognize them now.*

Just as I was about to lean over the front seat and change the radio station from that oldies garbage Lisa was listening to, I saw Matt coming toward me with Lisa wrapped around his arm.

"What happened to her?" I got out to help Matt with Lisa.

"I don't know, but she passed out for a minute. The store manager helped us." Matt shut the car door on the passenger's side and went to get into the driver's seat.

"It must be the stress. Are you okay?" I looked into Lisa's face. Her eyes were puffy and her hair was out of place. Not at all like Lisa.

"Yes, I'm okay. Let's just go home, please." Lisa reclined in her seat and put her head back against the headrest.

"Okay." Matt gave her one more glance before he started up the car.

"I'll be better when I get home," Lisa snapped.

"If you say so, but if you're not feeling better soon, I'm making a stop at the nearest emergency room." Matt kept one hand on the steering wheel and he held out the other hand to touch Lisa's hair.

"Don't be overly dramatic. I'm fine," Lisa pushed his hand away and started to fix her hair.

"He's right. You should be checked out." Although I was wearing my seatbelt, I managed to push my body forward in the backseat. I put my hand on Lisa's shoulder.

"Hey, why is everybody poking me? I'm the doctor here, remember? I know what I'm talking about." Lisa peeled my fingers off of her.

"All right, whatever you say," Matt said.

"I'll be fine once I get home and get a little food in me." Lisa motioned toward her mouth.

We pulled out of the service station parking lot and into the street.

"Yeah, food sounds good to me." Matt took out a cigarette and popped it into his mouth.

"Oh no, you're not smoking in my new car." Lisa snatched the cigarette out of Matt's mouth before he could light it.

"Sorry, I forgot." Matt took it from her and put it away.

"You should be." Lisa crossed her arms and folded her legs.

"You know Lisa don't play that." I smiled and tapped him on the head.

"It has been a long day. Don't tick me off, you two," Lisa said.

"I ain't making no promises." Matt stuffed a stick of peppermint-flavored gum into his mouth instead.

"Very funny." Lisa didn't smile.

I didn't comment because I was already lost in the drive. Soon I began to see streets lined with evergreens, larger houses and wider spaces between properties. Children played in their backyards instead of on the pavement. Expensive vehicles decorated the driveways. I was home.

It was always a beautiful neighborhood, but I never liked the cookie-cutter sameness that ran from driveway to driveway. Same luxury cars and SUVs, same brick faces, same two-piece suits and designer attaché cases. The air, although fresh, was one of blatant conformity and seemed to stifle any sense of creativity I could ever think of having.

As we pulled up to the red brick colonial house, I took a deep breath.

"It has been a long time since I've seen this house." I put my hands over my mouth.

"Too long." Lisa looked back at me briefly.

"When was the last time?" Matt opened his door and walked over to open mine.

I climbed out, but not without hesitation. "The last time I was here was the day I moved to my own studio apartment in New York City," I said.

"Sounds cool," Matt said.

"It was cool. I had two other roommates, but it was still nice." I stared straight ahead. "I had just graduated from high school and I was really excited about going to F.I.T."

"I'm sorry I missed that." Matt took his backpack out of the trunk.

"Me too," I said.

"Did Phil and Lisa help you move out?" Matt helped Lisa out of the car.

"No. They were too busy. A few friends from school did," I said.

"I remember it like it was yesterday. She arranged for two hoodlums to help her because Phil and I had to work," Lisa said.

"I'm surprised you remember. That was ten years ago. And those guys weren't hoodlums," I said.

"Whatever," Lisa said.

"And I thought I packed light." Matt took my purse from me and held it up high.

"My bag is at the hotel," I answered, but his words and mine had vanished.

"Oh, I thought you were staying here with us," Matt said.

"No, I'm sorry I didn't tell you." I kept walking toward the door.

"There is plenty of room." Lisa opened her arms wide.

I paused. "Thanks, but I think it's best this way."

"Excuse me?" Lisa put her hands on her hips.

"I mean it's easier for me to get some work done, and I left all my stuff at the hotel," I said.

"I see." Lisa unlocked the door, disarmed the alarm and led the way.

I took a deep breath and followed Lisa, relieved by my narrow escape. My surroundings were captivating. The sturdy mahogany front door, the scent of fresh flowers and polished wood filled the foyer.

Matt followed behind us. Then he took our coats and hung them in the hall closet. He may have looked like a thug, but he was still a gentleman.

Slowly I turned into the living room and looked up at the vaulted ceiling. Surprisingly, the room didn't seem as big as it used to. The antique grandfather clock still stood in the corner and Mama's portrait still hung over the fireplace.

I walked over to the Queen Anne high-backed chair, slipped into it and rubbed my hands against its soft fabric. The first few years Mama was gone, Lisa wouldn't let anyone sit in this chair, Mama's chair. As time went on, though, it became less and less sacred. Eventually Phil and Lisa both took turns sitting in it to watch the evening news.

Everything was neat and in place, much different than the way I kept my villa. A few pieces of the furniture were new, but even the style of those reminded me of growing up here. Everything did. The way the ferns hung from the huge bay windows, the way the pictures were arranged on the armoire and the color of jade that Mama loved so. It was everywhere. Lisa disappeared into the kitchen, while Matt followed me in and stood facing me.

"It feels good to finally be home, doesn't it?" Matt looked directly into my eyes.

"I guess so." I wasn't so sure.

"If only Mama could be here with us," Lisa said when she came back with a bag of chips and a doughnut. She took off her shoes and sat down on the couch.

"That would really be something," I said.

There had been a time when all I wanted was for Mama to come home, but that dream faded long ago. All that was left were her things: her crystal candy dish and porcelain china dolls sitting in the china cabinet amongst the precious breakable dishes. If they were moved too much, like the dream of Mama coming home, they would be shattered forever.

"If Mama was here now, she'd probably have a pot of shrimp gumbo on." Matt joined Lisa on the couch. "I sure miss that Cajun cooking."

"All of this while preparing legal briefs, chatting with the district attorney, and fighting for some community cause." Lisa smiled at me and waited for me to smile back. *Mama's image is everything.*

Everyone had such good things to say of Tanya Cambell-Hunt—everyone except me, that is. The talk was always about Mama "the outstanding lawyer" or Mama "the pillar of society" and about how she worked magic in the household and the community until the manic monster took over her soul.

Most of me wanted to know what went wrong, what traumatized her, but a small part of me wanted the answer to be buried forever. I closed my eyes, trying to flush away the recollections, but they came rushing in. *Not the Mama I remember.*

I remembered being five years old, peeking in through the half-cracked door of Mama's bedroom and smelling the nasty tobacco smoke as it crept into my nostrils. Going in without a sound, the heels of my shoes were careful not to touch the well-polished hardwood floors. Moving up closer through the fog, I saw her. Her face could hardly be seen through the darkness. All of the lights were off and the satin curtains were drawn. Another typical Saturday. My small hand moved toward the shaded lamp, but she grabbed it with hers and pushed it away. Then she told me she didn't like light, that some things were better hidden in darkness.

I walked out of her bedroom, stopping only to look back at the lump under the satin comforter. From then on, I wondered what she thought I looked like in the light.

A tear tried to make its way out as I sat there, but I squeezed it back into my subconscious.

"How are the boys, Lisa?" I decided to change the mood.

"You know that Phil Jr. graduated summa cum laude and will be finishing up on his masters at Stanford this year, and Andrew is a senior at Princeton." Lisa stuffed her mouth with potato chips. She passed the bag to each of us, offering us some.

"Impressive." I took a few chips just to be polite.

"Johnathan is only a sophomore in high school, but he is in the honor society, of course."

"Of course," I said. "Is he around here somewhere?"

"No, actually he's staying at Phil's parents' house for a couple of weeks. I needed a little break during this time." Lisa uncrossed her legs and leaned forward as if she was about to stand.

"Right, with all the running back and forth to the hospital and everything," I said.

"Exactly. So between all the Raquel stuff, then transporting him to and from school and to and from his various activities, I was burned out after a day." Lisa walked over, reached behind me and adjusted the velour throw pillows.

"I don't know how you manage all that career, wife and motherhood stuff, even under normal conditions," I said.

"It isn't easy, I'll tell you that much. You guys want some real food to eat or something to drink? You're my guests now."

"Just a little something maybe." Matt never could resist Lisa's cooking. "But take it easy. Remember what happened earlier."

"Oh, don't worry about me. I'm just a little under the weather, probably coming down with the flu or something." Lisa hunched her shoulders. "I feel better now that I have something on my stomach."

"Just a little water for me, please." Food was the last thing on my mind.

"Water? Child, please. You never did eat much, did you? Too bad. You're going to eat something. You're home now." Lisa started toward the doorway.

"I'd like to use the bathroom to freshen up first," I said.

"Well, go right ahead. You remember where everything is. Use the one in Mama's room since it's downstairs and it's the best one in the house," Lisa said.

Immediately, I was tense. My heart started beating faster and the inside of my palms started sweating.

"No, that's okay. I'd rather use the downstairs guest room." I headed toward the French doors.

"Now, don't be silly. I want you to see all the work Phil and I did in there. We redid everything. I don't mean to brag, but it's gorgeous." Lisa stood in front of me and gently guided me in the direction of the master bedroom, Mama's room. "Besides, you're my baby sister, and I insist that you use the best." She reached over to pick up my bag, but I grabbed her hand.

"That's really not necessary."

"If I redecorated it, it's necessary," Lisa said.

"Well, if you insist." I lifted my back and walked slowly into Mama's bedroom. The décor drifted past my notice because the master bathroom was my problem. By the time I turned the knob, I was perspiring profusely and I thought I wouldn't make it.

First, I stuck my head in, carefully examining the three golden swans hanging on the wall, and the jade toilet seat cover. These were objects that transported my mind to a time when living had not been easy.

Then I made my entire body enter against its will.

The antique white paint and mahogany trim was fresh, but the painting hanging on the wall was the same. The same Victorian painting of the lady with the deep green eyes, framed in genuine mahogany. Then there was the antique tub with the golden legs. Finally, there was Mama's antique toilet. I had really hoped they had gotten rid of it.

Less than a minute later, I came out. Lisa and Matt were still standing in the same position.

"Well, that was quick. You must be on European speed, huh?" Lisa let herself smile.

"I can't use that bathroom." I didn't smile back.

"Don't be silly. Why not?" Lisa sounded like she had lost her patience.

"Because I was almost drowned in there."

"What are you talking about?"

"I'm talking about Raquel and how she almost killed me." I fell into my seat.

"Child, what do you mean by she almost killed you?" Lisa pressed.

"I'm talking about when I was seven. You and Phil had gone out of town and Raquel was high as usual." I went on to explain to them how Raquel almost took my life.

It wasn't the first time I was hit in the face, because I was used to Raquel's reign of terror on me, but it was the first time the sting of it was different. Her hands seemed like weapons of the severest kind, like steel knives that could slice my heart into a thousand pieces. But after the day she tried to drown me in Mama's antique toilet, my fear turned into disgust. I began to look at Raquel and the world through tainted eyes.

"Girl, what are you saying?" Lisa's eyes were a bulging red.

"Man, is this true?" Matt came up close to me.

"Would I make up something like that? For a long time I was angry with Mama for leaving me here with her crazy daughter," I said.

"I'm so sorry. I had no idea." Lisa's pupils were swollen with horror.

"I don't want your pity. I know you didn't know about this, but you knew she was beating me up all the time." I couldn't back down.

"Not like you say. I mean, we believed in discipline. Mama did too. But not like that." Lisa lowered her head.

"Yeah, well, this had nothing to do with discipline. Apparently no one explained the difference to Raquel." Perspiration ran from my forehead down my nose.

"Why didn't you say something?" Lisa was still calm.

"Would it have mattered if I told you that one thing?"

"Of course it would matter." Lisa turned away from me.

"You all knew she was smoking that pipe, and yet as long as she didn't do it around the house, as long as she didn't mess up the fine furniture, it was all hush-hush." I threw up my hands.

"Phil and I never condoned Raquel's behavior." Lisa walked toward me, raising her hands and her voice. She wasn't calm anymore.

"But you never put her out either. No matter how many times she messed up, you never put her out." I pointed to the door.

"Mama was against it," Lisa yelled.

"Why would you listen to her? Mama was insane." I picked up a throw pillow and threw it to the floor.

"She was not insane." Lisa picked up the pillow and placed it back on the couch.

"Mama is insane." I took up the pillow again and squeezed it to my chest.

"You take that back." Lisa shook her index finger at me.

"Whatever. You knew Raquel hated me." I wiped my tears with my hands.

"That's not fair." Lisa pulled the pillow from my arms and once again placed it on the couch.

"Fair?" I just knew she wasn't talking to me about what was fair.

"Raquel didn't hate you. You don't know everything," Lisa said.

"You should have told us and gave us a chance," Matt said.

"A chance? You had years of chances. But you went running off to your PTA meetings, and little league football with the boys, and the never-ending medical conventions with Phil and—" I stopped when I noticed Lisa's expression.

"And you blame me?" Lisa's eyes and mine met for a moment.

"No, I don't blame you. I blame myself for not putting a bullet through Raquel's head when I had the chance," I said.

"Makaeli." Matt touched my shoulder.

"Oh, come on, Matt. You weren't even around back then." I resented and resisted any signs of affection.

"I would have been if I could have," Matt said.

"Now, I don't believe that either. You got out on parole, walked into my life, pretended to be friendly, but did you stay around?"

"I couldn't. I—" Matt stuttered.

"You couldn't? You made yourself needed, made yourself trusted and then three years later you disappeared as suddenly as you came," I said.

"I had my reasons for leaving." Matt's voice quivered.

"Yeah, I'm sure you did, but I don't want to hear them. I'm not seventeen anymore," I said.

So fired up, I walked out of the living room, down the hall to the kitchen. Its mahogany cabinets and marble countertops looked the same, but the color scheme was different. I was relieved that there was no jade in the room. Lisa had decorated the room with lilac and lemon yellow flowered curtains, dishtowels and matching canisters. Lisa and Matt followed me in and sat at the mahogany table.

"We're sorry." Lisa reached across the table for my hand.

"I know you are. So am I." I took her hand.

"Raquel was apparently mentally unstable," Lisa said. "Can we please get past this?" Lisa held up two fingers as a peace symbol.

"We're sorry." Matt also held up two fingers.

"This isn't the sixties, but I accept. Peace is what I need, so—" I managed to bring up a hint of smile through my tears.

Lisa handed me paper towels to blow my nose. Then she led us back into the living room where we settled down in front of the big screen to watch television. Each of us sat on separate couches. Lisa flipped the channels with the remote until she stopped at a Lifetime movie. *How appropriate.* We watched in silence until the mood softened.

"Well, let's talk about something pleasant. Tell us all about Italy." Lisa smiled, showing her pretty white teeth.

"Well, it's more beautiful than you could ever imagine." I smiled back at her, grateful for the opportunity to bring her into my world.

"More beautiful than New Jersey?" Lisa spread her arms out and laughed heartily.

"I work in Milan. It's a busy city, and my place of business is located in a villa-styled building, much like where I live. Except that I live in Venice." I walked over to the window and opened the curtains.

"I've been to Paris and London, but I've always wanted to travel to Milan." Lisa came behind me and fluffed out the open curtains.

"Sounds cool, I guess." Matt leaned back in his chair.

"I live in Venice where the streets are mostly rivers," I said.

"Well, you always did like the water." Lisa shook her head.

"Being by the water in Venice is much better, though." I sat down across from them and changed my position as my excitement level increased.

"It sounds great, but you know how I hate the water." Lisa frowned.

"There is a lot of boat traffic, outdoor cafés, lots of pasta, and romantic nights by the water." With each sentence, I visualized what I missed so much. Especially Antonio.

"Romantic nights, huh? Anyone special?" Lisa was ready.

"No. I'm just speaking in general terms. It's a really nice place to live." I leaned forward in my seat.

"I don't think I could ever be tempted to leave the U.S., but if I did, I'd probably give it a try," Lisa said.

"The people there are much more liberal and more accepting of some things." *More accepting of me.*

"Like L.A." Matt put his hand out I gave him a high five.

"You and your L.A." Lisa turned to me. "Anyway, tell us about your company."

"Well, Designs by Makaeli is my life. It's a small company now, but I worked hard to get it." I spoke slowly, enjoying each word. "After grad school, I worked for many fashion houses."

"That sounds like fun," Matt said.

"It was anything but fun." I shook my head, remembering my hardships.

"Really?" Matt seemed surprised.

"Believe me, this little black girl did everything from dressing mannequins to sewing toilet covers before I finally got my break." I snapped my fingers three times.

"Your work got you noticed." Lisa clapped her hands.

"No, actually it was my legs that got me noticed, but after this dude named Mario Vitelli, who is big stuff in

Italy, took his eyes off of those, I was able to show him my work." I smiled.

"If you got it, flaunt it." Matt started to laugh.

"Well, you're resourceful," Lisa said. "That's great. And here you are."

"Here I am, and you'll be seeing my label in the U.S. very soon, hopefully," I said.

"It's good to know you've made it. I'm still waiting for my lucky break," Matt said.

"I wouldn't say I've made it, but my stuff is selling fast in Milan," I said.

"We're proud of you." Lisa patted me lightly on the head.

"Yeah, we are," Matt said.

"Thanks. I'm a little surprised that you approve." I was puzzled.

"Why?" Lisa seemed uneasy.

"There was a time when I thought you'd have been happier if I had chosen something more conservative, like law or banking." I focused my attention on her response, anxious to hear if she finally accepted me.

"Or medicine?" Lisa asked.

"Yes, or medicine." I wasn't sure her sentiments were genuine.

"Didn't I always encourage you to go for your dreams?" Lisa looked disappointed that I doubted her.

"Yes, but sometimes you made me feel like my dreams were your nightmares," I said.

"Oh, come on, stop." Lisa waved her hand.

"No, really. You used to suck your teeth whenever we talked about the college application process, like if I didn't go to Harvard or Cornell, I was doomed for life." I put my hands around my throat as if I were strangling myself.

"So dramatic," Lisa said. "That's not true. I did no such thing."

"Just for the record, I wouldn't have ever gone to any of those preppy ivy leagues even if I wasn't going to F.I.T. Those campuses just aren't my style. Maybe Penn State, Howard or Syracuse, but that's as stuffy as it gets for me." I looked into her eyes as I spoke.

"Your grades could have gotten you in, but it was that attitude of yours." Lisa jumped out of her seat.

"You're right. I had an attitude. Still do. Those ivy league people are just a little too stuck up for me. No offense." I could tell that even after all these years, Lisa couldn't stand to hear me talk like this. *Same old image-loving Lisa.*

"That same rebellious attitude." Lisa was trying hard to maintain her cool, but bits and pieces of anger were leaking through.

"I prefer to call myself independent," I said.

"I have another name for it." Lisa came right up to my face.

"Hey, hey, let's not get too serious, ladies. We're just having fun," Matt shouted.

"You always were a character." Lisa looked at Matt then sat back down.

"Yep." I was determined to taunt her.

"When seasons meant sporting events and proms to most kids, you marched to the beat of a different drummer," Lisa said. "In fact, a whole other band."

"Yeah, the seasons meant colors, cuts and prints to me. I was just weird that way, I guess," I said.

"Very weird," Lisa agreed.

"Leave her alone." Matt pretended to punch Lisa's arm.

"Fool, have you lost your mind?" Lisa really punched Matt's arm.

"Nobody took my designer goals seriously. Nobody except Mrs. Pearl," I said.

"You're lying. That's not true either," Lisa said.

"Just because I was a little taller than average, everyone at school wanted me to be a model. That used to make me so mad." I clenched my teeth in mock misery.

"It sure made you mad, but it shouldn't have. Look at you." Matt waved his hands. "Voila."

"Like I care about any of that." I sucked my teeth.

There was that so-called beauty element again. What was it with people and their preoccupation with the visual? Didn't they know there was more going on underneath a person's skin? My looks had never done anything except complicate what would have been otherwise simple situations. Sexual harassment, lost companionship, broken hearts, misinterpreted intentions, and a lack of professionalism amongst my male peers all stemmed from this so-called "runway look" of mine.

Lisa, who was obviously trying to hide her annoyance at this point, excused herself to the kitchen to make lunch.

I pulled out my ballpoint pen, took out my planner and began to scribble the theme for my new clothing line:

> *You look at me and all you see*
> *Are angles and lines, angles and lines*
> *Not the real me.*

This time I sat on the couch while Matt sat in Mama's chair with his feet on the mahogany center table. *Same Matt.* He playfully took off his baseball cap and placed it on my head.

"Lot of memories in this house." Through the window, I could see the backyard where Matt and I used to shoot hoops.

"Got that right." Matt stood next to me and looked outside.

"This room reminds me of the day Lisa told me you

were gone. I was sitting right over there." I pointed to the couch.

"That was a long time ago."

"I've been to hell and back since then." I was determined to be honest today, something I hadn't done very often.

"You took it hard, huh?" Matt looked surprised.

"Well, you never called to find out how I took it, did you? I know it has been a while, but to me it seems like just yesterday."

"To me too." Matt hung his head down.

"I took it very hard," I said.

"I'm sorry." Matt looked up for a moment, and then dropped his head again.

I wondered if he was really as ashamed as he looked.

"You don't have to be. That's just the way life is." I sat down again and folded my hands in front of me.

"You're right, but it isn't fair."

"Life isn't fair." I fought to contain my tears.

"You're still angry with me."

"Not really. It's just a sensitive topic for me. I mean, you were my defense and then you were gone." My reserve was melting.

"I doubt if you needed a defense with that mouth of yours." He attempted a smile, but I couldn't reciprocate.

"I was so lonely back then." I began to shake.

"I know."

"I had no real friends worth mentioning," I said in my softest voice.

"I remember," Matt said.

"I'm still lonely sometimes."

"I didn't know that." Matt looked troubled when he said this.

"And did you know I started drinking heavily on the day

you left and wasn't able to stop until years later?" I felt the emotion building up in me.

"What do you mean, drinking?" Matt raised his eyebrows.

"Just what it sounds like. I drank until I couldn't feel anything anymore."

It took years before I recognized that I had a problem and before I had the strength to get help. With the help of an Italian group for alcoholics, I was able to leave that part of me behind and get on with the business of designing, and designing my future, in particular.

"I didn't know about the drinking."

"I know you didn't," I said.

"I feel bad about that." Matt put his hands over his face.

"Don't."

"No, really I—"

"Don't worry. It's too late now." I walked to the other side of the room and sat down.

Matt didn't follow.

He'd never know the guilt and condemnation I felt, drowning myself in wine coolers and strawberry daiquiris and being useless to God. Matt would never know how not measuring up had brought me down.

Lisa called us in to the kitchen as she set a silver tray of turkey and cheese sandwiches, salad and a two liter bottle of Pepsi on the table. She was so domesticated. Cooking, cleaning and serving were her specialties. Nothing ever out of place or time. At the same time I admired her flair for order, I wanted to wrinkle the tablecloth, leave a few dirty dishes in the sink and throw a few articles of clothing around. That would make it all more human. Maybe even make her human.

Lisa sat in a high-backed chair at the head of the table with her carefully placed napkin and dainty silverware in front of her. Matt and I sat on each side of her and faked the etiquette we each knew Lisa expected. The awkward silence made the food go down like paste, and I washed it away with a cup of Pepsi. The hands on the clock seemed to stand still in this house of stone.

"I think Mama's visit went pretty well, considering," Lisa said, dipping salad into her bowl.

"Considering what, that we're still breathing or that she's still breathing?" I didn't want to sound harsh, but the truth was the light.

"No, considering her condition." Lisa wasn't smiling.

"It was good to see her anyway," Matt said.

"Yes, it's always good to see Mama, isn't it, Makaeli?" Lisa gestured for my response.

"Yeah." I didn't want to make any more waves.

Conversations were bittersweet and urging me to move on, to give up. Too much had gone on here. Some known things and some unknown things. What a family: psychotic Mama, stuck-up Lisa, dangerous Raquel, disappearing Matt and unlovable me.

Maybe there was something about this house with its cold crystal chandeliers and mocking marble arches. Maybe these were the things that ran Mama, Matt and me away. Who wanted to live in the perfect façade of this three-story house anyway? I didn't mean to yawn, but my dissatisfaction was rising up from the inside.

"Sweetheart, are you tired? You can take a quick nap before we go back to the hospital." Lisa looked at me hard.

I'm definitely no one's sweetheart. "No, thanks. I'm all right." But I wasn't. Hurt surrounded me in every possible way.

However, I didn't want to get into it with Lisa. She never did anything to me intentionally, so I didn't hold the fact that she didn't understand me against her. She was one of those who thought that everything important would be found on the surface—surface-driven superficial.

Excusing myself from the table, I walked into the foyer and sat on the middle step of the spiral staircase. I decided to call Antonio. This was my first opportunity to talk to him, and he sounded relieved to hear from me. Joy spilled over into my voice, betraying me.

"Antonio, it's me," I said.

"I miss you."

"I miss you too. You're the only one who is real. Everyone here is just a hypocrite." My voice was a little more than a whisper.

"I'm sorry to hear that. What about Raquel?"

"No change thus far. She's still at Newark Medical. I'll keep you posted." I didn't have time to engage him in the details.

"I'll be in New York tomorrow for a shoot," Antonio said.

"Really? For how long?"

"Probably a day or so. Aren't you staying at the Marriott?"

"Yes, in New Jersey, not in New York."

"That's no problem. I can run right across to Jersey and get you."

"But I won't have any free time to socialize."

"We don't have to socialize. I just want to see you."

"I can't." I wanted to see him, but I didn't want my family to see him.

"If I can't see you then, when will I hear from you again?"

"Not sure, but I've got to go."

"So soon?" Antonio didn't like to be rushed.

"I don't want these people in my business," I said.

"And what business is that?" He loved to toy with me.

"My personal business. I'll talk to you later." I felt my cheeks turning a hot pink.

"Wait a minute. Why do you care what they think or what they know?"

"Bye, Antonio."

"Goodbye," he said.

While I slipped my cell phone back into its case, Lisa and Matt strolled through the foyer.

"You look flushed. New boyfriend?" She smiled and then winked at me.

"Not exactly." I wasn't in the mood to explain my relationship with Antonio. Besides, considering Lisa's secretive nature, she was the last person I owed any words.

Matt went into the living room without a word. Lisa grabbed a sweater from the hall closet, gave me a weird smile and walked back to the kitchen.

She's smothering me already. Lord, I've got to get out of this house.

I reached into my purse and pulled out the crumpled piece of paper. Today the words seemed bottomless.

If anyone was owed an explanation, it was me.

The decision was made. Now was the right time to ask Lisa about the note. I stirred up all the courage I needed, but just as I was about to march in to the kitchen, the doorbell rang.

Chapter Twelve

Lisa

I walked back into the kitchen wondering who Makaeli was talking to on the phone. Her secretiveness was a reminder of just how little we knew about each other. I didn't know her friends or lovers, if she had any. I didn't know about her present or her future; only her past, and that wasn't anything we could celebrate over. Every time I'd push, she'd close up on me. I wasn't trying to offend her. Pushing was just my way; yet I knew I had to find a different way if Matt and I were going drop the bomb on her that we planned to.

I had just picked up my dishcloth when my troublesome brother walked into the room.

"Don't start," I said.

"Now is the time." Matt walked right up to me.

"All right then, fine. Let's do it. I'm tired of arguing with you."

"That's a first." Matt shoved a piece of gum into his mouth.

"Do you want a piece of me today?"

"No, let's just go do what we know we've got to do."

"Okay, let's go." I put down the dishcloth, swallowed my spit and mustered enough courage to look in the direction of the kitchen door. If only my feet had cooperated, it would have gone smoothly. For some reason, my legs felt like lead as my mind raced with the possible consequences of our intended actions.

Matt walked past me and I could hear his footsteps on the hardwood floors. I had no choice. As my legs lost their stiffness and I moved in what seemed like slow motion toward the living room, the doorbell rang.

Chapter Thirteen

Makaeli

This place is getting to be busier than Grand Central Station. I stood up, straightened my blouse and walked back into the living room with Matt. I stood over by the fireplace as Lisa walked by to answer the door. She hadn't mentioned that anyone would be stopping by, and Lisa, whose every move was planned, never catered to surprise visits. So I was intrigued about the visitor at the door.

But that's when I heard a familiar voice and I took off running behind Lisa. *Could it really be her?* Just as I suspected, it was Mrs. Pearl.

"Mrs. Pearl, I'm so happy you're here." I gave her a tight squeeze. "Lisa, you really got me this time."

"I just wanted to add a little joy to a very long and depressing day, and I figured a visit from Mrs. Pearl would do the trick," Lisa said.

"Well, I can't argue with that. Please come in, Mrs. Pearl, and sit down with me." I must have been glowing.

"All right, but just for a little while. Your sister called me just as I was about to go to New York—Brooklyn, in fact, to see my grandchildren. I had to see you before I leave tonight." Mrs. Pearl smiled her classic smile, the one I had missed over the years.

"It has been so long." I hugged her again, taking in the softness of her arms.

Good old Mrs. Pearl. By senior year of high school, I worked at Pearl's Cloth World, where I could get all the fabric I wanted at half price. At least that was my original intention, but after working there, I liked everything about it: the customers, the discounts, and the training. Most of all, I loved Mrs. Pearl.

She was a short, heavy-set widow in her mid-sixties who wore a different wig every day of the week. Sometimes different lengths, textures and colors, but always stylish. She was a shrewd businesswoman and an awesome seamstress in her own right. Her creative energy was almost contagious. On top of that she was an awesome woman of God who had the love of Christ in her heart.

We walked into the living room where Matt was still sitting.

"Mrs. Pearl, this is my brother, Matt. Matt, this is the infamous Mrs. Pearl. I don't think you two ever had a chance to meet." I gave her my biggest, most perfect smile.

"Good to meet you, Matt. Your sister sure did brag a lot about you back then," Mrs. Pearl said.

"I'm pleased to meet you. Makaeli has said a lot of good things about you over the years," Matt said.

"If you two will excuse us, Matt and I are going upstairs to watch a little TV so you two can talk. It was nice seeing you again." Lisa pulled Matt by the hand and they both waved goodbye.

"Thank you, sweetheart." Mrs. Pearl waved back.

"I can't believe you're here," I said.

"Girl, you're still as beautiful as you ever were. Grown now, though."

"Yes, I'm all grown up." I spun around.

"I've missed you." Mrs. Pearl smiled.

"Me too," I said. "How is the store?"

"It's just fine. Not as busy as it used to be, but I get by."

"It was always such a nice store."

"It sure would be nice to have you around again from time to time," Mrs. Pearl said.

"If I didn't live so far away, I'd come by."

"I'm sure you would, darling."

"How is your brother, Mr. Paul?" I was only being polite. Never did like her fraternal twin, and he never paid me any attention.

"Paul is still being himself. You know how that is," Mrs. Pearl said.

"Does he still wear his glasses on the tip of his nose while he does payroll?" I recalled the days I worked at the store, enduring Mr. Paul's pessimistic attitude and stringent policies.

"He's still walking around with that evil look." Mrs. Pearl frowned. "I'm still praying for him to change his life."

"Oh, I'm sorry to hear that."

"But never mind him. Let's talk about you." Mrs. Pearl adjusted her red wig.

"Not much to tell. I'm still the same me," I said.

"What about your designs? Tell me all about them," Mrs. Pearl said.

"Designs by Makaeli is really doing well. They're catching on in Milan." I was excited to finally be able to share my accomplishments with my mentor.

"Oh, I'm so happy for you."

"You should have gone with me. You're so talented yourself." I touched her sleeve and admired the craftsmanship in her self-designed clothes.

"Child, that time has passed. This is your day." Mrs. Pearl laughed.

"But you add so much flair to your store and to everything you do. You live for fashion, know your craft and your sewing—you can really hook it up."

"I'm too old for that now. I give my time to the Lord and let the young folks do the rest."

Her personality matched her rhinestone boots. She lit up every room with her milk chocolate skin, eyes like warm coals, deep dimples and perfect white teeth. Her hefty laugh was neither offensive nor raucous, but it invited others to join in. Mrs. Pearl truly got a high off people, different people, all people.

"I miss those days at the store. I learned so much from you." A sadness came over me because I had left Mrs. Pearl behind and she would never be willing or able to catch up.

"I knew you'd make it big one day. God had already showed me and I knew it would come to pass."

The best thing about Mrs. Pearl was that she was a born-again Christian, not like a lot of the so-called Christians I knew. She had a very no-nonsense view of the world, an attitude she attributed to the Bible. I never had to guess what she thought was right, because she didn't just talk about it, she lived it. Her consistency, if nothing else, won my respect.

My eyes glanced at the oriental rug. I was ashamed to tell her that I had not been to church since I left the U.S. and that the whole idea of God was so foreign to me now.

"You haven't been serving, have you?" Mrs. Pearl could always read me. I didn't know if it was the prophetess part of her or the mother part of her, but she always knew.

"Excuse me? Serving?"

"Serving the Lord, girl. Don't play with me, Makaeli Hunt."

"I'm sorry . . . I—"

"I still remember the first time you came to church with me."

"I was nervous that day."

"I could sure tell that. You were shaking."

"It was the only time I had ever been to church except for a couple of weddings or funerals."

"Now, I knew that was a crying shame." Mrs. Pearl shook her head.

"But when Pastor Brown talked about Jesus dying to wash away all my sins, no matter what they were, I knew I had found something special," I said.

"You've got that right."

"I knew I had a lot of sin in my heart, and if this Jesus could die for me—"

"I used to tell you to keep your heart with all diligence." Mrs. Pearl threw her hand into the air and waved it gently.

"For out of it come the issues of life." I finished her sentence.

"That's right, girl."

"And I knew I had to get my heart right, 'cause that's what I had—issues." I smiled.

"Don't we all, sweetie." Mrs. Pearl stretched out her thick legs. "Then you got all choked up one day and came running up to the altar with your hands in the air, tears running down your face."

"I was pathetic."

"No, you were beautiful."

"I remember like it was yesterday."

"So do I."

"Pastor Brown had preached about God's perfect love." I felt tears about to overflow onto my face. "That was the best day of my life."

"If that's true, then why haven't you been serving the way you promised the Lord you would?"

"That was so long ago."

"So what?"

"I've been pre-occupied with my sister Raquel. She's sick, you know?"

"Lisa already told me about Raquel when she called, but what does that have to do with your relationship with God?" Mrs. Pearl was never the type to play games.

"Oh, but you don't understand. I've been working so hard, trying to break color barriers and gender barriers and trying to do good in Italy and—"

"You can work 'til you drop and do all the good you think you can do, but good without God is in vain."

"You're right. I've been avoiding the issue, but lately I've been feeling different."

"Really now? Different how?"

"Like feeling really empty and knowing I need the Lord."

That was an understatement. God was all I ever thought about lately; how I wished I was worthy of His love.

"It shouldn't have taken you that long to figure that out. You were already saved."

"I know."

"All you have to do is rededicate yourself to Him. He'll take you back."

"I'll be going back soon, I promise." I felt like such a disappointment.

"It's not me that you need to promise anything." Mrs. Pearl leaned forward in her chair.

"I know you're right." But how could I tell her I was ashamed to go back?

"I can't believe you're that same bitter little girl with broken posture and chapped lips that could hardly form a smile."

"I don't think I had a lot to smile about back then."

"Not at first, but after a while I began to see you grow. I began to see something in you that used to be in me—but better."

"I don't know about that," I said.

"You're an overcomer."

"I don't know about that either."

"You can live out all your dreams if you have faith."

"Faith isn't always easy to come by. There were so many days when I wanted to die." I looked directly into her eyes.

"I know you did, but I said you were too young."

"You said I was too young to die."

"God wasn't finished with you yet, honey."

"But sometimes, when things got really bad, I figured I was finished with Him."

"I don't know why you were so hard-headed." Mrs. Pearl smiled.

"I don't either, but somewhere along the line I made up my mind that God couldn't help me." I sat there shaking my head for a minute.

"It's a good thing you were wrong."

"Yeah."

"Oh my goodness. Look at the time. I've got to get going." Mrs. Pearl looked at her watch. "I hope I'll get to see you again before you leave town."

"I hope so too."

"When are you leaving, dear?"

"I'm not sure, but Mrs. Pearl, I'll never forget you." I knew the kind of relationship I had with her was found only once in a lifetime, and I wanted it to last forever.

"Don't worry about me. It's God I don't want you to forget."

"How can I?"

"I've got to go now, but I want you to always take the Word with you." Mrs. Pearl rose from her chair and grabbed her rhinestone-trimmed handbag.

"Well, I didn't pack my Bible, but I'm sure there is one back in my hotel room," I said.

"No, that's not what I mean. Carry it always in here." Mrs. Pearl put both her hands over mine and pressed my hand against my heart.

"Thanks so much for coming." I began walking her down the hall and into the foyer.

"Thanks for entertaining me. You know I'll be praying for your sister." She handed me a piece of paper.

"I know you'll be praying." I looked at the paper. "What's this?"

"That is my new address and phone numbers. I hate that we lost touch when you moved."

"Me too, and let me give you mine." I took out one of my business cards and wrote my address and home phone number on the back.

"But you pray for your sister also."

"That might not be the best idea," I said.

"The past is the past. We can't change that. I know about your differences and all, but Romans 12:14 says 'Bless them that persecute you. Bless them and curse not.' Remember that." Mrs. Pearl stopped at the front door and hugged me with her wide, soft arms. She had the same smell of jasmine she had when she comforted me on so many occasions.

"Thank you." As I opened the door to walk her to her vehicle, a million memories flooded my mind. Faithful, honest Mrs. Pearl. I always loved her because she never gave up on me. Even now, she was like no other person known to me. And although it was probably selfish of me, I secretly wished I was Mrs. Pearl's daughter.

I wanted to express my love for her, but I couldn't find the words. *Do I even know what love is anymore?*

"I'll still be in Brooklyn, but maybe you can stop by the

church on Sunday. Do you still remember where the church is?"

"Yes, I remember."

"I'm sure Pastor Brown would love to see you." Mrs. Pearl grabbed my hand and squeezed it.

"I'll see what I can do."

"Don't see what you can do. Make it your business to be there," Mrs. Pearl said.

"Goodbye, Mrs. Pearl."

She looked into my eyes, but she didn't say goodbye. "What can separate you from the love of God? Nothing."

She shut the door of her Dodge Caravan, and with a quick wave of her hand, she rolled out of the driveway.

I walked back to the house and looked at my watch. It was almost time to go back to the hospital—7:35 P.M. Visiting hours began again at 8:00. Standing in the foyer, I could hardly believe Lisa and Phil had lived here all these years. Never ventured out to buy a house of their own.

I figured it must have been the finality of shutting down Mama's home, of giving up on Mama's coming home that kept them in this house. Year after year, child after child—number one, number two, then three.

I walked into the hallway, peeping into each room on the ground floor. Neither Matt nor Lisa were in the den, living room, dining room or kitchen. I knew they were upstairs watching television.

It was easy to see that the study was still where Phil spent most of his time. The smell of the new leather and expensive cigars mingled in the atmosphere. The *New York Times* was open on his desk. Probably the financial section, but I didn't have time to look, so I turned off the light.

Then, like iron to a magnet, I was drawn to Mama's room. I pushed the door open gently, flipped on the switch, and the overhead light allowed me to search the room with my eyes. It didn't seem at all like it did earlier.

Much less intimidating. Maybe because in my mind the beautiful jade bathroom was blocked out.

The Victorian paintings on the wall were vaguely familiar. Probably worth a lot, although I'd never cared much for that kind of art work. I was more of an abstract person. The curtains were jade-and-cream chiffon. *Typical.*

I went over to the dresser first and fumbled among the many perfumes. Lisa had done a good job of keeping everything well dusted and in its proper place. There was an assortment of black and white photographs, mostly of Mama and her first husband. One was of Mama with the four of us. None were of my father.

I touched the rounded edges of the huge mirror and I heard a key fall to the hardwood floor. I carefully picked it up. *It must've fallen from behind the mirror.*

I began to look around for the corresponding lock. My eyes stopped at the walk-in closet. I opened the double doors and frowned from the smell of moth balls. There were rows of suits and evenings gowns, silks, cottons and minks. Kneeling down under the second line of hanging clothes and crawling amongst her shoes brought me to a new low. What was I looking for?

I leaned against the wall, ready to push myself up, to walk away from this room and all of its secrets. Just then, I saw a small trunk on the other side of the closet. There was a quilt sitting on top of it.

I carefully placed the quilt on the floor and checked the size of the lock. Not knowing whether the key would fit made my teeth chatter. Relief came over me when the key turned smoothly in the lock. But at the same time, I heard footsteps and voices. *Too close.*

Chapter Fourteen

Lisa

Matt and I sat in what used to be Matt's old room, which I made into a guest room, talking and trying to pass the time. It was decorated with huge bouquets of flowers and antique vases. Nothing at all like the dreary, unsanitary room Matt used to live in; when he filled it with basketball posters, soccer trophies, and comic books. Both the flowered comforter and the brass floor lamp brightened the room with the smallest window. We never received much sunlight in there.

Matt sat in the suede recliner by the window and I tried to sit Indian-style on the bed until the pain in my varicose vein-streaked legs reminded me of my age. The room was a comfortable place to visit, thanks to my impeccable interior decorating skills.

Matt flipped channels nervously as he popped pretzels into his mouth. He looked so much like our father when he did that. I really missed our father.

"I like what you've done to this room," Matt said.

"Thanks. It took a lot of work to get this room back to normal."

"Back to normal?"

"Are you kidding me? After I finished peeling gum and Janet Jackson posters off the walls, and then picked up all your dirty underwear and jock straps . . ."

"Come on, Lisa. It wasn't that bad."

"It was worse." I laughed.

"Have you seen all my soccer and basketball trophies?"

"When you went away, I packed them all downstairs in the basement. One day when you have time to sort through your things, you can take what you want with you."

"Yeah, I will," Matt said. "I'm glad you invited that nice old Pearl lady to come over."

"Her name is Mrs. Pearl."

"Whatever. No disrespect intended."

"I know, but watch yourself, regardless."

"Same big sister."

"You better believe it. We walk a chalk line in this house."

"I don't blame Phil for staying at the hospital." Matt laughed.

"What?"

"I'm just kidding. Hey, loosen up a little."

"I'm as loose as I'm ever going to get." I fixed my collar. How dare he ask me to loosen up. Everyone was always asking me to do the impossible. "Loosen up, loosen up," they'd say, but didn't they know I had to stay in control? I had to be the example. He reminded me of Phil when he begged me to go to those filthy football games with him. It was clear I wasn't cut out to be loose.

"What about this Makaeli thing?"

"I don't want to talk about that now."

"We've got to do it." Matt squinted his eyes and wrinkled his forehead.

"I know that. I just haven't figured out how yet."

"You don't have to figure it out. Just do it."

"Listen, you don't tell me what—" I heard noises outside, went over to the window and peeped out. I saw Mrs. Pearl shut her van door and drive away. The velvet curtains brushed across my shoulders.

"It's time to go downstairs," I said.

"Okay, but just give me a minute to get myself together."

"Get yourself together? Take your feet off my furniture, put on those raggedy sneakers of yours and let's get out of here before it's too late." I was only half joking.

"I see you haven't changed a bit." Matt jumped out of his seat, clicked off the television and started squeezing into his shoes.

"Nope, I haven't. Not going to either."

"I can see that."

"Not so people like you can relax with their feet up, while people like me do all the work. I think not." I turned off the light, opened the door, and walked out into the hallway.

"Same old Lisa."

"You've got that right. Now hustle."

I could never let them believe that I'd softened, even if I had just a little. Tough was the only way I knew how to be, and it was the only way I knew I could keep their respect.

Matt led the way down the stairs. Before we reached the bottom, we could see Makaeli coming out of Mama's room. I wondered what she was doing in there. My heart stood at attention as she walked through the hallway into the living room.

Signaling for Matt to go ahead, I waited until it was clear, then went into Mama's room. My eyes took quick inventory and nothing seemed out of place. Besides, anything questionable was removed long ago.

"I'll be ready just as soon as I clean up the kitchen." I

held up the bottle of dishwashing liquid as if proof were needed.

"I'll help you," Makaeli said.

"No, you can sit with me, but I insist that you two spend this time catching up. I'm fine, really." I went into the kitchen and they came behind me.

I let the sink fill up with warm, soapy water and dipped my tired hands into the soothing Palmolive mixture. I needed all the help I could get.

Before I could start the dishes, the phone rang.

When I answered it and heard Dr. Lieberman's voice, I kept my eyes on the stainless steel pots hanging overhead.

"Mrs. Jackson?"

"Dr. Jackson. Yes, this is me."

"I'm sorry to have to call you at home, but I'm afraid your sister has taken a turn for the worse."

The sunlight came in through the window and although its warmth was evident, I began to shiver.

"How so?"

"Your sister has internal bleeding, and although it hasn't been confirmed yet, I believe she may be bleeding from the brain. Unfortunately, it's quite common in these cases."

"Yes, I know," I said.

"In any case, we've given her a blood transfusion, a few pints, but we will need more by tomorrow."

"A blood transfusion?"

"Yes, she has lost a lot of blood already."

"Of course. My family and I were about to come back anyway. Thank you," I said.

"You're welcome. Goodbye."

Hearing this report seemed to make the lemon yellow walls cave in on me. I hung up the phone and turned to face Matt and Makaeli. *No time to figure out how to say it; just say it.*

"That was the hospital. They're giving Raquel several pints of blood because she's still bleeding internally." I knew what the medical repercussions were. "They're probably going to have to give her another blood transfusion."

"That's really serious, isn't it?" Matt put his head down on the table for a second.

Makaeli didn't say a word.

"They might need us to give blood." My stomach flipped.

"Oh." Makaeli finally had a response.

"I'm ready. What blood type is she?" Matt's intentions were always heroic.

"She's type A," Lisa said.

"Good, that's me," Matt said.

"Me too," Makaeli said.

"You've read her chart, Lisa. What do you think?" Makaeli's gray eyes locked with mine.

"Well, her vital signs aren't good and the doctor thinks she might be . . ."—I lowered my head—"bleeding from the brain."

"Oh no," Matt said.

"Wasn't her brain already in trouble from the deep sleep she's in anyway?" Makaeli always asked one question too many. I could tell that Makaeli was trying to understand Raquel's condition, but I was in no mood to play teacher.

"The bleeding from the brain is an effect of the cocaine overdose. She's not exactly in a deep sleep. The brain activity during a coma is different from being asleep," I said.

"Oh," Makaeli replied.

"She can't respond to stimulation. It's as if she's trapped inside her own body." I shook my head. "So yes, her brain was always in trouble, but now with the bleeding, she's in more trouble."

"A nurse told me she might be able to hear," Makaeli said.

"That's absolutely true. Some say they can even visualize things, but in any case, Raquel is not getting better. She appears to be . . ." I wasn't sure how to say what needed to be said.

"Dying?" Makaeli didn't cut corners.

"Yes." I forfeited my other chances to tell the truth. This moment was all I had.

"Let's hurry and get back to the hospital then," Matt said.

"Go on. I'll be right out." I dried my hands with a paper towel and looked up at the clock. Each minute was precious. I looked back at the sink full of dishes, wanting to drown my sorrows in the suds, but being the tower of strength that I was, I knew I couldn't. I couldn't let life break me. I wouldn't end up like Mama.

Matt left the room first, but Makaeli stayed behind. From the corner of my eye I saw her biting her bottom lip, something she had always done when she was under pressure. I saw a wrinkle in the middle of her forehead. I wondered if the stress was that visible on me. *Oh Lord, where are you now? If you're real, then please reveal yourself to me.*

"Okay, guys, are you ready?" I walked past the living room into the foyer and grabbed my coat from the hall closet.

Makaeli was right on my heels, taking her coat also. "I'm ready."

I went out first, followed by Makaeli and Matt.

"I'll drive." Matt was already bundled in his jacket with his New York Yankees hat pulled over his ears.

"No speeding in my new car please." I shook my head.

"Don't worry about it. You're in good hands when I'm behind the wheel." Matt hopped into the driver's side of my car.

"This is a BMW five speed, not your nineteen eighty-five Chevy Cavalier automatic."

"Oh, so you've got jokes."

"I try," I said.

Makaeli laughed from the back seat.

I tried to participate in the lighthearted chatter of Makaeli and Matt, but when I thought about how weak Raquel was and about her blood transfusion, I couldn't concentrate. Bleeding of the brain was a serious matter, and as a doctor, I knew precisely what it entailed. No one could sugar coat it, not that anyone had even tried, and I was ready to face the challenge head on. So we rode back over the potholes to Newark Medical Center, not knowing what condition we would find Raquel in when we got there.

Chapter Fifteen

Makaeli

When we arrived at the hospital, Matt and Lisa went in to see Raquel immediately. I waited outside the room for a while, trying to summon strength I knew I didn't possess. Finally, I got myself together and went in for a few minutes.

Looking at Raquel's face made me remember and want to fight, to pay her back for all those years she fought me.

"High yellow heifer." Raquel raised her hand to slap me. I could almost feel her long, witch-like fingernails before they hit my face. Her movement was so swift and powerful that I felt the air it created against my skin.

"Don't touch her. She can't help it if she's Mama's little mulatto." Lisa grabbed Raquel's arm before it reached me.

Raquel jerked away from her and rolled her red eyes. Her funny-smelling cigarette still hung from her black lips. I wondered if it would drop and burn a hole in Mama's oriental rug.

"Don't you pay any attention to her. She's just ignorant, that's all. I'd put her out if I could," Lisa said.

Lisa retied my ribbon, patted me on the head and walked out carrying her Luis Vuitton suitcase. As soon as the door closed be-

hind her, Raquel passed by, mumbling under her breath. I smelled the alcohol as she came closer. Casually, she took the lit cigarette from her mouth, rolled it around between her fingers and then placed it ever so gently against my thigh. The burning seared my soul and I let out the loudest sound my little body could make.

I squeezed my teddy bear tighter as my eyes filled up with tears, but it was no use. Lisa was already out of the driveway, on her way for a weekend away with Phil, and I was left with Raquel, alone. She didn't even look back at me before stomping out of the room.

I fell to the floor by the steps and wished with all my nine-year-old heart that Mama could come back home. Just then, I looked down at the cross pendant that hung around my neck. Oh God, if you're real, please rescue me.

When I was tired of staring at Raquel's scrawny, deteriorating body and tired of listening to Lisa's medical analyses, I left the room. Then one at a time, Matt, and finally Lisa, followed.

Every time I walked away for a minute, Matt and Lisa huddled together in the hospital chairs, whispering and looking at me out of the corner of their eyes. Lisa frequently had her finger in Matt's face, but whenever I came over, they became quiet.

The perfectly white walls and the silence were like a prison for my mind. I wanted so much to get out of there and to never come back.

"What's going on? You two are so serious." I knew something was going on, but I wasn't sure of what.

"This is serious. Raquel is . . ." Matt shook his head.

"Oh my goodness. She's not . . ." I clasped my hands over my mouth and fell into a chair.

"No, she's not dead. We're just very worried. Her condition is very unstable," Lisa said.

"You scared me for a minute there." I exhaled.

"Oh, sorry," Matt said. "We do need time to talk, though."

"Are you sure this is the right time?" Lisa squinted her eyes.

"What's a better time?" Matt clenched his teeth.

"I don't know. You tell me," Lisa said.

"How am I supposed to know?" Perspiration dripped down Matt's forehead.

"I thought you had all the answers. If not, then why get anything started?" Lisa batted her eyelashes.

"It's already started," Matt said.

I had never seen these two go at each other like this. They were always a team, always in sync with each other, like Donnie and Marie Osmond. Now they were uptight. I wondered what made the natives so restless.

"But should we play judge now?" Lisa wrinkled her eyebrows.

"That's old," Matt said.

"Wait a minute—cut. You two are talking in riddles. I don't know why you're so mad at each other and I'm too tired to try to figure it out. I'm going back to my room at the Marriott to get some sleep." A yawn came out of my mouth as I stretched.

"Oh, we're sorry. You can go back to the house and stay." Lisa handed me a key.

"No, thank you," I said.

"Take it anyway. It's a spare. You might need it for tomorrow," Lisa said.

I was about to refuse it again when I thought about the trunk in Mama's closet. I reached out to accept the key with my hand shaking, but I hoped she didn't notice.

"We'll see you here in the morning, then?" Matt stood up.

"Bright and early. I just need a little beauty rest." I couldn't take my eyes off of the curious pair.

"You don't need beauty anything, but we'll see you tomorrow," Matt said.

"Phil won't be home until late anyway, so Matt and I are staying here all night," Lisa said.

We were getting nowhere with this phoniness. It was clear that they needed a chance to get themselves together. They were pathetic.

"I'll see you guys tomorrow." I dropped the key into my purse, slipped my purse on my shoulder and walked away. Knowing they were watching me, their eyes seemed to burn a hole in my back.

"Tomorrow." Lisa sounded unsure if there would even be one.

"Good night," Matt said.

"Good night." I halfheartedly threw up my hand in a backward waving motion without ever looking back. I walked to the elevator.

They were certainly acting strange. I thought that maybe the doctor told them something about Raquel while I was in the restroom; that maybe Raquel wasn't going to last until morning and they knew it. Whatever it was, I knew I'd find out eventually. The real issue at hand was Mama's trunk. I had to quickly get back to it. I had no time for Lisa and Matt's foolishness when a mystery could potentially be revealed.

When I exited the hospital, there was a row of cabs parked in front. I quickly hopped into one of them.

The driver was an African man with a heavy accent, and I was glad when he finally figured out the directions to New Brunswick. He maneuvered his way through the streets and despite getting lost on several occasions, managed to drop me off at the house. I walked up the driveway and went in cautiously. Luckily, Lisa hadn't bothered to set the alarm before we left.

My time was limited, because although Lisa and Matt were safely stuck at the hospital, Phil could unexpectedly come home at any time. Within minutes of getting in, I was back at the place where I started.

I flung the quilt aside, pushed the key into the lock and flung the trunk open wide. There were scattered pictures everywhere. I looked through them briefly and determined that I had seen them all before. There were some pictures of Mama and her first husband, wedding pictures, some of him and Mama on the beach, some of him in the military, then some of our school pictures and pictures of family outings, most of which were taken before I was even born. Nothing new or special. I dug through the pictures to the bottom and found a labeled lock of Matt's baby hair, Lisa's baby booties, an unidentified baby blanket, and Raquel's baby footprints. Frustration set in. I didn't see anything with my name on it.

Deciding to give up, I closed the trunk and sat down with my back against the wall of the closet. It was then that I felt something sharp scraping against my lower back and I turned to identify it. It was a small metal compartment almost at the base of the closet. It was about the size of my fist, and it was painted to blend in with the wall. When I picked the little door open with my fingernails, I expected to see electrical wiring or some other technical apparatus, but instead I saw paper. I reached my hand in and pulled out a small sealed envelope. The paper was so old that it had turned brown and brittle.

I hurried to peel it open. It was another picture, but unlike the others, it disturbed me. It was a picture of a tiny pink casket trimmed in pink roses. On the back was written "love no more" in scrawled, almost illegible penmanship. My heart rose and sank in the same instant. I placed the envelope back inside the compartment and put the picture into my purse, but that didn't end my search. I frantically looked around the closet for any other information. *Nothing.*

I didn't know if this picture was at all related to the note I kept all these years, but I didn't have time to find out. Everything was put back into place, and I quietly left the house of my childhood without feeling that I was ever home.

With my heart still beating fast, I locked the front door and called a cab from my cell phone. While I waited outside, I tried to study the picture I had taken, but it was dark outside. Before long, my cab took me back to the Marriott. I walked past the concierge and other attendants, anxious to be alone in my room.

Once I reached my destination, the first thing I did was throw off my clothes and hop into the shower. When I was done in the bathroom, I sat on the plush carpet and called Antonio.

"Hi," I said.

"It's good to hear from you," Antonio said.

"Good to hear you too."

"How is Raquel?"

"The same. Well, actually worse." I closed my eyes when I said it.

"I'm sorry to hear that."

"Yeah, well, I don't want to talk about that. That's all we've been thinking about and talking about the whole time."

"I understand," Antonio said.

"I saw Mrs. Pearl tonight."

"Good. How is she?"

"Beautiful. She was unmistakably the best part of my day."

"Good."

"She always makes me feel so special."

"You are special." Antonio's voice was warm and inviting.

"No one accepts me the way she does, just the way I am. The total me, not the way I'm expected to be."

"What about me?"

"I don't mean you don't. I—"

"I'm just teasing. I know what you mean. I'm glad you saw her."

"So am I," I said. "I don't always understand everything she says, but the way she says it with such affection and confidence makes me always believe what she says."

"And what did she say?"

"She said, 'Bless those who persecute you.' " My emotions almost prevented the words from coming out.

"Did she? And who does she think is persecuting you?"

"She knows how I used to feel about Raquel because I confided in her."

"Used to?"

"I guess I'm changing a little. I want Raquel to live, at least. But I didn't get a chance to talk to Mrs. Pearl about that."

"Now, that's progress. So you want her to live?"

"Yes. You should see what all of that repeated drug use did to her body."

"Drugs are a serious matter."

"She used to have caramel skin like Mama's and Lisa's, but now it's more of a burnt sienna. Lisa says she's very weak and vulnerable to infections."

"It doesn't sound too good," Antonio said.

"No, it's not. She probably won't live through the night." Suddenly, I didn't feel like talking anymore. "Listen, I'm a little tired now, so I'll call you tomorrow and fill you in."

"Why do I feel like you're trying to get rid of me?"

"Believe me, I've already tried to get rid of you. I don't know how."

"Good for me."

"Bye for now." I placed the phone back into its cradle.

Not only wasn't I in the mood for talking, but I wasn't in the mood for thinking either. Yet I couldn't stop obsessing about Raquel. I couldn't stop the images.

When I closed my eyes, I saw her buried in a coffin, with a tombstone that read: RAQUEL CAMBELL WAS A DAUGHTER, SISTER AND LIFELONG ENEMY. I saw myself attending her funeral, wearing a little black Versace dress with matching shoes and purse.

Tears rolled down my face and the heat from my skin created a mist. I looked at my swollen eyes in the bathroom mirror. I recalled Raquel's evil eyes the last time I saw her conscious.

I went back to the bed and curled up into the fetal position, holding my knees against my chest and waiting for the pain in my heart to stop. Flooding my pillow with years of anguish was the only thing I could do. Eventually, my memories and my tears took me into a deep sleep.

The next morning was Sunday. As the sun poured through my hotel room window, I awoke with a strange feeling. *Is Raquel already dead?*

As I picked up the phone to call the hospital, I began to tremble. I put the phone down and decided I would just go instead.

Peeling off my silk pajamas and forcing myself into the marble tub was self-indulging under the circumstances. Aromatherapy usually did the trick, but today was the exception. I hopped out of the tub, dried myself off and began to cream the tired curves of my body. Brushing my hair, spraying it with oil sheen and pinning it into an updo didn't soothe me either. I applied my foundation and a light pink lipstick. No eye shadow or blush today.

Dressed in a wool pantsuit, I attempted to get out early, but suddenly I felt extremely warm. I took two sips from a half empty glass of water that had been set on the nightstand, and then splashed the rest of it on my face.

I sat at the little cherry wood desk across the room. A look in the drawer satisfied what I knew I needed. Sure enough, in typical American hotel style, there was a King James version of the Bible in the top drawer. The gold letters felt warm under my fingertips.

Reading Psalm Ninety-one comforted me.

He that dwelleth in the secret place of the most high shall abide under the shadow of the Almighty. I will say of the Lord, He is my refuge and my fortress: my God; in him will I trust.

I picked up my sketch pad and began to doodle, first with no understanding, and then the creations came to me. In the midst of catastrophe, I was creating. Even in death there was life.

Then I prayed. "Dear Most High God, I know you remember me even though I haven't talked with you in a long time. Please let my sister be okay. I know I didn't always want this in the past, but I'm sorry for that now. I'm not exactly sure why, but I need her to live. Please take away this bitterness I feel. Help me to forgive, if not in whole, then in part. Amen."

Even though my attempts at forgiveness had failed yesterday, I was determined to try again today.

Chapter Sixteen

Lisa

Matt and I ate dinner in the hospital cafeteria, exchanging worries and harsh words until we could barely stand each other. Then we emptied our trays and went right back up to ICU.

It was still busy even late at night, just like it used to be when I worked the night shift. Overworked nurses, doctors and medical technicians walked back and forth with equipment and medications, flipping through pages on charts and entertaining themselves with mindless chatter as they went about their routines. I heard the doctors' whispers and I could imagine what they were probably saying. Raquel was in a dangerous position. No medical authority would dispute that.

Then there were the visitors who roamed the hallways, some crying, some moaning and some praying for their loved ones who, for one reason or another, lingered on the brink of death. I pitied them, really. I pitied their random displays of emotion, their lack of self control. *Pull yourselves together, people.*

After all, ICU only meant the possibility of a life ending,

and given my life lately, the ending of life didn't sound so bad. Mine was over anyway, just like Mama's was when she had her last child. No husband, no love, no life. I didn't want to end up miserable and insane like Mama. I just wanted to be in control again. I looked over at Matt, who had his feet on the center table and was rubbing his mustache.

"I'm telling you. She keeps staring at me." I hit his feet with my fist and he dropped them.

"So what?" Matt turned his cap backward.

"You love to taunt me, don't you?" I took off his cap and threw it into the chair beside him. "It's almost as if she knows something."

"That's impossible," Matt said.

"Then why does she keep looking at me with those cat eyes?" Just the thought of a cat's anything made me shiver.

"What else is she supposed to look at you with, her feet?"

"You know what I mean." I gave him one of my sternest looks. I was in no mood for his foolishness.

"It's all in your head." Matt picked up his cap, threw it into the air and caught it.

"I'm not paranoid, just tired."

"I'm tired too. Tired of playing these games with Makaeli."

"What are you saying?"

"Now that I'm full, I'm ready to call her, meet her at the house and tell her everything." Matt grabbed me by both arms.

"I can't do that." I pulled away from him.

"Why not?"

"I'm not ready yet." Suddenly, I was flustered.

"Oh, come on, Lisa. You've been stalling ever since I got into town."

"Things are just not right."

"Everything doesn't have to be in your little schedule book to be right," Matt said.

"That's not what I mean."

"What do you mean then?"

"Just give me one more day to get myself together and to make it right." I put my coat over me, stretched out and closed my eyes.

"All right, one more day, but the clock is ticking." Matt touched his watch.

Now it was official. There was pressure from every side.

Chapter Seventeen

Makaeli

Five minutes was all it took to adjust to the bumpy cab ride. The sidewalks and cars were covered with fluffy white snow. Most of the streets had already been cleared and salted for driving, so I arrived at the hospital without a hitch.

Since bad news had been my constant companion lately, I almost expected to hear it. On the elevator I held my breath, but I stopped when I became lightheaded again. I realized I should have stopped for breakfast, but it was too late.

When I turned the corner, I saw Lisa and Matt asleep in the waiting area. Matt's shoes were off and he was stretched out peacefully on one of the couches. Lisa sat in one of the chairs with her legs crossed and her head slumped over as if it was her intention to stay awake the whole time. Her linen pantsuit barely had a crease in it, and her small Coach bag's strap was wrapped tightly around her arms. I walked past, careful not to wake them.

I looked at my watch and saw that it was too early. Visiting hours hadn't started yet. But there was no nurse in sight, so I walked straight up to the door of Raquel's room and pushed it open.

It wasn't easy to tiptoe in Donna Karan stiletto boots. The overhead clock ticked away, with every minute seeming like an hour. Clearly her condition had neither improved nor worsened overnight.

I walked over to Raquel and put my hand on her rough, swollen ones. Her hair was one of the only places free of tubes and wires, so I touched it hesitantly, almost expecting her to sit up and slap me.

The bright lights alone seemed like they would kill her, not to mention the "sick room" smell. She was lying there like a slab of meat, not moving or speaking. I knew she was surrounded by strangers day and night, poking her with long needles, taking from her the one thing she needed so badly—blood. She couldn't even say as much as "ouch," if she could even feel anything. I knew she couldn't see me, but I wondered if the comatose could really hear.

I pushed my face so close to hers that I could hear her heartbeat.

"Come back, Raquel. I don't know where you are right now or what you feel about the past. I'm not even sure how I feel about everything, but something inside is telling me to forgive." I spoke, but I didn't expect her to respond.

I had to hurry to say what I came to say because I knew within minutes someone would come in to check Raquel and they would find me. It was a consistent intensive care ritual.

"I don't know who or what hurt you to make you so mean, but I do understand hurt, if nothing else. I know it well. And I don't want to hurt anymore. If coming back to us will cause you more pain, then by all means, make your peace with God and go to your Maker. But if you want to live and to be forgiven, then come back to us. We may not be a perfect family, but we're your only family. Please come back and please forgive me for hating you all these years." My heart beat faster than it had in a long time.

Fear gripped me, barely allowing me to move. I took a deep breath and wiped the sprinkled tears from my face with my hand before searching my purse frantically for my package of Kleenex.

Before I could pull out a tissue, the buzzer went off. Through a blur of tears I saw the line on the heart monitor go straight, and like clockwork, I was rushed from the room.

"Code blue," the nurses announced as they ran in with the doctors.

The buzzer was still going off in my head. They were trying to revive Raquel. One, two, three, zap. One, two three, zap. What beautiful, sequential harmony they had. Everything was a blur now. No heartbeat. No life.

Chapter Eighteen

Lisa

Matt and I woke up because of the commotion and went over to find out what was happening. Nurses and doctors sped past us with clipboards and gadgets. I wondered what was going on.

Then I saw Makaeli being pushed from the room. She was paler than usual and she was breathing hard.

"Makaeli, what happened? What were you doing in there? No visitors were supposed to be in there yet. It's too early." I glanced at my watch and then back at her, hardly believing what I was seeing.

"I know, but I had to see her." Makaeli was shaking.

"Before visiting hours?" I know there was a hint of accusation in my tone and disapproval in my eyes, but I didn't care. *She has gone too far.*

"I needed to see her right away. I couldn't wait, and no one was around to stop me from going in." Makaeli wiped her cheeks with her hands.

"So you just went in?" I grabbed her by the arms and shook her.

"Yes, she's my sister, remember? Isn't that why I flew

thousands of miles just to be here?" Makaeli pulled herself from my grip.

"Yes, but—" I was breathing hard.

"But you think I tried to kill her," Makaeli said.

"I didn't say that." But I was thinking it.

"Well, I didn't, if that's what you're thinking." Makaeli got right in my face.

"Lisa didn't mean that," Matt said.

"We know you have every right to see Raquel, but . . ." I said.

"We were just surprised that you were here so early and that you went in." Matt spoke calmly.

"You mean that I went in *alone*?" Makaeli threw her hands into the air.

"I'm sorry, but I'm all wound up right now." I extended my hand apologetically.

She let me hold her hand for a second and then she dropped mine. How dare she? I wanted to choke her for being so irresponsible, for going inside Raquel's room totally unattended. No permission, no supervision. I knew how she really felt about Raquel. *Did she try to kill her?*

"I didn't do anything wrong," Makaeli said.

"Well, what did you do?" I needed to know.

"I asked Raquel to forgive me for having bad thoughts about her, and I asked her to come back to us, back into the land of the living," Makaeli said.

"Maybe she wanted to go," Matt said.

"Or maybe she was trying to come back but couldn't do it on her own," Makaeli said.

"Maybe. I just don't know," I said.

As I watched the scene unfold, I felt helpless. They pumped and pumped until finally, Raquel was breathing again. She had a faint heartbeat, but a heartbeat nonetheless. We were all grateful that she had decided to cling to life.

When the doctor came out of the room, I walked over to meet him.

"We've managed to temporarily stop the bleeding, but she had another convulsion and I'm concerned about the succession of them," the doctor informed us.

"So she's been having them frequently?" I was shocked to hear that.

"Yes, and if she continues to have convulsions one right after another, I'm afraid it's possible she might never regain consciousness," he said.

"Right," I said.

"There is also the possibility of her having a stroke as well. So we're monitoring her closely and hoping for the best."

On the surface, I responded well to what he was saying, speaking in medical terms and agreeing with his precautions. Yet on the inside, the pressure was building. I was sure my pulse was racing.

We dried our eyes before Matt and I went in to see Raquel. Makaeli stayed in the waiting area, peeping through the glass window, following us with those cat eyes. The nurses and doctors allowed us to see Raquel only for a few minutes before they chased us out.

Then we fell into our seats, wet-faced and exhausted. Needing time to be alone, I offered to get the coffee. The walk to the cafeteria gave me additional time away from Makaeli, time to think. And additional time to pray, for whatever that was worth. *Help me, Lord.*

My cell phone vibrated in my pocket, interrupting this rare moment I spent with God.

"Hello," I said.

"How are you?" Phil's voice was stable.

"I'm okay now, but Raquel flatlined a little while ago."

"Oh no," Phil said.

"I can't believe we came so close to losing her."

"I'm glad they were able to save her, but I wouldn't want to lose you either," Phil said.

"What do you mean lose me?" *What is he talking about?*

"I talked to Matt earlier and he said you fainted at the gas station yesterday. Why didn't you tell me?"

"With everything going on, I just forgot."

"Fainting? That's not like you. What's going on?"

"Oh, nothing. Just probably stress. When I got some water and a little rest, I was fine. I am fine."

"Are you sure?"

"Of course I'm sure. Matt shouldn't have worried you." I hoped he wouldn't probe any further.

"How was the visit with your mother?"

"Unfortunately, it went as expected." I held the cell phone tightly in my hand as I paced back and forth.

"Not so good then?"

"No, not at all. I was hoping that I would see you last night, but—"

"I had emergency surgery and didn't get in until very late. When I did, I noticed you weren't home." Phil sounded tired too.

"I'm still here at the hospital," I said.

"And Makaeli?"

"She is here too."

"Have you talked to her yet?"

"No, I haven't had time." I wanted to throw the phone far from me.

"No time?"

"When exactly do you propose I do this, in between trips to the insane asylum and the ICU?"

"You're stalling and your time is running out, Lisa. Tell her."

"I'll talk to you later."

"Tell her before it's too late, if it's not already."

"Bye, Phil." I had enough of him.

Our phone calls used to be magical. Now they were just downright antagonizing. I rubbed my hand over my blouse and wished my womb was empty. New life was such a responsibility.

My boys, Phillip Jr. and Andrew, were grown now, and Johnathan was getting older each day. Phillip, as he said on many occasions, looked forward to starting his own practice and he looked forward to me helping him. He wouldn't be pleased with this setback.

My cell phone vibrated again. *Why is he calling back?*

"Listen, I don't have time to talk to you right now." I was about to press the end button, fearing he would antagonize me again.

"That's fine. Then just do the listening. About your fainting yesterday, I know you've been under a lot of stress, but . . ."

I had wanted to talk to Phil for days. It was interesting how God seemed to intervene in his own time.

"But what?"

"I would like to think I know your body."

"Okay, so?"

"You're not pregnant, are you?"

Chapter Nineteen
Makaeli

After Lisa brought us coffee, I sat back in the armchair and sipped it. Yesterday had been a long day and today seemed to be following the same pattern. Matt and Lisa peered at Raquel through the glass window, whispering.

I stood up to stretch my legs, but I remained a few feet away from them, feeling like a hypocrite. Without warning, I felt an arm slip around my waist and a hand over my eyes. I knew these hands.

"Guess who?"

I turned on my heels to that familiar sultry voice. Every fear came true before me. Antonio stood in front of my family like a white knight in shining armor.

"What in the world are you doing here?" I faked a smile, grabbed him by the arm and pulled him to the side.

"You wouldn't return my calls. I tried to reach you on your cell. Aren't you happy to see me?" Antonio's lips drooped.

"Happy? Surprised is probably more accurate." My words were merely whispers.

"I hope you mean that in a good way."

"You know I don't want this." I stared into Antonio's dark eyes.

"This what?"

"These people to know my personal business." I discreetly pointed to Lisa and Matt behind me.

"These people are your family." Antonio's eyes were serious.

"So what?" I rolled my eyes.

"So what exactly are you hiding?"

"I'm not hiding anything. It's just that—"

"Is it that I'm white? So what?" He lifted his hand to touch my face, but I blocked it.

"Well, they certainly can see that now, can't they?"

"You're ashamed of us, aren't you?"

"There is no us, remember?" I really wanted to kick him where it hurt.

"There is a you and there is a me and together, we're an us."

"Okay, okay, but I've made you no promises," I said.

"Not yet."

"You're impossible." I saw disappointment in his dark eyes.

"Impossible to resist, hopefully."

I couldn't believe Antonio was doing this to me; embarrassing me in front of the enemy. I already explained to him how they felt about interracial relationships and about my parents' racial struggles within the family structure. Yet apparently that meant nothing to him because here he was, grinning the widest grin in front of them.

"Please just go. I appreciate you coming, but I don't have time for this drama."

"I didn't come to bring drama." Antonio touched my cheek with his fingers.

"But I just spoke with you last night." I quickly removed his hand from my face.

"I arrived here by jet early this morning. My client wanted an early photo shoot."

"Photo shoot?"

"Yes, in New York City, remember?"

"Yes, how could I forget? But I never invited you to come by here," I said.

"I wanted to stop by and be supportive." Antonio held my hand close to his chest.

"You came to test me." I pulled my hand away.

"I'm sorry you feel that way. I'm heading off to the city now, but if you need me, I'll be staying at the Trump Towers." He walked over to the elevator without a second glance.

"I'm sorry," I said. I made up my mind to make it up to him later.

I didn't really want him to go away. Inside, I wanted him to stay, but the heated stares into my back dictated otherwise. I could imagine the race going on in Matt's and Lisa's hearts and minds. I knew their disappointment.

After all, they were once civil rights warriors in their day, the offspring of a former Black Panther. I wondered why I was such a coward and why I didn't stand up to them. What was I afraid of? I didn't want their approval, but I wasn't sure what I did want. Their pathetic version of love? Maybe. I caught a tear as it drifted toward my very Anglican nose.

Sadness overcame me for the first few minutes after Antonio left, yet I didn't move to stop him from leaving. In fact, I didn't move at all. Instead, I stood still with my back toward them and watched Antonio turn the corner.

"Makaeli, are you all right?" Lisa's voice was startling.

I didn't answer.

"Girl, answer me," Lisa said.

My head began to ache. I was filled with regret, but it was too late to run after Antonio. And it was too late to pretend that my life was normal. I didn't know what to do, so I waited, and as Matt and Lisa surrounded me, Mrs. Pearl's words resurfaced. *"What can separate you from the love of God? Nothing."*

Although I was unsure of the answers to everything, I was sure of one thing: I had ignored God long enough. He was calling my name. He was the only one who could heal my heart. Mrs. Pearl was right. It was time for me to get back in church.

I threw my coat and purse over my shoulder.

"I'll see you all later. I've got to make a run."

"But Makaeli," Lisa said.

"We've got to talk," Matt called out to me.

"Later." Within minutes, I was out of sight.

Chapter Twenty

Lisa

Matt and I witnessed the unthinkable—a rescue attempt by what appeared to be Makaeli's significantly white significant other.

"Did you see that?" I put my hand on Matt's shoulder.

"I couldn't miss it," Matt said.

"She ran out of here so fast."

"Lightning speed."

"I'm hungry and I'm sick of this cafeteria food. Let's go to that pizza place we passed on the way here last night," I said.

"You want something as messy as pizza?"

"Oh, don't be ridiculous."

"And this early?"

"Sure, why not?" I shrugged my shoulders, anxious to get on with the business of eating.

"Let's go," Matt said.

We left the building and walked through about an inch of snow to Angelino's Pizzeria, a block away from the hospital. It was a tiny take-out place with pictures of ancient Rome on the wall. There stood only a counter and a few stools, leaving barely enough room to stand; however, the smell that came from the oven outweighed any discomfort. So we ordered two slices of pizza and two Sprites to go. Then we went back out into the cold.

"So, who do you think that was with Makaeli?" I sucked down my first piece of mozzarella cheese, holding it carefully as we walked.

"I don't know, but they looked kind of close." Matt lifted his slice to his mouth.

"Close can't even begin to describe what I just saw. I definitely doubt they're business associates." I trudged through the snow slowly.

"She didn't even introduce him." Matt tried to pull his Knicks cap down over his ears.

"Introduce him? She practically ignored him. And where is she going in such a hurry?" I shook my head.

"Probably to go hang out with homeboy," Matt said.

"He's no homeboy. Didn't he look Italian to you?" As we neared a patch of ice, I grabbed Matt's arm to support myself.

"As Italian as this pizza."

"Maybe she brought him with her from Venice," I said.

"You mean hiding him at the Marriott all this time?"

"It's possible."

"Maybe," Matt said.

"I don't know what to think." I really didn't.

"I don't either."

We weaved in and out of parked cars, passing by a number of open stores and passing by many people. It was always busy in the city, even in inclement weather, yet I hardly noticed any of the details; it was all a blur.

With one hand on my hip and the other on my head, I moaned to make my misery evident. "I know, but this has been one of the hardest times for me."

"You've been acting a little crazy lately. What's up with you?"

"You mean besides the obvious, the sister in intensive care, the other involved with a white man, and this secret that's looming over our heads?" I stopped to lean against a fire hydrant.

"Yeah, you look different."

"That's because I'm pregnant." I gave up the secret as easily as it came to me.

"Congratulations." Matt saw the look on my face.

"At forty-eight? Save it."

"What?"

"It's bad timing."

Now, that was an understatement. Not only were Phil and I on the verge of divorce, but I was so depressed I couldn't even do anything about it.

"Well, how did this happen?" Matt put on his gloves and bent down to make a snowball.

"The usual way, and don't you dare throw that snow. I'm in no mood."

"No, I mean—" Matt let the snow fall through his fingers.

"I know what you mean. We hardly talk to each other anymore."

"Well, your condition has nothing to do with talking." Matt gently touched my stomach.

"I'm not laughing." I gave him one of my looks. "We weren't careful and here we are. Ironically, we've had separate rooms for about two months now."

"I'm sorry to hear that. Does Phil know about the baby?"

"He figured it out. I confirmed it. He panicked."

"That doesn't sound like my buddy Phil." Matt stopped in the middle of the sidewalk.

"This is a new day and a new Phil. Things aren't the same between us anymore." I grabbed his arm, urging him to keep walking.

"Why not?"

"I don't know how or when we started to drift apart, but it happened. We were always working, and then we were always consumed with all these family problems and never had any time for ourselves. Mama, Raquel, you, Makaeli, our own children. It never ends."

I thought about the last six months of virtual silence, the heated arguments over Makaeli, the extended working hours, and then there was my own depression. Just like Mama, I slowly slipped away from who I was. Phil tried to get me to go away with him, to loosen up and have some fun. I kept refusing, focusing only on perfecting my work and my home. Somehow, I probably let my duties as a wife slip. Somewhere along the line, I began to resent Phil and I think, as a retaliation, he began to resent me. It was as if all our years together, all the closeness we shared had deteriorated to nothing.

"You guys have had a lot to deal with," Matt said.

"Then to top it all off, Phil blames me for this whole mess with Makaeli, and I don't even know how to reach either of them. I don't even know how to reach myself." It was so cold I could see my breath when I sighed.

"I feel ya."

"This pregnancy is just added pressure to an already volatile situation." At that moment, I knew where I needed to be.

We were just a few feet from the hospital when I turned away from the direction we were walking.

"Matt, I'm going to have to talk to you later." I started walking toward the parking lot instead. All of a sudden I knew what I needed, what was missing in my life the whole time.

"Hey, where are you going?" Matt started to follow behind me.

"Home first. I've got some business to take care of. I'll meet you back here at about four o'clock, okay?"

"Okay, but—"

"I'll see you later." Directions never seemed as clear as they did now.

Chapter Twenty-one

Makaeli

Everyone at Calvary Missionary Deliverance Church looked happy. The ushers greeted me at the door wearing their stoic white uniforms, stockings and white gloves. The deacons, missionaries and church mothers sat on opposite sides of the front row. The quaint sanctuary was welcoming with its fluffy dark gray carpet and silver accents. The cushioned seats were softer than I remembered them.

The choir sang their hymns in harmony, rocking back and forth in their burgundy-and-gray robes. Their voices boomed like thunder against the stained glass windows, and the rhythm was familiar to me. They sang "Our God is an Awesome God." Clapping didn't seem as natural as it used to, but I did it anyway.

Well, Lord, I'm here. Now what?

Sitting next to me was a lady in her mid sixties with a huge red feathered hat. Whenever she shouted "hallelujah!" her chestnut brown wig rose around the edges of her silver gray hair. People were steadily fanning. *What a spectacle.*

Then a younger group came up to sing; three women and two men dressed in matching orange-and-brown outfits. Two of the women, obviously in their early twenties, wore caps on top of their braided extensions. The third woman wore nothing on top of her curly 'do. Both the men and the women wore brown boots and brown leather blazers. I wasn't used to this kind of youthful, hip look in church, but I liked it. They sang a song about God being a refuge, which I didn't recognize but that was understandable considering the length of time I was away from church.

Taking in all of the details, including the colors and fabrics that the congregation wore, kept me mildly amused. But mostly I waited for God to speak through Pastor Brown.

His six foot seven inch frame towered over the maple wood pulpit as he grabbed hold of the microphone. As usual, the Word was enticing yet firm.

" 'There is no fear in love, but perfect love casteth out all fear: because fear hath torment. He that feareth is not made perfect in love.' I John 1:18. I want to talk about how some of you are afraid today, living in the past, afraid of the future. Can I get an *amen*? Jesus came to us with God's great love that we read about in Ephesians 3:19," Pastor Brown said.

Pastor Brown preached, broke it down in many different ways. When the sermon was over, the congregation roared with *hallelujahs* and *amens*. The organ chimed in and the Holy Ghost took hold of the choir.

At the end of the service, just as I was about to sneak down the aisle, Pastor Brown came up to me and shook both my hands.

"How have you been, sweetie?" Pastor Brown said.

"Just fine, thanks," I said.

"It's good to have you back at Calvary Missionary, Sister Hunt." Pastor Brown gave me that deep-dimpled smile.

"I'm surprised you remember me. It's been so long," I said.

"Yes indeed, it has, but I never forget a young person's face. Especially a young person that was once on fire for the Lord. That is until you stopped coming. What happened?"

"A lot of problems at home, Pastor," I said.

Suddenly, the memory of me trying to squeeze myself into the pantry while Raquel poked me with a broom broke my concentration.

"I hope things are better for you now. And if not, you're in the right place."

Overwhelmed by his straightforwardness, I let my lips form a smile, but there was resistance behind it.

"Mrs. Pearl told us about your sister and we've been praying for her. How is she?"

"Still comatose."

"I see." Pastor Brown pulled on his beard.

"We're hopeful, though," I said.

"Oh yes, there is always hope," Pastor Brown said.

"Our hope is built on nothing less than Jesus and his righteousness." A lady I recognized as one of the missionaries stopped and threw her arms around my neck.

She asked me where I had been all these years and I explained that I lived in Italy. Then she gave me a puzzled look and said she had to meet with one of the elders.

"You take care, baby." She grabbed an older lady as she passed by and walked away with her.

"Thank you for a meaningful sermon." I turned back to Pastor Brown.

"All of God's Word has meaning if you seek Him," Pastor Brown said.

"Well, I've got to get back to the hospital now. Being in this sanctuary brought back a lot of old memories."

"They don't have to be just memories. Jesus is still real for today." Pastor Brown pointed to the altar.

"I know. But I'll be going back to Italy soon," I said.

"You're a designer, right? Mrs. Pearl always talks about you."

"Yes, sir." I looked directly at him.

"Well, you can certainly visit, but make sure you find a church home in Italy. They do have some, don't they?"

"Yes, sir. Most are Catholic churches, but I do know of one non-denominational one." I wasn't sure what reaction he would have to this information, but nevertheless, it was the truth.

Pastor Brown raised his eyebrows. "Get in church and get in God."

"Yes, sir." I agreed to what I had already agreed in my heart to do.

"You take care now," Pastor Brown said.

"You too, Pastor Brown." I wondered if I would make it back to God in time.

He walked away slowly and then blended into the congregation as if he were never there.

I was about to sneak past the hugs and roaming eyes, but as I approached the last row, a familiar head of wavy hair startled me. *What is she doing here?*

Chapter Twenty-two

Lisa

That place was the epitome of bad taste—the polyester curtains, the dull color of the carpet—but I'd keep my opinion to myself. After all, I wasn't there for aesthetics. I was there to feed my hungry soul. My desperate soul.

Pastor Brown delivered an interesting sermon. Something about fear interfering with love, and that certainly was me these days. Lately, I was afraid all the time. Afraid of Phil leaving me, afraid of having another baby at my age, and afraid of telling Makaeli the truth. I hadn't heard a sermon like that for years, or any church sermon for that matter, since Phil and I visited Aunt Lucy's church one Easter Sunday about ten years ago.

At the end of service, I remained seated in the pews, feeling a little awkward, looking around to see if I recognized anyone, but I didn't. I looked at the ushers, the choir and the clergy going about their business, laughing and talking as if this church thing weren't a serious matter. I couldn't understand their joy; not when trouble was all around me. Feeling out of place, I held my mink coat snugly around me as if it were a shield protecting me from this unfamiliar experience.

When most of the crowd had cleared out, as I bent over to pick up my matching mink hat, I noticed a familiar scent rising in my nostrils—peach body butter, Makaeli's scent. When I raised my head, I saw her standing in the aisle beside me. She was wearing a sleek black dress and black leather boots.

"Makaeli, what are you doing here?"

"Well, I can ask you the same thing."

We both laughed at the irony of the situation and decided this was not the ideal place to talk.

Within minutes, Makaeli and I found the nearest coffee shop, Jenny's Java House. It was a greasy little place with abstract paintings on the wall, polka dot tablecloths and miniature abstract sculptures on each of the tables.

"Pretty eclectic, huh?" Makaeli smiled and I knew she was comfortable in her element.

"It's a mess, if you ask me. I'm not with all of this artsy stuff." I dusted off a stool and sat at the counter.

One waitress with an earring in her nose stood behind the counter and took our orders. Another waitress walked by wearing low cut hipster jeans and a polka dot T-shirt tied up to reveal a butterfly tattoo on her lower back, right above her buttocks. I shook my head in dismay.

"Nice dress," I complimented Makaeli.

"Thanks. I designed it," she replied.

"You're very talented."

"So what were you doing back there at Calvary? Did you follow me?"

"Follow you? Of course not. I didn't even know you were there until I looked up and saw you after service."

"Oh, I thought maybe—"

"Believe me, I was as surprised as you were," I said.

"I'm sorry. It's just that when I saw you I—I never knew you went to church."

"I don't. This was the first time I've been in years. Never saw the need for it really until now."

"I see," Makaeli said.

"What about you?" I wanted to bond with Makaeli, to feel like her sister again.

"Gradually, I saw the need, but I kept putting off going back. Something kept holding me back, I guess." Makaeli stared at the table.

I wondered what she knew about setbacks. I gave up my whole life for her and this secret I was carrying.

"Mmmm," I said.

The waitress set down our coffees in record time. Uncomfortable in each other's presence, we drank them in record time also.

"Pastor Brown really brought that message about love home, huh?" Makaeli looked up as if it were a test question.

"Oh yes, he did. It was just what I needed to hear." Surprisingly, I aced the test.

"Me too."

"Are you going back to the hospital now?"

"Where else would I go?" Makaeli stood up and fumbled around in her purse.

"Okay, let's go." *Thank God the interrogation is over.*

We walked toward the exit.

"Lisa," Makaeli said.

"Yes?" I stopped short of opening the door.

Makaeli held a photograph out to me. "By the way, do you know anything about a dead baby?"

Chapter Twenty-three

Makaeli

Lisa did not answer my question but promised she would once she reached the hospital. First we stopped at home so she could change out of her fancy clothes. She offered to take me to the hotel to change also, but I convinced her I was comfortable enough in the clothes I was wearing. I didn't want any more delays in getting to the truth.

We drove through the streets to the hospital in almost total silence.

The only thing she told me was that she and Phil were expecting a baby and that it wasn't a good time for it. She didn't explain the details, so I didn't pry. I figured it had something to do with her age, though. After all, in less than two years she would be fifty.

When we finally reached the hospital, Lisa stayed in the restroom for quite a while. So much so that I began to be concerned. When she came out, she walked directly over to me as if she had been practicing how to approach me. Matt was already waiting.

"Sit down, Makaeli. I'm going to answer all of your questions, as hard as this may be for me," Lisa said.

"Nothing is ever hard for you," I told her.

"That's not true. This is very hard for me. I don't know where to begin." Lisa wiped the sweat from her brow.

"How about at the beginning?" I suggested.

"Well, it all started with Mama and your father," Lisa said.

"Okay, go ahead." I nodded.

Standing over me, Lisa appeared to brace herself, stiffening her neck and shoulders. She sat down across from me. Matt plopped down into another armchair.

"Two years after our father died, Mama met Oliver Hunt." Lisa's voice was as steady as it always was.

"Right, my father," I said.

"Yes, he was a senior partner at a rival law firm," Lisa continued.

"I know that already." I was instantly annoyed.

"He was infatuated by Mama and she was—lonely. Oliver wasn't a bad looking older guy. In fact, I thought she hit the jackpot when he pulled up into our driveway in his red Porsche." Lisa folded her legs, revealing a run in her silky stockings.

"That is, until we learned he was white," Matt said.

Now there was that color issue again. I wanted to crawl inside myself and pull my skin behind me. If I was turned inside out, all they would see is blood, tissue and bones. We all looked the same underneath.

"But they looked good together, and Oliver was spoiling Mama with expensive gifts, so I guess we all dropped our guard just a little." Lisa was perspiring around her hairline. "No, we dropped our guard a lot."

"All Mama's friends and colleagues thought they were the perfect power couple. Everybody except us, of course.

After we got to know him a little, we knew." Lisa continued, barely pausing to breathe.

"Knew what?" I wanted to know.

"That he really wasn't the man he should have been; not that he ever pretended that he was. But after he broke Mama off with that five-carat rock, what could we say? She took the bait," Lisa said.

"What do you mean 'bait'?" It was getting interesting.

"You know, the good looks, charm and—" Lisa rolled her eyes.

"Plenty of dead presidents," Matt finished Lisa's sentence.

"Okay, so he had a little bling, and?" I was already getting hot.

"Mama was hooked, and looking back on it now, I can't say that I blame her. The man was a very eligible bachelor. So after a whirlwind romance and a two-month engagement, the wedding was on," Lisa said.

I imagined my father, a man I saw only in one wedding picture, towering over Mama's five foot eight frame, and yet ruggedly handsome. I remembered that he had dark hair and dark eyes, nothing like mine. He also had a smile that said "winner." *Too bad it seems as though I'm about to hear he's a loser.*

I quickly jumped back into the flow of conversation.

In the minutes that followed, they explained how my father was a cold and calculating attorney. How his father was a judge and his grandfather was a district attorney back in Detroit, implying that he had inherited his passion.

For a minute, I thought I missed him. But it was impossible to miss someone I never knew.

Then they told me how he never liked them, and how he and Mama argued over sending them to boarding school in Maine. It was almost too much information to absorb.

"Only six months into the marriage, Mama got pregnant and the honeymoon was over. In his demented mind, I don't think he ever saw himself as a father at all," Lisa said.

My head dropped in despair. Just as I'd always suspected. My birth was a burden and inadvertently, the cause for Mama's condition. Not only that, but I had probably run my father off as well. To me, that explained why he never tried to make contact with me before he died. Vomit crept up into my throat, but I held it back by will. I should have let them continue, but I needed a break from this baring of the soul.

"I'll be right back. I've got to go to the ladies' room," I said.

In the restroom, I splashed cold water on my face. I pulled my hair up into a ponytail and reapplied my lipstick. I leaned against the sink and stared at myself in the mirror. *Am I ready for this? Is it time to bring out the note?* I patted my purse the same way people pinch themselves to see if they're dreaming.

Two women entered the restroom. Beautiful women, actually. They had cocoa brown skin, the kind I wished I'd had for so long. One wore a short Halle Berry style bob and a denim pantsuit, and the other wore long braided extensions and a denim skirt outfit. Both wore thick-heeled boots. I looked down at the black dress and boots I was wearing, and felt out of place. I had originally planned to wear this outfit to Raquel's funeral. Who would have imagined I would've ended up in church?

I dialed Antonio's cell, hoping he would comfort me with his kind words; hoping I could meet him in New York, where he could soothe me with his gentle hands. Just hoping that for a little while things could be normal and I could feel beautiful and loved. Even if it wouldn't last. His phone rang again and again. No answer. I didn't bother to leave a message.

I walked out of the restroom, not knowing what awaited me. My feet were tired from walking in these heels, so I limped slowly back to the waiting area. I grabbed the sides of the same arm chair I sat in before and fell back into it.

"Are you okay?" Lisa asked.

"I'm fine. Now, go ahead." I moved in closer and positioned myself so that my eyes were fixed on theirs. I hung onto every word, intensely waiting for this sacred something they wanted to drop on me.

Just as I was about to catch the words as they dripped from Lisa's tongue, Phil came up behind Lisa.

"Hello, everybody," Phil said. He tapped me gently on the shoulder. I don't remember exactly what Phil said because I was still focused on what Lisa and Matt had to say. After a few minutes, I saw Phil turn his back to us and go in to see Raquel. Lisa went with him and Matt went to the vending machine down the hall. I, on the other hand, spent the remaining minutes pacing the floor until Matt returned with the sodas. Then Phil emerged from the room with Lisa close behind him. Finally, without hesitation, Phil said goodbye and was gone.

Lisa looked like she felt awkward around her husband. "He just came to check on her during his break."

"I figured," I said.

"Well, I imagine you're ready to continue with the matter at hand," Lisa said.

"Yes, please," I told her.

"Okay, let's see. Where was I?" Lisa scratched her head.

"Mama's marriage wasn't going too well," Matt reminded her.

"Right. Now I remember. Since I was away at Cornell, I missed most of the drama," Lisa said.

"I was right in the middle of it," Matt confirmed by nodding his head.

"I came home for two weeks in July and found the house empty. Raquel and Matt had been sent off to a camp in Pennsylvania for the summer. Mama was round like a beach ball by then." Lisa bent her arms to look round like a ball.

"Life looked great on the outside." Matt was chewing and smacking his gum like it was his last chance to do so.

"But it wasn't?" I questioned, being drawn in deeper and deeper.

"No, it wasn't," Lisa answered in her usual bold voice.

Although Lisa's speculations were interesting, it would have been nice to hear all of this from Mama, to hear any of this from Mama. Poor, missing Mama. *What about the note?*

I motioned for them to stop talking because I couldn't hold it in any longer. I unzipped my purse, reached into my wallet and unfolded the note. Without a word, I handed it to Lisa. She looked at Matt, examined the words and began to read it aloud.

"Dear Lovechild, I'm sorry about how I let you down, how I let you die and how a part of me has died with you. Mama."

"Where did you get that?" Matt seemed to tremble.

"I found it in Mama's room the night before I went away to college," I said.

Lisa handed the note back to me. "I've never seen this particular note before, but—"

"But what?" I watched her face for clues.

"But I do know what it means." Lisa looked at Matt.

"Well, what does it mean?" I could hardly hold it in.

"When we finish our story, you'll know what it means too," Lisa said.

"Okay, I'm ready for what happened next." My eyes

quickly scanned both of their faces. They looked as if they had the air knocked out of them.

"It was the last day of summer camp. Lisa came to pick us up because the drive was too long for Mama." Matt unbuttoned the top of his shirt as if he was too warm.

"Mama was seven months already and feeling badly." Lisa began to speak slower, quieter, not at all like herself. "So Raquel and Matt stuffed their bags into my Volkswagen."

"We were rushing because it was raining so hard," Matt said.

"There was a severe storm watch going on. It was a mess," Lisa said. "So here they were wrapped in raincoats and smelling like camp, in my opinion. I drove really fast so I could beat the storm, drop them off and still get a little rest before heading back to school in the morning."

"We were through." Matt started fiddling with his mustache.

"I kept looking back at their pitiful faces in the rearview mirror and neither of them looked too healthy. Matt's face was too skinny and Raquel's was too plump. They both looked miserable to be going back. Raquel wanted to know why I didn't take Mama's car, and she was whining about having a bad headache. I had to endure so much complaining."

"Okay, so . . ." I sat on the edge of my seat.

"I ignored Raquel because I figured she was just depressed." Lisa took a deep breath. "Anyway, I hoped that Oliver wouldn't be home, but when we pulled into the garage, I saw his little two-seater. I knew he was probably in his office, his usual hiding place. Snakes always need a place to hide."

"Got that right." Matt stuffed another stick of gum into his mouth.

"So Matt and Raquel sneaked upstairs with their bags

and I left them to unpack. I went to check in on Mama because sometimes she took afternoon naps. That's when I heard their voices." Lisa frowned up her face as if the memory hurt her.

"Whose voices?" I was almost afraid of the answer.

"Mama and Oliver were arguing again. So I turned on the automatic coffee maker and waited. A few minutes later, I heard him zoom away," Lisa said.

"So he left?" I uncrossed my legs and adjusted my body in my seat.

"Yes, Oliver left. I decided to give Mama a little time to recuperate before I came busting in, so I went upstairs instead. Unfortunately, before I hit the top step, I heard a scream," Lisa said. "That's when Matt ran out of his room to see what was going on. He ran straight into me as I was coming up the stairs."

"Bam." Matt slapped his hands together.

"We didn't knock." Lisa's eyes became wide with the memory. "We just ran into Raquel's room together."

"What happened?" I was hooked.

"When I pushed the door open, that's when I saw . . ." Lisa squeezed her eyes shut as if she was in pain. "That's when we saw the blood."

Chapter Twenty-four
Lisa

"Blood?" Makaeli covered her mouth with her hands. "Yes, blood. We didn't know it yet, but Raquel was pregnant and about to give birth," My voice was getting louder as the intensity of the story increased.

"Pregnant? What?" Makaeli leaned forward in her seat and shook her head in disbelief.

"Yes, she was pregnant. Apparently, she had been able to hide it from everyone while she was away at camp. She was carrying very small, and even though she had gained a little weight, none of it looked like it was in her stomach area, so . . ." I didn't dare look at Makaeli's eyes. Instead, I looked up but brought my voice down a notch. "So she was trying to make it to the door to call us for help when . . . when the baby started to come out."

"That's so gross. I don't believe this," Makaeli said.

"Believe it. I was only a pre-med student then, but I managed to deliver her baby—a feisty little baby girl." I swallowed hard.

Makaeli held the sides of her head as if it was spinning. I watched a familiar doctor walk past us into another patient's room, and I lowered my voice again. Then I took a deep breath and continued the story, knowing there was no turning back.

"Next thing we knew, by the time I got Raquel settled down with that situation, we heard a loud bump downstairs," I said. "So we rushed downstairs and it turned out to be Mama. She had fallen and you're not going to believe this, but—"

"But what?" It was obvious that Makaeli was fed up by now.

"She had fallen and had gone into premature labor. Her baby was born in distress."

"What about the paramedics?" Makaeli's eyes glistened under the overhead lights.

"They were on their way, but it all happened so fast, almost simultaneously. And don't forget that we were in the middle of a terrible storm."

Matt's eyes were bulging. "There was no other way and no time."

"What a nightmare," Makaeli said.

"The worst is yet to be told. Mama's baby stopped breathing and couldn't be resuscitated." I had to look into her eyes now. "She died. The baby died."

"Died? What do you mean Mama's baby died? I thought the baby you were referring to was me. Did Mama have another baby besides me? What about the baby in the picture?" Makaeli put both hands on the center table as if to brace herself.

"No. Mama was only pregnant once since Raquel was born, and that baby is deceased." I looked down, wishing the floor could just swallow me up. "You, Makaeli, are alive and well."

"You are very much alive and well," Matt said.

"What are you saying?" Makaeli's eyes looked haunted. "I don't understand."

"We explained to Mama about Raquel's situation upstairs, that she had just delivered a healthy baby girl. Then we told Raquel about what happened to Mama's baby. Then Matt and I took Raquel's baby and placed her in Mama's arms." I put my hands over my mouth. It was so hard to push the words up to my throat.

"When the paramedics finally arrived, we all told them that Raquel's baby died." Matt looked directly into Makaeli's eyes, something I wasn't yet able to do.

"So you lied? But I don't—" Makaeli began to tremble as she fought to hold back the tears.

A million thoughts were running through my mind all at once as I imagine many were running through Makaeli's.

"Mama did not have another baby. The baby that Mama birthed on that night, the baby from the picture, was gone from us forever. I'm sorry. But you are Raquel's baby." I reached out my hand for Makaeli.

Chapter Twenty-five

Makaeli

"Oh no. Oh no." I stood up. My head felt light on my neck. I let out a wail from the pit of my soul. All the horror of my past began choking me. Lisa's words were like hot grease being poured over my skin, burning and seeping through my pores to my internal organs. The nightmare infiltrated me.

"We're sorry, Makaeli, but we didn't know what else to do at the time." Lisa stood up and held out her arms for me, but I didn't move from my chair.

"We're sorry," Matt said.

"You're sorry?" I couldn't believe my ears.

"Raquel was so young and scared, and Mama was so devastated, we—We didn't know Mama wouldn't recover and never be able to mother anyone again. The post-traumatic stress and—"

The incandescent lights were too bright. The laughter of the nurses was too loud. Everything around me was heightened. Images were blurred and contorted. Everyone faded until finally, so did I.

When I came back to consciousness, there were nurses all around me.

"Is she all right? If you all keep up this commotion, we'll have to admit her or call security," the head nurse said before going back to her desk.

"We're sorry, ma'am," Lisa told her. "We're just trying to settle a little family issue. It won't happen again, I promise." She lied so naturally.

A little family issue?

"Makaeli, are you okay?" Lisa tried to help me up off the floor.

The nurses stood in their places, watching and whispering to each other.

"Get your hands off me." I stood up straight, reached into my pocket and threw her spare house keys down on the table.

"Raquel wouldn't have been a good mother." Lisa lowered her voice.

"Oh, now, that's an understatement, don't you think?" I was fired up. "You all deceived me, deceived everybody. You, Matt, Mama, Raquel—all of you. What a joke. I guess the joke is on me," I said.

"Makaeli, please listen," Lisa said.

"Listen to what? More lies?" I said. "Now I know why no one wanted me around all those years. Now I know why." I walked toward the corridor, away from the waiting area, away from my mother's sick room.

"It's not like you think. Raquel used to be sweet. She was never the same since," Lisa said.

"Since me, right?"

"She was destroyed over it," Matt said.

"Yeah, I'm sure she was all broken up about it." It was time to torture them a little now.

"I'll get you some water." Matt walked over to the water fountain with a paper cup and began to fill it.

"Sweetheart, please," Lisa said.

"Sweetheart?" Her words made me sick.

"Calm down." Matt ran up behind me with the cup of water.

"Calm down? Don't tell me what to do. How dare you two," I said.

"Try to understand—" Matt reached for me, but I turned away.

"Understand? I understand that you two have been judge and jury over my life." I took the paper cup and threw it at him.

"Look, none of us ever spoke of that night again. It was as if Mama's delivery had been normal and as if nothing bad had ever happened at all," Lisa said.

"But something bad did happen. I'm here, aren't I?" The roof seemed to be caving in on my chest. I couldn't breathe.

"You're right; it did happen. At first we felt guilty, but as time went on, we realized it was really for the best," Lisa said.

"For the best?" I wiped my wet face with my hands.

"Raquel was only sixteen years old and didn't know what in the world to do with a baby," Lisa said.

"But Mama was mature and . . ." Matt said.

"We didn't know she would break down after that." Lisa looked down and shook her head.

"Well, I think this is enough truth for one day. I'm speechless." My tears stung my eyelids.

"Wait. There is more you've got to know about Oliver." Matt sighed before he began.

I sat down again, not knowing what I would hear. They continued to stand.

"Oliver Hunt, whose last name I have? Mama's husband? You mean the one who, up until a little while ago, I thought was my father?"

"Yeah, he showed up at the house a couple of days later. He never asked anything about his baby or about Mama. We caught him packing his things, leaving Mama stranded." Matt balled up his fists. "We had words, got into it, and I ended up stabbing him in the chest."

"Luckily for him, the knife missed any major arteries or he would have bled to death," Lisa jumped in. "The doctors credited the alcohol in his system for actually saving his life."

"So I went to jail for attempted murder, and the rest ain't worth talking about except that I wasn't tried as an adult." Matt frowned up his face, but I was unimpressed.

"Thank goodness for that," Lisa added.

"What about my real father?" I asked.

"We don't know much about him except that he was Caucasian also and that Raquel knew him from school." Lisa wiped a solitary tear from her eye.

I finally got the strength to stand up. "Okay, let me see if I've got all this straight. Oliver Hunt, who is now dead, who I always knew as my father but never knew, is not my father, but is actually my step-grandfather. The mother I knew as my mother but never knew, is really my grandmother and my real mother is the sister I've known and despised all my life." All the little pieces to the puzzle were swimming around in my head, trying to make sense out of nonsense.

"Yeah, and we're sorry it went down like this." Matt opened his arms for me, but I walked away.

I took a deep breath. "Why tell me now after all these years?"

"We thought you should know in case Raquel—doesn't make it." Lisa's eyes seemed to plead with me.

"Oh, so we get to have one shining mother and daughter moment on her deathbed, is that it?" I asked.

I picked up my coat and purse. Matt tried to grab my arm, but my purse fell instead. I punched him in the stomach and then bent down to pick up my things. When a platinum card fell out of my wallet, I threw it at him. "Buy yourself a conscience."

Matt ran after me, but Lisa called him back. She was always the sensible one. I ran in and then out of the elevator, into a taxi and then back to the hotel, breaking the heel on my boot along the way.

The ride was unbearable, with my heart feeling chipped away like the ice we were rolling over. Time and space seemed to lapse and I exited the taxi in a daze, tipping the driver far more than I intended to. Nothing mattered. I ignored the greetings of the hotel personnel, took the elevator up, walked unsteadily down the hall and fell against my room door when I came to it. My hands were shaking and I barely kept my key card steady enough to open the lock.

Once I was inside, I threw off my coat and slid down to the floor.

It was the darkest day of my life when they told me the truth. It was like the lights went out in my soul. After all I had gone through, this was the final punch to the throat. I was numb.

Nothing could have prepared me for what I heard, for the anger and disappointment I had to swallow, not even my already hardened heart. Nothing.

I thought about the notion that Raquel, the dreaded one, was my birth mother, and I cried as the wounds of abandonment were reopened and the pangs of neglect were revisited.

I cried again for the loss of my mother, Mama, who was

now my biological grandmother. I cried for Raquel, the one who had unwillingly brought me into the world. Then I cried for this whitish-black skin I was in, for the way it confused the issue, isolated me and made people choose sides. Mostly I cried for the betrayal by Lisa and Matt, the only family I had left. *Why is such a loving God allowing me to suffer so much?*

I lifted myself up slightly and crawled over to the small refrigerator in search of a cure. I wanted serious alcohol in my system immediately, but all I saw was soda and beer. I thought about going downstairs to the bar. Some Bacardi would do the trick, but I decided to settle for the Budweiser instead. After years of trying to tame myself, I was giving up the struggle.

I sat down on my queen-sized bed and popped open the can, visualizing the buzz I would feel. Every nerve inside my body seemed to scream for its burning sensation. I wiped away my tears with my sleeve and lifted the can up to my mouth. Before my lips touched the aluminum, I heard Mrs. Pearl's voice in my head. I put down the beer and reached for the drawer of the nightstand where I pulled out the Bible. Then I flipped to the Twenty-third Psalm. *The Lord is my shepherd; I shall not want.*

"Lord, I thank you for being where I can't be and for seeing what I can't see. Amen."

Frustrated by my temptation, I emptied the alcohol into the toilet. Then I rolled up into the middle of the bed without even taking off my coat. I flipped on the television just in time to see a guy named Smokie Norful perform on a gospel awards show. I drifted off to sleep listening to him sing "I Need You Now." *Come rescue me. I need you right away.*

Chapter Twenty-six

Lisa

When I walked through the electronic doors of the local food mart, I was heavy with the burdens of this particular Monday, the day after we had told Makaeli the truth. I looked ahead of me at the tunnel-like row of shopping carts and saw a dead end, like my life. I chose a sturdy one for myself and kept moving. I looked over at my son, Johnathan.

He plodded behind me in his usual teenage fashion, loose fitting jeans, at least as loose as I'd allow, nothing too sagging. I wouldn't stand for his pants to dangle around his knees with his underwear showing like most of the common people. No, I wouldn't stand for that, not then, not ever.

I waited for him to catch up to me and we started down the aisles, each one of us in our own world, each of us probably oblivious to the other. The apricot-colored walls, bright lights and colorful displays should've lifted my spirits, but my spirit was another story these days.

I gathered up the usual: low fat milk, whole grain cereals and bread, a few steaks, some coffee, a rack of lamb, fruit juice and an array of leafy green vegetables.

I stopped in the middle of everything and thought of my unrelenting husband and how detached he was from me lately. There I stood in the middle of the aisle with green peppers in hand, and despite my usual resolve, I took a deep breath and allowed myself to cry. My eyes filled up with tears, and before I could wipe them away, Johnathan turned to me.

He frowned up and said, "What's wrong, Mom?"

"Oh, it's nothing. I've just been handling these onions." I grabbed a huge yellow one and held it close to my face.

"Oh," he said.

But Johnathan was a bright boy, and in his eyes, I saw his father's curiosity. I knew he probably didn't believe me, but I was grateful that he didn't question me further.

My left eye began to twitch slightly and I covered it with my right hand. Were Mama's symptoms invading me? I hoped Johnathan hadn't noticed anything. I had barely noticed anything myself and I was living in this body. A little pressure here and there had made the difference, but hopefully not to inexperienced eyes.

"Mama, you forgot the cake mix for Dad's birthday next week."

"Right, but I'll have the entire affair catered, cake and all." I sighed. "Believe me, I'm in no mood for baking."

"Whatever," Johnathan said.

"On second thought, maybe I'll bake a special cake for him."

"Cool."

I looked into his eyes and saw his father's. "I hope so."

Then he walked away from me looking like his father,

sounding like his father, and reminding me that I still loved his father.

I didn't want to be this vulnerable, but I was. So I continued down the aisle and to the checkout counter. I walked past the young, vivacious woman with the perky breasts and firm thighs, past the wrinkled, hunched over elderly women and past the unshapely, invisible middle-aged women who, like me, were trying to mask their broken lives with food and familiarity.

I smirked at the twenty-something-year-old cashier, who smiled at me with a mouth full of braces and a head full of weave. Then I left the store, dropped Johnathan and some of the groceries off at my in-laws' house and started my own lonely drive home.

After putting the groceries away, I went down into the basement to do the laundry. There was a pounding in my head that nearly drowned out the sound of the washing machine. This dark, dreary room was my least favorite part of the house.

Over in the corner I saw my sons' ten speed bicycles, baseball helmets, bats and football equipment, and I smiled as I remembered when my life was simpler.

Although I enjoyed having Johnathan help me with the shopping, I was glad he was still staying with his grandparents, and I was also glad that Matt would be leaving soon so Phil and I would finally have the opportunity for privacy. I doubted it would be beneficial, however.

I started the long journey upstairs, desperate to at least start a normal conversation. Phil barely looked up from his newspaper when he saw me come into the room.

"Well, at least Makaeli knows now." I began to fold the clothes from the laundry basket, one by one.

"Don't you feel better now that she knows?" Phil pulled his glasses farther down on his nose.

"I don't even know," I said.

"Why don't you know?"

"I guess I feel a little freer, but I also feel like I've lost my sister." I stopped folding and sat down on the bed. Phil and I hadn't been this close to the bed at the same time in weeks. Tension was building.

"You had already lost her. Now you have the chance of getting her back."

"Maybe," I said.

"She'll come around now that she knows some things." Phil always had the right answers.

"You're right as usual." When I put my hand on top of his, I noticed his wedding ring was gone, but I was too afraid to comment.

He switched on the television and flipped to a basketball game. I sat next to him on the bed, afraid to move around on the mattress, afraid he might mistake this nearness for intimacy and run to his office for safety. I watched the back of his balding head move back and forth with enthusiasm as he shouted for the New York Knicks.

I remembered that in a few months we would have a new baby, and I sighed at the thought. *Imagine, a woman of my age with a baby.*

My toes accidentally brushed across his leg and he quickly moved to the armchair. Just as I was about to confront him about it, Matt knocked on the door.

"Come on in, Matt." I opened the door for him.

"After I leave the hospital tomorrow, I'm heading to New York City to pick up a few things for Carmen and to take care of some business, but I'll be back in a day or two," Matt said.

"We understand. There is nothing else you can do here anyway." I was ready to give up the fight. "We'll probably be burying Raquel soon."

"Don't say that." Matt plopped down on my bed.

"There has been no progress. In fact, her condition seems to be rapidly declining." I put on my most serious doctor face.

Phil looked over his glasses. "That doesn't mean things won't turn around."

"But she might not even have the will to live." I pushed Matt off my bed and started to straighten up the covers. "No one sits on my bed except me."

"We don't know for sure if Raquel has given up." Matt sat down on my cherry wood bench.

"I wouldn't blame her after all she has been through." I continued to fold my clothes.

"I haven't given up on Raquel just yet. She's a tough cookie." Phil folded his newspaper. "Where do you think Makaeli gets that fighting spirit from?"

"What about Makaeli?" Matt looked sad now.

"Like Phil told me a few minutes ago, she'll come around. I don't know how or why, but I'm praying she will," I said.

"But what if she doesn't?" Matt walked through my bedroom door and peeped back in.

"Then I'll do what it takes to make sure she does," I yelled out at him.

A few minutes after Matt left the room, Phil put on his shoes, took his wallet off the nightstand and went downstairs. I didn't bother to ask where he was going. Instead, I let the warmth and coziness of my room, along with my own depression, lure me into a much-needed rest. When I opened my eyes from my nap, I focused in on the ceiling fan. With a yawn of frustration, I climbed out of bed and looked at my alarm clock. This sleeping in the middle of the afternoon was definitely not my style.

I dialed Makaeli's cell number and listened to it ring.

When the voice mail came on, I didn't know what to say.

"Makaeli, give me a call when you're up to it." I hung up the phone.

Looking outside the window, I saw that Phil's Range Rover was gone. When I peeped out into the hallway, I heard the big screen television with surround sound blasting downstairs. So I put on my snow boots, tiptoed down the steps, walked past the living room where Matt was probably laid out on my couch, and grabbed my coat from the hall closet. Then I walked quietly out the front door.

I closed the door behind me and began to walk up the ice-covered sidewalk. I put my hands into my pockets because I hadn't remembered to bring my fur-trimmed gloves.

I walked until I couldn't feel my hands or feet anymore. Then I ducked into the nearest store to buy a Snickers bar. I'd been craving one all day. As I was about to go up to the counter, I felt a hand on my shoulder. I turned around to see what was going on, and that's when I looked into the face of a dark-skinned bearded man.

"Lisa Cambell, I thought that was you. Don't you remember me?" He smiled, revealing a mouth full of perfectly even teeth.

"I don't think I do." Before I could finish paying the cashier, I recognized him. *Trouble.*

"From South Brunswick High School, remember?" He pushed open the door.

"Yes, it's just that I'm Dr. Jackson now," I said.

"Oh, I'm sorry. I didn't know."

"Don't be. How have you been? Darrius, right?" I followed him outside.

"That's right. Darrius Johnson. Me and Matt used to shoot hoops together after school—I mean Matthew."

"Yes, I do remember you. You used to come by the house sometimes."

"That's right."

"I used to wear braces." He smiled so I could see his straight teeth.

"I remember." I shook his hand and started to walk away. "It's good to see you again."

"How is he? I mean, I heard he got into some trouble during senior year."

"Yes, it was all over the news." My upper lip tightened. "That's how I first found out about it—from the news."

"Well, that was a long time ago. It was an accident, really." I swallowed hard.

"Oh?"

"But Matt is fine. He lives in California now." My eyes avoided his.

"Really? I travel out there to do business from time to time. Maybe I'll look him up."

"Yes, you do that. I've got to run." I started walking away from him.

"If you speak to him, let him know I asked about him."

"Will do, Darrius." I crossed the street and slid into the doorway of a storefront where I couldn't be seen. I had to catch my breath. That one threw me for a loop. I hadn't gone through anything that embarrassing since Matt was paroled from the state penitentiary thirteen years ago.

From my hiding place, I watched him use his remote to unlock his car door and drive away in his black Mercedes Benz.

As I began the long walk back to the house, I remembered those high school years and all the popularity we had, Matt, Raquel and I, before the incident. Naturally, after Matt's picture was plastered all over the country, the neighborhood began to swarm with rumors, gossip and innuendos, all circling our family. That's when the end had begun.

Walking was normally something I loathed, yet today I knew my bloated body needed the exercise. So I walked, breathing hard the entire time, until I reached the cold, icy front step. I was so out of shape. Before going into the house, I thought about Makaeli again and wondered if she had returned my call.

I'd have to try her again and then make my way back to the hospital.

Chapter Twenty-seven

Makaeli

When I opened my eyes, the first thing I saw was the sun peeping through the burgundy drapes. It was a beautiful Monday morning. My room was so nicely decorated with ornate vases of fresh flowers and sweet little landscape paintings. Under normal circumstances, I would have enjoyed the luxury of it, but the days weren't normal anymore.

Sunlight beamed down on my forehead as if it were burning a hole in my brain. I looked at the clock and saw that it was almost noon.

I had a terrible headache, so I climbed out of bed and took two aspirin. Then I sank back into the covers, sighing and crying, but I realized that neither would change my predicament. While I wrestled with self-pity, feeling like life spat on me once again, I was suddenly compelled to pray. So I crawled out of bed and dropped to my knees.

"Please, Lord, show me what I need to do next. You filled me once before. Please fill me again because I'm empty. Please fill me again. Amen."

After a quick shower, I hurried to get dressed, packed and ready to go. The phone rang again and again, but I knew it was the traitors. They couldn't disguise their ring. I gathered all my belongings and walked out of the room with the phone still ringing.

When I turned in my room key and settled my account, I called a cab from the front desk.

"Thank you for staying with us, Ms. Hunt. It has been our pleasure serving you," the hotel clerk said.

"Thanks," I replied.

The cab came and whisked me to the hospital. Although the wind threatened to unravel my neat hair bun, I didn't care at all. I was determined to see Raquel, the sister-mama, at least one last time.

The elevator door opened and I took a deep breath before stepping inside. A medium-built man with olive-shaded skin and low-cut black hair was already in the elevator. He eyed me sensuously from my lime green sweater to my snug-fitting jeans, but the glare he received in response was no invitation. *Brother, don't even think about it.* I guess he knew not to approach me after that one.

All I cared about was that the sister-mama would live long enough, at least, to tell me the truth.

Lisa and Matt were sitting in the same spot I left them in the night before. I wondered if they had even been home. The sound of their voices made my stomach turn. I trusted them with my life, and that is exactly what they stole.

I walked by their apologetic faces, holding up my hands so they would stay away.

"Makaeli, honey, I—" Lisa started.

"I think you've said enough." I opened the door to Raquel's room and went in.

There was a seat fairly close to the bed. The tubes didn't

scare me anymore. Life was the scary part, not death. All of the hiding, all of the secrets, all of the lies, all of the years. Life was more than scary.

I brought my head close to Raquel's and outlined her chapped lips with my fingernail. Her hands were about the same size as mine, only mine were nicely manicured and soft. Her bitten-down nails were a disgrace. Her nostrils were widened and full of tubes, and her arms had holes where needles were and where needles were no longer. Her face was a stony brown. Her wavy hair was without luster or form, and her body was like a long arrangement of bones. Some parts were swollen, while others remained slim. I touched the side of her cheek and it felt cool to my palm.

"It's me, Makaeli. I'm here and I know who you really are to me. I mean, I know I'm your daughter. Lisa and Matt finally told me yesterday. Even though I know how I was born, I need to know a lot more. There is so much more I need to know. Please come back to us so I can know," I begged.

Exhausted, I put my head on the bed rail. My eyes were closed. Just a few seconds of rest would ease some of the pain. Despite my best efforts to hold them back, those dreaded daydreams drifted in.

I imagined Mama wearing a long white dress with flowing white hair. She was twirling and dancing barefoot in a field of daisies. She was in no one's institution, with no bars or straps to hold her. Mama held a small, wavy-haired child in her arms, and I thought it was me. But when she turned around, it wasn't Mama at all. Underneath the wig and a wicked smile, it was Raquel.

I started sweating. *Maybe a pill will help.*

When I finally dug up an aspirin from my purse and looked up, Raquel's eyes were open. They were red and glossy, not at all like I expected.

"Oh my goodness." I didn't know what to do.

"You're . . . you're . . ."

She blinked as I stood over her, staring. She moved her left hand about an inch. I grabbed it to stop her from moving too much.

"Don't move. Save your energy. I know you can't talk to me, but I know about my birth. I just want to know . . ."

A tear ran down Raquel's face. My own face was red and wet as well.

"I just wanted to know what happened. I want to know why. I know you can't talk right now, but whenever you get better, I need to know why. Please just tell me why so I can let go." I dropped my head against the bed rail again.

Another tear fell from her eye. She lifted her hand to my arm. Her fingers seemed like ice on my skin. Her eyes rested on mine, but I couldn't bear to look into hers.

Seeing her eyes open sent a chill through me. Memories of her pulling me by my hair across the hardwood floor began to resurface. Images of my bloody fingerprints on the kitchen counter after suffering a busted lip clouded my vision.

I shivered in the cold room. Suddenly, I wasn't sure if being there was such a good idea. After all, what did I possibly expect to accomplish? So I decided that taking the first flight back to Italy was a better idea, where designs could be hidden behind, and where things made sense.

I dried my face with a Kleenex, left my chair and left the room without looking back.

Matt and Lisa stood when they saw me.

"She's conscious. You can go see her now." I walked by them both.

"Conscious?" Matt scrambled to his feet.

"Makaeli, please. We can't go on not talking," Lisa said.

Matt grabbed me by the arm, but I pulled away and ran down the corridor.

I heard Lisa say, "Let her go. She's a grown woman," as the elevator doors shut in Matt's face.

At hearing that particular comment, shame came over me, but not enough to make me turn around. I knew they would rejoice over the miracle and prepare for what would probably be a shaky recovery.

Before I left the building, I stopped at the chapel again. The chaplain was there talking with another gentleman. I slipped into the back row and bowed my head. After about two minutes, I felt his presence next to me.

"I'm glad you came back."

"Me too," I said.

"How are you?"

"I'm okay." I didn't look him in the eye, hoping he wouldn't notice that I had been crying.

"Have you resolved everything?"

"No, but I've been taking your advice." I rubbed my hands together, over and over again. Listening and waiting for answers.

"My advice?"

"Talking to God about it."

"Well, now, that's progress. What about your sister?"

"She's out of her coma," I said.

"That's good news."

"Yes, it is. I just wanted to stop by one more time before I go back home."

"Where is home?"

"Venice, Italy," I said.

"You're a long way from home then, aren't you?"

"I'm further away than you know." I thought I would break down right there, but I managed to hold on.

"Are you sure everything is all right with you? We can talk about it if you like."

"No, I don't want to talk about anything. I just wanted

to say thanks to you for being kind." I looked up and we caught each other's eyes. His eyes were chestnut brown.

"You're welcome," he said.

"An old friend of mine told me to get in church and get in God, so I figured I needed one more visit. If God is going to help me, I need to give Him something to work with," I explained.

"You have a very wise friend and you're getting wiser yourself." He smiled.

"Goodbye." I stood up and turned toward the door.

"Goodbye, dear."

I stopped before going out, but didn't turn to face him. "Do you really think God can work out anything, no matter how bad it is?"

"Yes, no matter how bad it is."

"No matter how much it hurts?"

"No matter how much it hurts, dear."

"Okay."

I nodded my head without turning around, wiped away the tears, walked out of the chapel, and out of the building.

When I was younger, I used to wonder why bad things happened, but by the time I was grown, I began to accept most suffering as normal. After a while, I hardly noticed the bad things because they rolled off my conscience like wax.

I decided not to call for a ride to the airport. I didn't want to be an executive pampered in luxury, cushioned from the world. I wanted to take the train this time, to walk and think and feel free like ordinary people.

So I started walking with my eyes toward the ground. The next thing I knew, I was watching the feet beside me, brown ones, beige ones and whitish pink ones. Some slow, some quick, but none that matched mine. Groundless. I felt like I was groundless, walking on air, like nothing was beneath me. Feeling faint, I stopped to lean against a lamp-post.

A middle-aged woman, whose face was framed by an afro, stopped to offer me assistance. I thanked her for her concern and started walking again.

My heart felt like someone had placed an eighteen wheeler inside my chest instead of a heart. As I approached the station, I remembered the one time Matt and I rode the trains together from Jersey to New York City and back. Matt was thirty-two, fresh out of prison and very angry back then, which, as an angry teenager, fit perfectly with my agenda.

My cell phone rang, bringing my mind back to the present. I turned it off, stifling their attempts at reconciliation. I didn't want to be reminded of Matt or Lisa. I just wanted to go home. I thought of something Mrs. Pearl said to me about God being my refuge and strength, a very present help in trouble. I couldn't remember which scripture in Psalms it was, but I knew I was in trouble and needed help.

So I took the train to Mrs. Pearl's neighborhood and walked the two blocks to Pearl's Cloth World. I took one look at the rusted iron security gate, which was still locked, and realized the store was closed. I should have called first.

An old man sat on top of a milk crate in the abandoned lot next door. I watched him pick up a paper bag with a bottle in it and pour the contents into his mouth. His eyes were beady and red, and his voice was scratchy.

"Are you some kin to Mrs. Pearl?" he asked.

"No, sir, I'm just an old friend," I replied.

"You remind me of her."

"Oh?"

"Yep, you got this way about you. Anyway, she ain't here.

Won't be open 'til tomorrow. Gone out of town, I think."
He put the bag down beside him.

"Are you a friend of hers too?"

"Me and her go way back. But everybody around here knows Mrs. Pearl. She's an angel, that's what she is. Nicest woman I ever met, except for my mama."

"She's the nicest woman I've ever met too," I said.

I watched him pick up that bottle and remembered my own days of addiction, the passionate urging for alcohol that threatened to take me down for so long.

As I walked away from the store, I observed the deterioration of the neighborhood, crumbling walls of abandoned buildings, and the streets piled high with garbage. I pulled my coat closer to my body as a strong gust of wind cooled my skin.

I continued walking through the neighborhood, dodging broken glass thrown about on the pavement and watching the people who watched me. Their eyes seemed to follow me, but I didn't catch on right away. Then I realized it was my look, the one that was so deceiving.

"What is that white lady doing around here?" one teenaged boy said. He had one pants leg up and the other down, his cap turned backward and a cigarette hanging out of his mouth.

"She can't be white." A teenaged girl with a small afro rolled her eyes.

"Sure she is." The boy kept his eyes on me.

"Maybe she's Spanish or something." The girl eyed me as if I were a basket of fruit or a novelty of some kind.

I sucked in my breath and kept my thin lips pressed tightly together as if I didn't hear them, as if it didn't feel like pins and needles pricking my skin, as if I hadn't heard this my whole life. "Mama's little mulatto," they used to call me to my face. Never mind what they used to call me behind my back.

Then the teens moved closer to me. Noticing their smooth brown faces, thick noses and coarse hair, I knew they'd never identify with the pale, anonymous skin I was in.

Just as I had that thought and emotion seemed to drain from my heart to my head, the girl yelled out, "Hey, she's no white lady." Then she looked at me so hard it was as if her eyes were peering into my soul, as if she could hear my heart shattering into a thousand pieces, ones it had taken the last few years to patch together. But patchwork was my life.

"You're a sister, right?" the girl asked.

"I am." And I smiled a fake smile, walking away with a false dignity. From the back of my head I felt their eyes and I longed for a covering, an African robe or headdress; something that would hide my shame. *Lord, help me.*

As I went through an alley and up a dead end street, I heard footsteps behind me. My heart began to beat fast and I turned around quickly to see if the teenagers were following me.

I stared into the face of a brawny built man.

"Makaeli Hunt, I thought that was you," the man said.

"Yes, I'm Makaeli, but I—" I didn't recognize him at all.

"Well, I've gained a few pounds since I saw you last. Don't you remember me now?" He licked his thick lips.

"I'm sorry."

"We used to go out sometimes—a whole group of us at F.I.T."

"Oh, I remember now."

"Think hard. I know you missed me," he said.

"William?" I tried so hard to forget certain people and events, to detach myself from myself, and yet one had slipped through the cracks.

"Yes, it's me," he said.

"Good to see you," I said.

"What are you doing around here? I saw your sister a while back and she said you moved away, far away." His eyes were moving up and down my body.

"I did. I moved to Italy. I've only been in Jersey a few days."

Feeling uncomfortable, I buttoned up the top of my coat and tied my scarf around my neck.

"Oh really? What brings you home?"

"I had some business to take care of, and I'm on this side of the city to say goodbye to an old friend."

"So you're leaving so soon?"

"Unfortunately, I've got to get back to work."

"You went into fashion design, right?" He lit a cigarette.

"Right. What about you? Did you do whatever it was you were studying to do?"

"No. I haven't worked in over a year. I never did complete my degree." He took a step forward.

"I'm sorry to hear that." I took a step back.

"Personal problems."

"I understand."

"You know the way we used to party. Well, it finally caught up to me."

"Believe me, it caught up to all of us," I said.

"You look like you've done well for yourself, though."

"That's because I put that stuff down. I had to get some professional help, but I haven't taken a drink in over five years."

"Good for you." He reached out to touch my shoulder, but I slid to the side. I couldn't stand the thought of him touching me anymore. I was no longer a naïve girl looking for love in all the wrong people. Those days were over.

"Look, why don't you stop by Calvary Missionary Deliverance Church one of these days and ask for Pastor Brown. Tell him I sent you." I reached into my purse and pulled out the program from Sunday's service.

"What good will that do?"

"Pastor Brown is a very resourceful man and the church has a lot of programs to help people."

"That's nice, but I don't know."

"Just go there and see," I said.

"Did they help you?"

"Yes, a long time ago. Since God is in control, I'm sure they can help you." I wondered how I could give advice I wouldn't take. "I've got a plane to catch, but you take care."

"Maybe next time you're in Jersey, we can hang out like the old days."

"I don't really hang out anymore, but we'll see." I threw up my hand in a waving fashion and left him standing there as I walked down the street and around the corner back to the train station. *I need a flight out of here ASAP.*

The old days. Who even wanted to remember those? A sister was still struggling with today.

Chapter Twenty-eight
Lisa

The moment Lashawn and I walked into the swanky seafood restaurant she chose, I knew I'd have no regrets about accepting her invitation. The surrounding aroma of fresh lobster and shrimp took me back to Mama's Creole cooking.

"Oh, it smells good up in here. I'm ready to get my eat on," I said.

"I know that's right," Lashawn said.

It was Monday evening and normally I would've been too tired by this time to go anywhere. Since I took a few weeks off from work, my schedule was totally free, and since Phil and I weren't on speaking terms, I was lonely.

We sat down on one of the padded benches in the lobby, waiting for our names to be called. Looking ahead at the black lacquer tables, the shimmering chandeliers and the white stone fireplace over by the bar, I began to wonder if I was underdressed. I fussed with the pearl pin on my very conservative navy blue pantsuit while Lashawn, decorated in a form-fitting apple red skirt suit, a black silk blouse, complete with knee-length boots and a red-and-black beret, rummaged through her purse.

Within the first few minutes, I told Lashawn everything that had gone on between Makaeli and me. She sat with her mouth open for a few minutes, then consoled me as if it were all old news. Before I knew it, we were comfortable with each other again. Good old Lashawn. Nothing shook her.

"Here you go." Lashawn handed me an envelope.

"What is this?"

"Just open it." Lashawn smiled.

I ripped through the paper quickly, anxious to see what the occasion was.

"A gift card to a spa?"

"Initially it was just for a girls' day out, but after what you've just told me, you deserve it."

I waved the card in the air. "Thanks. I guess you're right. I could use some relaxation time."

"And this is not just any spa. It's Le Merou, a very trendy, exclusive spa."

"Have you ever been there?"

"Nope, I've never been to that one, but I love the spa experience, so since I've got some time off, count me in."

"I hear you," I said.

Finally, a middle-aged waiter led us to our table and within minutes, we gave him our orders. As soon as he left our table, a short, stout gentleman sat down at the shiny grand piano and began to play a slow ballad.

"This place is really nice. I'm surprised you haven't mentioned it before."

"John and I just discovered it recently. Besides, I'm allowed some secrets, aren't I?" Lashawn gave me that typical "you should've told me" look.

"Touché."

"Have you heard from Makaeli yet?"

"No."

"I still can't believe you never told me about all this family drama before—all these years."

"That's the key word right there: *drama.*"

"So? I mean, I know you're a private person, but goodness, I'm your best friend."

"I know, but I just wanted to forget it ever happened."

"I understand. Baby switching is some deep stuff."

"Girl, it was a hot mess."

"You can say that again."

"It was buried as far as I was concerned. It wasn't until Raquel got sick that I even considered telling Makaeli."

"So you had no plan to ever let her know?"

"No. I would have taken it to my grave," I said.

"Ooh, now, that's deep."

"I didn't feel like it was my place. I always thought Mama or Raquel would tell her one day, but that one day never came, and then it seemed like it was almost too late."

"It almost was."

The waiter brought two glasses of water with lime, rolls, butter and salad. We thanked him and he went away.

"I didn't plan any of this, and that's not like me. I live by my plans and schedules, but this was different."

"Heck yeah, it was different." Lashawn stuffed a piece of roll into her mouth.

"This one threw me off course."

"That's understandable, I guess."

"I was so young back then. I certainly never expected Mama to get sick like she did."

"That was a rough time." Lashawn's ebony eyes seemed to sparkle under the lights.

"Very rough. I kept hoping she'd come home. So Phil and I would stay at Mama's house for a while and she'd seem to be better. Then she'd relapse again."

"That couldn't have been easy."

"Oh, *easy* never entered into my vocabulary, believe that." I smirked.

"I remember. You were a nervous wreck back then."

"But when Mama went in that last time and Phil and I decided to move in permanently, I didn't know what I was in for."

"Who ever knows what they're in for until they're in it?"

"I thought raising Makaeli would be easier than it actually was." I took a sip of my water.

"Who are you telling?"

I picked up a roll and began to spread honey butter on it. "Not that I had any experience with child rearing when she was born, but I watched Mama do it with us with such ease."

"Yes, I thought motherhood would be easy when Tashika and Tashira were born too. I stand corrected."

"I never dreamed Makaeli and I would have this rift between us, though."

"I know what you mean. Children don't always end up the way you want them to."

"Shoot, I guess all that was minor considering the size of this major family disaster." I bit into my roll.

"Girl, I don't know how you did it."

"I don't either. I just remember the secret kept getting bigger and bigger the more we covered it. Then finally it started leaking out from the sides like too much jelly on a peanut butter and jelly sandwich."

"Peanut butter and jelly. Now you're really reminding me of my girls." Lashawn smiled. "I'm surprised the stress alone didn't kill you."

"It didn't kill me, but it did rip me apart. For a while I thought I was going to have a nervous breakdown myself."

"I can only imagine," Lashawn said.

"There were the times Makaeli started asking questions about her father and then there was that silence the year Matt came home." I shook my head, knowing that secrecy was a way of life for us. It imprisoned us, and no matter how we tried to shake loose, the foundation, built entirely on lies, kept crumbling.

"How is Matt anyway? I've got to make some time to get by to see him."

"He's fine. He has his new family and—it's just this Makaeli thing that's out of control."

"Well, at least it's over and you can start rebuilding."

"Rebuilding what?"

"Your life."

"What life?" I looked at Lashawn as if she were a crazy woman.

"It might look broken down, but you can't give up." Lashawn smiled, revealing thousands of dollars worth of cosmetic dentistry. Her teeth were perfect beyond all reason.

"I'm not giving up, but I'm not sure how to fix it either."

The waiter returned with huge platters. He set down our entrees and we thanked him once again.

"Look, you let the past be in the past and you move forward." Lashawn reached for her plate and began to eat.

"Forward? Where exactly is that?"

"You're smart, so you'll figure it out."

"If I'm not dead first." I widened my eyes and began to eat also.

"You're strong. Just keep putting one foot in front of the other until one day the pain is gone."

"You know what? You're right."

"Aren't I always?"

"I'm going to move forward, but this time I'm going to pray first."

"Pray? You've been doing a lot of that lately, huh?"

"I've learned." I didn't even look up from my plate this time.

"I see you've learned well."

When I finally did look up, I smiled. "I've learned to do a lot of things in the last few days. When you've been to hell and back, oh, you'll pray."

"You're not going to become one of those holy rollers, are you?"

"Maybe I will, girl. Whatever it takes." I laughed and threw my hands in the air in mock surrender.

We continued to talk and laugh throughout the evening as good friends do, but after we paid our check, tipped the waiter and went our separate ways, I was sad again.

I picked up my cell phone and tried calling Makaeli's hotel room first. Then I tried her cell phone again. No answer.

I was sorry she had to find out the way she did and sorry she hated me, but I was glad to be rid of the lies we carried and nursed and the ones we buried. Now that the truth was out and I had a taste of freedom, I never wanted to go back to deception.

I drove home and walked into the empty house. I felt a chill go across my legs so I adjusted the temperature on the thermostat before I climbed upstairs. I took off my coat and threw it over the banister. I took off my navy blue pumps at the landing and carried them with me into the bathroom.

I looked at myself in the mirror, the graying edges of my hair and the skin that was no longer taut and smooth. Then I took off my pearl earrings, washed away the makeup with Noxzema and dried my face. I took off my blouse and examined my stomach, already stretching, and my breasts, already heavier. The reality of the baby inside me sank in.

I filled the tub with water and then slowly stepped in. Instead of calming me, however, the warm water and pink bubbles made me nauseated. As I climbed out and began to dry my weary body, I felt dizzy. I sat down on the side of my Jacuzzi tub and dropped my head down between my legs until I felt like myself again.

The tears came as an expression of all that I'd lost and of all that was to come. I didn't know about tomorrow because things were out of my control today, but inside, I believed things would be better, that God would carry me.

Arranging and rearranging things according to my will used to seem like a good thing. Playing God for so long surely messed everything up. Now it was time to let God be God. The responsibility of holding the family together was too much to deal with. I realized I was never and could never be the Almighty God I heard so much about. And as late as it was, it occurred to me that this is what went wrong in the first place. A sister had a wrong perspective of herself. *Lord, please save me from myself.*

I went into my bedroom and decided to call Mrs. Pearl. There was no answer, but I left a message so she would call me back. Then I covered my head with my blanket and planned to take charge of tomorrow as I drifted off into an uneasy sleep.

Chapter Twenty-nine
Makaeli

It took the entire train ride for me to recuperate before I was back on a flight to Milan. I was on my way to my only real home, where there was only beauty and no pain.

Destiny finally caught up with me and stabbed me in the back. I didn't have any idea why these tragedies occurred, but I knew I'd have to give up all hostility, resentment and vengeance and give myself, in love, in order to recover from them. Forgiveness clearly required something I wasn't ready to give yet—love. *Vengeance is mine, saith the Lord. I will repay . . .*

Looking out the window of the plane, I whispered, "I'm nobody's lovechild." I wondered why Mama would play games with my middle name, with my identity and then with my life.

I looked at the crumpled note until tears took over my thoughts. When it was soaked and the blue ink ran down the paper, I shoved it back into my purse.

I walked down the aisle of the plane, noticing all the smiling faces. One lady held her little boy in her arms. Another woman appeared to be with her husband and three kids. There were families everywhere. It was unavoidable. *Too bad I left mine and will never have one of my own.* I used the tiny restroom quickly. Then I leaned against the sink.

"Oh Lord, I'm crying out to you for answers. There has got to be more to this than the way I feel. I made a commitment to you once and now I know I let you down. Please forgive me, Lord, and take me back. I need you now more than ever. Please take me back. Amen."

When I went back to my seat, I pulled the collar of my coat up high and covered my head with my scarf, wrapping it all so tightly, as if I were in a cocoon, as if, like a caterpillar, I could transform myself from who I was and come out beautiful like a butterfly.

Back in Italy, I stopped at the pier. I knelt beside the water and let the wind blow through my hair. Staring out into the distance, I contemplated ending it all right there. I leaned over the edge, hypnotized by the beauty, and longed to dive in head first and head straight for the bottom. I planned to open my eyes and mouth on the way down, sucking in as much water as possible and watching the magnificent sea creatures before my lungs burst with abandon. At least my body would float freely through the waves without pain and without horror, I thought. Then, as I reached out over the side and almost lost my balance, I remembered hell and knew my torment wouldn't end if I took my own life. *Lord, forgive me for thinking like that.*

I stood up, looked up into the star-filled sky, and as the dark clouds rolled forward, I stretched my hands to God and called out to Him. "Jesus, please help me." I decided that only He could deliver me from this anguish.

When I left the *riva,* I went to the Bancomat to withdraw some cash from my account before boarding the train for home. I was so miserable I wasn't even sure if home would feel the same anymore. Surprisingly, as soon as I hit the covers of my own bed, I was relieved. Thank goodness, sleep came quickly.

Since I didn't want to be alone with my thoughts, I went straight back to work early. It was the only thing that took my mind off my problems.

When I arrived at my building on Tuesday morning, everything was quiet. I went into my office through the back door because I wasn't ready to deal with anyone face to face yet. I set my bag down and sat down behind my desk, ready to immerse myself in fashion. I checked my messages, checked my schedule and spoke with Nina on the intercom. I didn't want to see anyone yet. With only the sound of my pencil marking on my sketches, it was too quiet. So I tried to drown out the voices in my head by playing my favorite Italian CD.

Then the phone rang. It was Antonio.

"Are you still in the U.S.?" His accent was heavy.

"No, I'm back in Italy." I was ashamed that I hadn't called.

"Why didn't you call me to tell me you were home?"

"It was so sudden. Anyway, I'm really sorry about what happened in New Jersey." My cheeks started to feel warm.

"I forgive you," Antonio said.

"Good." I breathed a sigh of relief and then put both elbows on my desk.

"When can I see you?"

"Look, I'm so busy right now I'm going to have to get back to you on that."

"So you'll get back to me?"

"As soon as I can, I promise."

"At least I've got a promise to hold on to." He sighed at my ambivalence.

"Bye."

"Makaeli, wait, I—"

I hung up while I still had the chance. Relationship issues were secondary. I had real problems.

I picked up my sketches and began to plan my season lineup. Angelik, Valeria, Frederique and Alek Wek were the super models I needed, but Gina would have to do for now.

I called Gina into my office and she walked in gracefully, with her thick, black hair hanging down her back. Gina was potentially the model of all models. Perfect hair, perfect skin, perfect body and a big head to match.

"Hi, boss. What will my gorgeous body be modeling next?" Gina chewed her gum like it was the last piece on earth.

"The new look focuses on hemlines." I rolled my eyes. Gina could be so conceited at times.

"Shorter. How risqué." Gina winked.

"Why not? You've got the legs for it." I barely looked up from my work.

"I sure do." Gina admired her six foot, size three frame in my full length mirror.

"Shorter skirt, longer overcoat—voila," I said.

"Oh I get it—contrast."

"Right. You're pretty smart for a runway girl."

"What is that supposed to mean, Ms. Hunt?" Gina's eyebrows almost met in the middle.

"You're nineteen years old and you don't want to be an amateur all your life, do you?"

"No."

"Then learn how to take criticism."

"Don't you mean constructive criticism?"

"Nope. I mean criticism, period, constructive or not." I wasn't normally this harsh, but I was hurt and therefore, today was the exception.

Gina turned to walk away. Without turning around she

said, "Mrs. Hunt, you know we missed you around here when you were gone. Did you enjoy your trip to the States?"

"My sister was ill, so it wasn't exactly a vacation." The memory of Raquel's piercing eyes danced around in my head.

"Is she better now?"

"Yeah, she's better now." At least someone was better. The inside of my stomach still burned with bitterness.

"You never even mentioned that you had a sister."

"I used to have two. Now I only have one." If Gina had any hope of connecting with me, I had to kill it now.

"Oh, I'm sorry to hear that." She gave me a curious look, but I was glad she let it go.

"So am I. That's all for now. Thanks." I watched her disappear through the doorway.

When she left the room, I put on my reading glasses. I studied the pictures on my desk, using precise aesthetic judgment. Every fabric, pattern, collar, pocket and fastening had to be perfect. The sketches of the knitwear, outerwear, trousers and overcoats were larger than life. *Watch out, Versace and Anna Molinari.*

My dreams were always big enough to escape my reality. When I began to feel a little tired, I took off my pumps and settled back into my red Italian leather chair. Before I could close my eyes, Nina called to tell me Antonio was here to see me. I told her to send him in. But before he opened the door, I put back on my shoes and straightened the papers in front of me.

"Hey, beautiful girl." Antonio came in with his camera on his shoulder.

"Just call me hardworking girl." I kept looking at the sketches on my desk until he sat on my desk. Then I looked up at him.

"Okay, beautiful, hardworking girl," he said.

I took off my reading glasses. "So funny. I'm very busy here, as you can see."

"Yes, I can see that, but why haven't you returned my calls since yesterday? And what are we doing about dinner tonight?"

"I spoke with you once," I said.

"I'm not talking about that patronizing little thing you call a conversation. I'm surprised you even answered your phone then. Now, what's going on? What really happened when you went home and why are you back so soon?" He leaned forward and took the papers out of my hands.

"I thought you might be happy to see me back sooner."

"I am."

"It's a long story," I said.

"Great, you'll tell me over dinner."

"I don't know what you're doing about dinner tonight, but I'm curling up with—"

"Me?" He laughed heartily.

"No, my sketches."

"Darn, lucky sketches." He gave me that sultry look of his and my body tingled.

"I've got a serious project to finish for next winter's line." *Don't give in.* I pointed my pen in his face and he smiled.

"Slow down a little. You just got back." He took the pen from me and secured my hand.

His hands were everything I remembered: strong, but gentle. He began to stroke my fingers one by one. I was losing the battle.

"You know that's how I operate. I've got to be ahead to win."

"And this is some of Lisa's teaching, I suppose?" He let go of my hand and chuckled.

I hated it when he mocked my family values, if you could call them that. "Yes."

"She was tough, huh?"

"A dictator, but nothing compared to—" I blocked out the memory instantly. "Listen, I don't want to talk about this right now."

"Are we going out this evening?"

"You still don't get it, do you?" I was in war mode again.

"Can I keep you company while you work tonight? I promise not to bother you."

"How sweet, but I wouldn't be able to concentrate." I shuffled supplies around in my desk, determined not to let his eyes catch mine.

"So you do feel something for me?" He cupped my face in his hands.

"I didn't say that." I had to look at him now. *Game over.*

"But you didn't say you didn't." His fingertips ran across the fullness of my bottom lip.

"Look, I don't want to play games with you. I didn't accept your ring because I'm not a candidate for a committed relationship right now, especially not marriage." I pulled away from him.

"I know. You've made that painfully clear." His jaws tightened.

"Okay then, what's the problem?" Tears built up underneath my eyelids.

"I'm sorry. I shouldn't push. I'm not used to being turned down." He walked toward the door.

"So you propose often?"

"You know what I mean. I'm used to getting what I want, and I want you." He turned around to face me.

"There is a first time for everything."

"I'll go now, but I'll be over at eight to watch you sketch. There will be no commitment. I promise I won't lay a hand on you."

"You're impossible." I could see the form of his muscular chest underneath his silk shirt. I was glad he wanted to be mine.

"They call me impossible back at the studio."

"All right, all right I give up. I'll see you at eight. Bye."

I waved my hand as he left the office. At least I could spend the evening with him, even if I couldn't marry him.

Chapter Thirty

Lisa

The paisley curtains blew open to reveal a sunny but cold day outside. Sitting on the edge of my bed with my textbook open and my highlighter at hand, studying for my upcoming exam was the goal for the morning, but my lower back tingled with pain. This kind of torture made me wonder whether I really wanted to continue practicing neonatal medicine. It had always been so easy for me, but now, with my mind in a hundred different places, it was a real challenge.

Concentration was key. Skimming each page for the most important content, my vision became blurred and the words seemed to run together in front of me. I rubbed my eyes with both hands. One more chapter outline and I could take a break. The phone rang.

I answered it, hoping it was Makaeli. It was Tuesday now, and every hour since she left us two days ago, I hoped she would call.

"Have you heard anything from her? Matt's voice was a husky mixture of raw masculinity and his inability to stop smoking.

"Not yet. She checked out of the Marriott, so I assume she went back to Venice."

"I see. Anyway, I called to let you know I'll be back in Jersey at about ten o'clock tonight. I'm finishing up everything here in New York so I can get back there, see Mama and then get back to L.A.."

"You had better hurry back before Carmen has that baby without you," I said.

"She has a couple of weeks to go."

"Still," I said.

"Okay, mother hen." Matt laughed aloud. "I'll think about that."

"Do you need me to pick you up?"

"No, I'm taking the Path train in." Matt cleared his throat.

"Well, hurry up then."

"How are things between you and Phil?"

"Wonderful, if you consider sleeping in separate bedrooms and meeting to sign checks a good relationship." I put the top on my highlighter and pushed aside my stack of textbooks.

"Maybe you should talk to him."

"Talk to him? Like I haven't tried." I swallowed hard.

"Maybe you two should talk to someone, a counselor or—"

"Or a shrink? No way." *I'm not crazy like Mama.*

"Whoever. Look, when I came out of prison, my parole officer hooked me up with someone and it helped."

"Actually, I think I'm beyond talking. I need more than some rehabilitation program. No offense."

"None taken," Matt said.

"Look, I need some heavy divine intervention at this point." My eyes and heart were heavy from the week's events.

"Divine intervention? Since when did you become so spiritual?"

"Spiritual? Since my life became a shambles. Since the physical, emotional and mental have failed me." I wanted to make it plain.

"You're serious, aren't you?"

"I wouldn't joke about something like this. I know that for my life to get better, it has to start with God."

"More power to you. Do what you've got to do." Matt gave me his blessing, not that I needed it.

"You know I will," I said.

The sound of a car pulling into the driveway alarmed me. I peeked through the curtains and saw that it was Phil.

"I've got to go. Phil is home."

"Good luck," Matt said.

"Thanks, but I need more than that. Bye." I hung up the phone and threw on my thick blue bathrobe. I ran downstairs and waited for him in the foyer.

As soon as his keys unlocked the door, I grabbed the doorknob and pulled, leaving us standing face to face.

Phil stepped back. "How are you?"

"I'm sorry if I startled you." I tried to sound demure, although I wasn't good at it.

"You did." Phil looked annoyed.

"I wasn't expecting you home so soon."

"I didn't expect to be home so soon either, but my last surgery went smoother than usual."

"Oh, you're the smooth one, a genius with a scalpel." I reached over to touch his hands, but he slipped by me.

"Piece of cake," he said

"I'm glad you're home, though." I made my voice softer than I usually did.

"I'm exhausted." Phil took off his coat and hung it on the wooden coat rack.

"I was hoping we could talk."

"Talk? Don't we talk all the time?"

"No, we don't. Not about the things that matter. We're always talking about business or about family, but never about us."

"We are a family."

"Phil, you know what I mean. Us, the man and wife us, the lovers us." I stood directly in front of his face

"Have you been watching *Oprah* again?" Phil walked around me.

"Please don't patronize me."

"Okay, I'm sorry, but can I at least get in the door first?" Phil turned his back to me and went into the living room. He plopped down on the couch and picked up the remote.

I walked behind him and snatched the remote from his hand. "Oh no, not tonight."

"What did you do that for? Can't a man have a little down time?" Phil threw off his tie and kicked off his loafers.

Tears began to form in my eyes, but I refused to let them fall. "Normally I wouldn't interfere with your down time, but I need—"

"What, woman? What is it that you need?" Now Phil's voice boomed out of control, louder and harsher than even I had been accustomed to.

"I need you, Phil, just you. I don't care about the money and the prestige and the stuff. I need us, you and me to be us again, like we used to be. Before this Makaeli thing and this Raquel thing and before everything."

"Well, I guess you're just going to have to talk to yourself, because I'm in no mood for this now." Phil left the room and started climbing the stairs.

I heard the guest room door slam and I knew I'd be

alone again tonight. I swallowed hard and took the stairs to our bedroom, the cold, brutal place where memories were like capsules—easily dissolved.

I started to call Lashawn, but knew that she and her husband were probably enjoying each other's company. After all, this was her second marriage and she was determined to get it right.

I remembered when marriage was fresh and sweet to me. Now that the children were gone, I felt like a maid service and a womb of convenience. Although there was only a wall which separated our rooms, the true distance was much greater, the distance between heart and mind. Somehow, throughout the years, we grew away from each other, and it seemed like neither of us knew our way back.

I took our wedding picture down from the dresser and stared at the young, wavy-haired bride whose wide smile was an indication of her happiness. What happened to that bright-eyed girl, never the enthusiast, but content in my pragmatism nonetheless? I took off my wedding ring and placed it next to the picture. *Where is my fairy tale ending?*

I opened the drawer to my side table and pulled out my sleeping pills. I wanted to sleep the day away. In fact, I wanted to sleep my middle-aged life away. But I remembered the baby and put the bottle down. He or she was already controlling my life—a life I wouldn't mind trading for someone else's.

On the other side of the wall, I heard Phil coughing. The television was turned up so loud I could hear the news word for word. Phil won the fight again.

I sat down on the side of the bed, buried my head in my paisley-covered pillow, and I let out a wail of frustration. Instantly, my head began to ache. I couldn't even take aspirin because it wouldn't be good for the baby, so I pressed the sides of my head with my fingers. What was a woman my age doing carrying a baby anyway?

I knocked against the wall with my fist and he turned down the volume without me saying a word. If he knew me so well, why didn't he know my heart was breaking?

As I was about to turn out the light and give up, the phone rang. I hoped it was Makaeli.

"Hello." I answered after the first ring.

"Praise the Lord, this is Sister Pearl speaking."

"Hi." I sighed with relief. "You received my message?"

"Yes, but you sounded a little shaky on my recording. Is everything all right?"

"No, everything is all wrong. Makaeli has gone back to Venice and she is not receiving calls from me or my brother, Matt," I said.

"Really? That doesn't sound like Makaeli," Mrs. Pearl said.

"You see, we hurt her very much by withholding the truth from her."

"The truth?"

"The truth is, Mrs. Pearl, that my mother is not Makaeli's mother."

"Not her mother? Oh, dear me."

"My sister, Raquel, is her mother. I'm really Makaeli's aunt."

"Oh, I see. That's a big truth."

"We feel really bad about it now, but I don't know what else I can do. She won't call us back and she's thousands of miles away."

"That's right."

"It's not like I can just drive over to her. I just—for the first time in my life, I don't know what to do."

"Give her time. She'll come around eventually."

"How can you be so sure?"

"I know how God operates, and Makaeli is ready to hear Him now."

"I hope you're right."

"Listen to me, Lisa. Whatever you've done in the past, Jesus died on a cross to wash it all away. And not just what you've done in the past, but anything you will ever do in the future as well. All you've got to do is to admit you're a sinner and receive Him as your Savior."

"I need saving."

"We all do."

"Believe me, I've tried life on my own and it stinks. How do I receive this Savior?"

"Just confess it with your mouth, sweetheart, that Jesus died and rose again for you. Believe it, repent and you will be saved."

"If you had talked to me a week and a half ago, I would have said you were crazy, but after all I've been through, I do believe. I do believe."

"Good, that's the first step to salvation. I've got my Bible right next to me and I'm going to read I John 1:9 to you. 'If we confess our sins, he is faithful and just to forgive us our sins, and to cleanse us from all unrighteousness.'"

"Oh yes, I confess that I'm a sinner." I felt more vulnerable than I had ever felt in my life.

Then Mrs. Pearl continued to lead me through the scriptures. "Romans 10:9-10 says that 'if thou shalt confess with thy mouth the Lord Jesus, and shalt believe in thine heart that God has raised him from the dead, thou shalt be saved. For with the heart man believeth unto righteousness; and with the mouth confession is made unto salvation.'"

"I confess that Jesus Christ is my Lord. I believe He died for me and was raised up for me. I believe He is the only hope I've got," I said.

"And the best hope you've got. Your life will be changed forever."

"Thank you, Mrs. Pearl."

"Now, I expect to see you at the church on Sunday. At least until you find a church home of your own."

"I'll be there. I've got no place better to be."

"Good. God bless you."

"No, God bless you." I put the phone back into its cradle gently, hardly believing the joy I felt.

The release from the pressure instantly cleared up my headache and my heartache. I lifted my hands and cried out before God, letting tears of remorse and of victory prepare the way for a peaceful sleep.

I was on a new spiritual path, and I promised God that nothing would turn me around.

Chapter Thirty-one
Makaeli

I freshened up in the ladies' room and anticipated Antonio's call. It was already seven-thirty. Finally the call came through. Since his last photo shoot was in the area, we decided to meet at the square.

I couldn't believe I put myself in the position of seeing Antonio when I knew I shouldn't see him. It was bad enough that I was battling with my mind. Now I had to battle with my body as well.

Didn't I say I'd be home working? So much for the word *no*.

While waiting for Antonio, an interracial couple walked by, followed by an older Asian man. Diversity was always an asset. Ever since the first day I moved to Italy, I was pleased with the acceptance and integration of minorities into the European culture. It was not like where I grew up. I was grateful that their welcoming environment helped me to pave my way into their world.

Many Italian women, as well as tourists, hustled about with shopping bags. I glanced across at the Piazza Duomo, which used to be the largest Christian church in the world. I tapped my leather boot against the mosaic tiled floor and looked over my shoulder for him again. It was getting late.

I went across the street to take a peek inside the Piazza. Its stained glass windows, paintings and marble floors were exquisite. I thought about Pastor Brown's words: "Get in church and get in God." And just like Mrs. Pearl always said, nothing can separate me from the love of God. I felt the urge to pray, right there in the lobby.

"Dear God, I don't know what's going on in this crazy world, but I wait and I look to heaven. I know there is a price to pay for deception, but it seems like I'm the only one paying over and over again. Please help me to understand and to get through this—to forgive. In Jesus' name, amen."

I looked at my watch, noting that it was exactly eight o'clock and started to get anxious about seeing Antonio. Just as I looked up, he walked up behind me and put his hands around my waist. Despite my feelings, I maintained my composure.

He put his lips up to my ear and whispered, "*Ciao, bella.*"

"Mr. Antonio Benzini." I loosened his arms from around me and extended my hand. He kissed it playfully. A sister was enjoying these European customs.

"Before dinner, let's stroll down to the Nap." He walked next to me.

"Via Nap? One of my favorite shopping areas. That sounds tempting." I licked my lips.

"You could pick up a pair of shoes and a purse to match." He put his arm around my shoulders.

"Now you're not playing fair." Without warning, I giggled, something I had not done for quite a while.

"We can stop by the Galleria Vittorio Emanuelle, too."

"Oh, so you're trying to bribe me." I turned to stand in front of him, leaned in close and then stepped backward. It was a little game I liked to play.

"With everything I've got." Antonio took my hands and pulled me closer.

"We have to see what you've got then." I reached up to adjust his collar. The heat from his breath stirred my senses.

"Don't tease me, *signora.*" He stared at me with those dark, mysterious eyes.

"I'm sorry."

"You ignored me in New Jersey and you were so uptight earlier." He took my hands from his neck and kissed them.

"I apologize again. I wasn't ready to start a color war with my color sensitive family."

"I'm sure it wouldn't have been as awful as you think if you had just introduced me."

"Let's just say you're wrong. If you had stayed, you would have seen the looks they gave me."

"If I had stayed, I would have died from the looks you were giving me."

"The results of my trip were catastrophic."

"That bad?"

"Worse," I said.

"Worse?"

"Brace yourself."

"Okay."

"My dearly beloved sister is out of her coma." I said it quickly and waited for his reaction.

"That's good news."

"Not necessarily."

"What do you mean?"

"Never mind. Let's enjoy the night and talk about this

another time." I put my hand up to signal for the conversation to stop.

"Okay, I won't push." He didn't sound convincing at all. He would continue to push. If nothing else, Antonio was persistent. It was one of those things I really respected about him. He never gave up. I was glad he let it go temporarily, though.

We walked, shopped and talked, but we didn't talk about my family. In each shop, I went through the motions of going through the racks, but my mind wasn't on fashion. It was on identity, and just like the tags on each of the garments, I was labeled. Labeled by family, by genes, and by circumstances.

Finally, we stopped at an obscure little café for dinner. This time, when I looked into Antonio's dark eyes, I remembered the day we met.

It was at a photo shoot in Milan about a year ago. I worked to perfect a model's silver embroidered ensemble while Antonio busily set up his cameras and lights. I hardly noticed him at all at first, and he barely said a word to me until after the shoot was complete. When he lifted his camera equipment, that's when I saw his muscular arms and legs in action. Then his eyes met mine, and there was so much compassion in them, I hadn't been the same since.

After dinner, Antonio and I took the train to Venice. He walked me to the door and put his arm around me. My shoulders tingled at the feel of his warm palms. He reached down to straighten my scarf and his peppermint breath mingled with mine. He was so close to me I wanted to taste his lips, but I decided against it. I didn't want to start something I couldn't finish. Something I could never finish. After all, he deserved better than that. So I turned on my heels, away from him, and pretended to search for my key. Then I said goodbye with my back still facing him, hoping my desire for him would go away.

When I entered my apartment, I focused in on the plushest red carpet and matching red-and-gold curtains available in Italy. The richness of color always made me smile. I walked by my abstract oil paintings and the African pottery collection to my bedroom. There, I sat on my orange canopy bed with the bright checkered quilts and turned my radio on full blast. Digging through the laundry piled in my favorite leather armchair, I found my most comfortable flannel pajamas. Then I walked to the bathroom, dropping off each piece of clothing along the way. Sitting on the edge of the tub, running my bathwater, I thought of Antonio and wondered if he was home yet. He only lived a few miles away from me.

The aroma and the lather of my peach body scrub seemed to take me to another dimension of myself— peace.

As I came out of the tub, I noticed that my answering machine was lit up. Checking the messages quickly, I soon confirmed what I already knew. It was Lisa and Matt calling to apologize again. What was wrong with these people? Did they expect their empty, pathetic words to rectify everything overnight?

I towel-dried myself and rubbed peach body butter onto my skin. Then I curled up underneath my down comforter.

Finally in bed, I found it difficult to sleep. My mind kept going back to the many drinks I used to have in the bar around the corner; the taste of each one going down my throat, creating a stinging sensation in my stomach and making every sordid memory more intense. I got up and searched for any alcoholic beverage, but of course, there were none. *You have a drinking problem, idiot, remember?*

During the search for the impossible, my old Bible sur-
faced. I dusted it off and opened it up. A few of Mrs. Pearl's
tattered scripture references fell from it. I looked up those
particular scriptures in the Bible and read them over and
over again.

I read until my eyes were heavy. I read until a peace
came over me and I fell asleep, meditating on the Word of
God.

Chapter Thirty-two

Lisa

I woke up on Wednesday morning with Mrs. Pearl's faith-filled words resounding in my mind.

Looking forward to visiting the day spa with Lashawn, I showered quickly and forced myself into a pair of Spandex exercise pants with a matching top. I hadn't worn these since I stopped making use of my Bally's membership. I applied a fresh coat of lip gloss and no foundation just in case. Since I expected a lot of pampering, I didn't want to put on anything that I would have to take off.

While I waited downstairs in the kitchen for Lashawn to come, I fixed myself a bowl of granola bran cereal. Finally she showed up, fifteen minutes late and honking the horn like she didn't have good sense.

I grabbed my gym bag and my down jacket, ran out the front door and jumped into Lashawn's fire engine red Lexus.

"What in the world is wrong with you, making all that noise this early in the morning?"

"I'm sorry," Lashawn said.

"You should be. You woke up the whole neighborhood."

"Sorry, sorry. I'm just running late, as you can see."
Lashawn looked over at me and smiled.

"Off to a slow start this morning?"

"Yes, my girls were giving me grief," Lashawn said.

"Yeah, well, that's what children do."

"Tell me about it. It was hairdo problems and outfit
problems."

"All kinds of drama, huh?"

"You have no idea how hard it is with girls. Wait 'til your
little girl comes into this world." Lashawn reached over to
pat my stomach.

"If it's a girl." I wasn't sure I wanted one.

"Oh, it's going to be a girl, and then you'll find out."
Lashawn rolled her eyes in a way that made me laugh.

Lately, she was the only one who could make me laugh.

"I'm glad you gave me this gift card." I shook it in her
face.

"And I'm glad I have a day off to enjoy it with you."

"I plan to do some serious relaxing," I said.

"Like you're the only one." Lashawn looked over at me
and raised her eyebrows, diva style.

She broke the speed limits throughout the entire drive,
paying little attention to the law or innocent passersby. A
few times, the car seemed to slide on the ice, but she was
able to brake and get her bearings. Needless to say, it was
too much adventure for me. Finally we crossed over the
bridge, entered New York City and arrived on the upper
East Side.

When we drove up to Le Merou, we were greeted by two
valets who took the keys to Lashawn's car and drove away.
Before we could pull the doorknob, we were welcomed by
a doorman and a tall, leggy blonde who wore fake eyelashes and fake fingernails.

"Hi, my name is Candice. Welcome to Le Merou, the ul-
timate luxury spa experience."

"Hi, I'm Lashawn and this is my friend, Lisa."

"It's good to meet you both," she said. "We have eight thousand square feet of pleasure for you to indulge in."

The lobby was decorated with a marble floor, natural stone walls, a huge Greek sculpture and accented with bamboo and giant palm trees.

"This is beautiful."

"Very beautiful," Lashawn said.

Candice took us through the first two floors, gave us a brief tour of the sixty-foot indoor lap pool and the high performance fitness center. Then she led us up a spiral staircase into the massage room and introduced us to our masseuse, Kira Lee.

"Ladies, I'm leaving you in Kira's hands now. Enjoy your stay." Candice waved goodbye as she walked through the double doors.

We waved politely, said our thanks and then turned to face our new guide.

Kira was a petite Asian lady who wore a ponytail that hung down to the center of her back. She showed us to the dressing room and pointed out the closets where we would leave our clothes.

I was a little nervous at first, but the other women seemed so calm and happy that I dropped my reserve faster than I anticipated. Everyone was wrapped in towels from head to toe. Some were already being massaged and others were having facials, manicures or pedicures. Everyone was being waited on hand and foot.

"All right, ladies, you're about to embark on a sixty-minute journey to paradise," she said.

"Paradise, huh?" I was a little skeptical.

"This is a hot riverbed rock, and what I'm about to do is to rub these on your skin using long Swedish strokes." She held up a couple of rocks.

"Did you say hot riverbed rocks?" Lashawn said.

"Never mind the rock part. Did you say hot?" I said.

"Yes, this is called a hot stone massage," Kira said.

"And how long did you say it would last?" Lashawn asked.

"About sixty minutes." She seemed confident about her craft.

"Does it burn?" Suddenly, this didn't sound like such a good idea to me.

"No, it creates a relaxing sensation."

"A relaxing sensation?" Lashawn stretched out her arms.

"Yes. When it's over, you'll feel warm and tension free," she assured us both.

"I hope you're right." I wasn't completely convinced.

"Don't mind her. She's not used to relaxing," Lashawn said.

"Look who is talking. Neither are you," I said.

"You two sound like classic workaholics." Kira smiled.

"Yes, we're doctors," I was proud to reply.

"Oh, doctors. Then you should really appreciate what our customized skin and body treatments do for your health."

"I'm sure we will," Lashawn said.

During that particular procedure and during the sixty-minute hydrating facial, I felt moisturized and rejuvenated. I relished in the atmosphere of tranquility, excited that these treatments would also protect my tired skin from the bitter winds outside.

"What's next on the agenda?"

"I think I'm going to get a bikini wax. They have an advanced system I've been reading about—Epilight hair removal."

"Well, with all this cellulite on my body and all the extra weight I'm about to gain, I won't be wearing anybody's bikini anytime soon."

"Oh please, you're in great shape. Besides, you never know." Lashawn laughed a hearty laugh.

"I do know. The thing I really need is an anti-age mask."

"Now, that's practical."

"And that's what I am—practical."

When we were done with the next procedures, although they offered many kinds of modern skin and body treatments I was curious about, such as micro-dermabrasion and acupuncture, the only one thing I knew I wanted was to sit in the sauna. I wanted to relax, thinking of nothing—no sister, no husband, no kids. It was going to be perfect.

"I'm going down to the sauna room while you get your hair done," I told Lashawn.

"Okay, but in the next hour, we meet back here and go for lunch." Lashawn was always excited about food.

"Sounds good. This greedy baby inside me wants food already." I circled my stomach with my hand.

"I know what you mean because I'm a little hungry myself. My blueberry pancakes are wearing off," Lashawn said.

"Blueberry pancakes? All I had is granola cereal."

"Oh, you poor baby. First you've gotten religious on me, now you're eating healthy on me too." Lashawn poked out her red painted lips.

"Oh, believe me, as hungry as I am, that was just an isolated incident, my sister."

"I hear you, girl." Lashawn went back inside the room.

I walked through the huge columns and continued down the corridor until I reached the staircase. That's when the dizziness hit me.

Trying to grab onto the railing was a good idea, but unfortunately, my consciousness was already fading. I remembered falling, but I didn't remember being carried away. It was my second collapse in a week, but this time I almost fell down a flight of stairs, except my leg got caught in the railway after the first two steps. Then the attendants came running in, but they couldn't wake me up right away. I couldn't shake it, and that's when they called for help. I don't know when Lashawn found out what happened.

Chapter Thirty-three

Makaeli

On Wednesday, I woke up early, threw on one of my winter white business suits and had a driver pick me up for work. I rode up, down and through mountains and tunnels. Riding in the square and traffic circles reminded me of Washington, D.C., back in the States.

Just as I arrived at the office, I saw Nina. She was short, with strong muscular legs and narrow hips. Her eyes seemed to fade into her dark brown hair. She smiled when I gave her the list of errands I needed her to run.

"I'm glad you're back, *Signora* Hunt," Nina said.

"Believe me, I'm glad to be back." I meant that with every fiber of my being.

"Was your trip successful?"

"Let's just say it was eventful."

"I understand. Traveling can be very stressful."

"You have no idea." I handed her a stack of papers. "Unfortunately, I still have a lot of loose ends to tie up."

"Will you being going back soon?"

"Probably not. There is something I've got to take care

of first before I consider going back." I thought about my mess of a life.

"I see. I'll take care of these for you. Let me know if you need me."

"I will. Thank you."

After going into my own office and settling down amongst my creations, the day came and went like any other. I sketched, answered calls, and had meetings. Hard work was the one thing that gave me the most satisfaction, and I let it try to fill me where I felt empty.

That evening, I drove home and met Antonio in Venice.

We chose a very cosmopolitan restaurant nearby and settled in with its savvy clientele. We were seated by a window. Unfortunately, the shallow fog disturbed my view. A young waitress sauntered over and took our orders.

"Okay, enough is enough. You promised to tell me what's going on and you haven't yet." He held my hand across the table and wouldn't let it go.

"You're good to me, but you don't deserve this. Get on with your life. Mine is a complicated mess."

"Mine is way too simple and I like mess. So humor me."

"I found out some really bad news when I was there." My tears seemed to have a mind of their own and ran down my face in wild abandon.

"Your mother?" He dried my face with his handkerchief.

"No, she's fine. Ironically, though, she's not my mother."

"Pardon me?"

"To make a long story short, my sister Raquel is my birth mother." *Strike one.*

"The violent one?"

"Yeah, that's her." *Strike two.*

"Are you kidding?"

"I wish I was. Raquel was young. Mama lost her baby, the real Lovechild, and here I am." *Strike three. I'm out.*

"Are you okay?" Antonio held one of my hands.

"No, I'm very angry." I pulled it from him, made a fist and pounded it on the table.

"Mmmm. I see."

"Shouldn't I be?"

"Maybe." Antonio unfolded his napkin.

"Maybe?"

"I guess that depends on the circumstances." He looked very serious, not at all like the fun-loving guy I knew him to be.

"Circumstances. Does that really matter? I wanted to know more, but I left. Lisa and Matt have been ringing my phone off the hook and leaving messages three and four times a day." I rolled my eyes. "I'm about to change my numbers."

"Don't do that. You need to talk to them eventually."

"I'm not ready to talk to them."

"I know you're hurt, but I think you still have a lot of people who care about you, who made sacrifices for you."

"Sacrifices? Through lies and cover-ups. I feel like I've been sacrificed. If Raquel had not overdosed, I still wouldn't know that I'm her daughter." The conversation stirred up all my raw emotions and I began to sniffle.

"Right or wrong, I imagine that they had their reasons." Antonio took a sip of water.

"So they say." I felt poison in my heart whenever I considered their reasons. When our food arrived, I practically dove into the arancini.

"I'm surprised you ordered the arancini." Antonio wasted no time digging into his plate either.

"Why? You know I love these fried dumplings." I stuffed another forkful into my mouth.

"True, but I know you're not crazy about the meat in it." Antonio tried to snatch a piece of meat from my plate.

I playfully stuck his finger with my fork. "Get back. It's not that I don't like the meat; it's just that I'd probably like it better with just the cheese and sauce."

"Exactly." He tried to reach into my plate again, smiling the whole time.

I grabbed his hand. "But I'm willing to make the sacrifice."

Antonio wrapped his fingers around mine and for a few minutes, we were lost in each other's eyes.

It was good to be home and eating at one of my favorite restaurants by the water. *Isn't this where it all started?* It reminded me of South Street Seaport in New York City. Matt and I had gone there once, sampling ice cream flavors and stuffing ourselves with gyros and pizza. It's funny how we had become so close in such a short time. *How could he have betrayed me?*

For dessert, I sank my teeth into the walnut cappuccino torte while Antonio had nothing.

"I can't believe you're still hungry. No one would believe you're able to eat like this, not by looking at you."

"Thanks. I don't do this all the time, as you know." I leaned over and punched him in the arm. "I haven't eaten well since I arrived in the U.S."

"I know," Antonio said. "You should call them."

"Not now." I didn't look up from my plate.

"So you'll call them?"

"Maybe." Our eyes met before my fork reached my mouth.

"Makaeli?"

"Eventually." I put down the fork.

"No, soon."

"Okay, okay. I will." He had a way of making me agree to things I had no intention of agreeing to.

"They're your family. A little dysfunctional, but still your family. You've got to be reconciled to that."

"*Reconcile* is not in my vocabulary right now. A sister is just trying to maintain."

"Maintain and remain in love with me." He threw a curve at me.

"Who said I was in love with you?" I stood up and put my hands on my hips.

"Your eyes gave you away." He stood up also and tilted my chin upward with his hands.

"Really? Traitors." I covered my eyes with my hands.

"When will you give in and marry me?"

"I told you that I've got too much going on right now and none of it is good. Besides, you know how I feel about this black and white thing. No offense." I sat back down.

"None taken, but we're not your parents."

"I know that." I put my hands face down on the table.

"What would it take to make you mine?" Antonio put his hands on top of mine.

"I am yours." I let my hands intertwine with his for a minute.

"All mine."

"It would take resolution of all my issues, the mess that is my life." I pulled my hands back.

"Consider it done. I can have you back on a plane tonight."

"That won't be necessary. I'm still working on me."

"You can't hide forever."

"I know I have to forgive, but right now it's a struggle."

We left the restaurant, walked through a narrow alleyway, over a quaint bridge and stepped into a gondola. I loved the intimacy of these little boats.

Antonio never mentioned another word about my family. We went on with our evening as though nothing had changed. And by sunset, the sky had turned a smoky gray violet.

"Let's go down to that new church and see what it's like," Antonio said.

"Which one?"

"The one down by the—"

"You mean the one we saw the other day?"

"Yes. I heard they have mid-week Bible study and I thought it would be nice to visit."

"Now?"

"Why not? A client of mine invited me once."

"Really?"

"Yes."

"Sure. Let's go," I said.

We walked down to the church and before we even entered the great cathedral, we were greeted by two ladies who looked like native Italians.

Once we were inside, I looked around and observed different nationalities. Although most appeared to be Italian, there was a healthy mixture of colors, nonetheless; blacks and whites together. Some people lifted or waved their hands just as some people were stretched out on the floor or kneeling. Others swayed back and forth gently in front of their seats, while others merely leaned forward and kept their faces in their hands. Everyone worshipped in unison in his or her own way. I was happy to see such a universal oneness. The atmosphere was different, but the spirit was the same.

We sat in the last row so we could easily duck out if we needed to.

The piano was melodic and subtle. The choir sang as if they were the heavenly host. Then finally, an Italian minister came forward and taught from the Word of God. Except for the occasional word I didn't understand that Antonio was more than happy to translate, everything went smoothly.

By the time we left the service, there were no cars stirring, no bicycles or taxis. There was only the occasional floating water bus, but the *vaporetto* wasn't popular at this hour. The ripples in the water made me feel like I was suspended in time.

The moonlight led the way to my huge portico. It was time to say goodnight and to send Antonio on his way.

"I had a great time tonight," he said to me.

"Me too." I turned away from his gaze.

"What's wrong?"

"I just wish I didn't feel like an ugly, tormented misfit." I grabbed his hand with one of mine and motioned for him to follow me with the other one.

But being the gentleman that he was—and I sometimes wish he wasn't—he didn't follow me in. I thought back to the time I tried to lure him into Villa Sampaguita, a deluxe bed and breakfast near Asti in Piedmont, but he turned me down. It was clear that he wanted more from me than just my body. He wanted a commitment, and that's what I wasn't ready to give.

I wasn't sure if it was that Roman Catholic background or his mother's conversion to the Pentecostal denomination that influenced him. We didn't discuss religion often. But I admired his willingness to wait for me to make up my mind. I had sure told him enough times I'd never marry him, yet he endured my confusion and never complained.

"You can't be ugly. You were created this way and you're perfect."

"Nothing about me is perfect, but you always know the right things to say."

"Don't be tormented either."

"I can't help it." I put my finger up to my eye to hold back the tears.

"Remember, God forgives us so we can forgive everyone else." He stroked my neck, kissed my forehead and backed away from the door. "You've got to forgive them and move on."

There was pain in his eyes as he blew a kiss from the other side of the huge arches. I was sure he was frustrated with me, though, and I wondered how much longer he would be around if I didn't make up my mind soon.

Upstairs, Antonio's words haunted me. I thought of Mrs. Pearl and decided to call her. She would know what to do. My heart raced as if it were trying to win its way out of my body. My long fingers wavered as I picked up the phone. My palms were moist with perspiration.

I waited while the phone rang, fondling the onyx pendant that hung between my breasts. On the third ring, she picked up.

"Praise the Lord. This is Sister Pearl," she greeted.

"Hi, Mrs. Pearl. It's me, Makaeli."

"Child, I know who you are. You sound like you've been crying. What's wrong?"

"Everything is falling apart. Raquel is okay, but I'm—"

"You're not okay?"

"It's not just my family. It's me too. I—"

"Honey, I see God calling your name. Been calling for a long time, but you've been resisting."

"I've started praying again." I wanted her to believe in me again, even if I didn't believe in myself.

"Oh, you've been talking, but you haven't been listening. God wants you to surrender. Do you remember Luke 6:36?"

"No."

"It says 'be ye therefore merciful, as your father is also merciful. Judge not; condemn not, and ye shall not be condemned. Forgive and ye shall be forgiven.' " Mrs. Pearl's voice was steady.

"Please, Mrs. Pearl. I don't need preaching. I need you to tell me what to do."

"Surrender."

"Surrender what? I don't have anything left in me." I paced back and forth across the floor.

"Surrender your will to His will. He'll rescue you, sweetie. No matter how alone or empty you feel, He'll rescue you right where you are."

"But you don't even know what happened in Jersey," I said.

"I do."

"You do?"

"Your sister Lisa called me," Mrs. Pearl said.

"She did what? How dare she get you involved in this."

"She was desperately worried about you. And I got involved a long time ago, remember?"

"I'm sorry—I . . ." I rolled over on my bed and pulled the covers over me.

"Besides, you'll be surprised when you talk to her."

"Surprised when I talk to her?"

"Never mind. We'll talk about that later. You go back, take God with you and take care of everything. You can't keep running away."

"I was so close, Mrs. Pearl. I even went by the church. But then it seems like it was all snatched away."

"What can separate you from the love of God? Nothing." Same old Mrs. Pearl, same words.

"I wish you were here with me." My tears got in the way again.

"I can't be with you, but God can, always."

"But how can I go back?"

"Start going and the good Lord will give you the strength you need along the way."

"But I—"

"No more excuses. Just go and handle your business. I'll be waiting for you when you're done."

"Thanks. I'll call you when I get back to the States." Again, I agreed to the unagreeable.

"I love you, Makaeli," Mrs. Pearl said.

"I love you too." Finally the words were able to come out. I placed the phone down gently.

First Antonio and then Mrs. Pearl. What was wrong with everybody? Didn't anybody care about what I was going through? *What shall separate us from the love of Christ?*

I slept on these words.

When the phone rang early the next morning, my first instinct was to ignore it. *It's probably Lisa or Matt again.* Fortunately, I answered it anyway.

"Makaeli," Phil said.

"Phil?" I heard the stress in his voice.

"I'm glad I caught you. There has been an emergency."

"Is it Raquel?"

"No, it's Lisa."

"Lisa? What now?" My heart sped up as his words came forth.

"I called before. You haven't been checking your messages. Lisa has been in the hospital since yesterday. It's the baby—"

Chapter Thirty-four

Lisa

The moment I woke up and looked into the eyes of an emergency medical technician, I realized my life was at a turning point. My ride in the ambulance was less than comfortable, and even though I didn't fear for my life, I did fear for the life of the child inside me. Everything had fallen apart; everything that I had come to depend on. I had no choice other than to trust God.

Mercy Hospital was much different than Newark Medical where Raquel was. Their emergency room wasn't as crowded, the cafeteria was a freshly painted sky blue and the patients were generally quieter. This was the upscale hospital I worked in. Yet, I never thought I'd wind up a patient here, whining like some abandoned kitten thrown by the wayside. I never dreamed I'd be stuck with a failing marriage and a distressed fetus, hooked up to monitors like Raquel and fighting for my freedom like Mama. Helpless and pathetic.

But then I remembered my new relationship with God. I was more than a conqueror according to what Pastor

James had said. So I forced myself to smile and I waited for the answers I knew would come.

On Thursday, my second day at the hospital, I sat on the side of my hospital bed, fully dressed and waiting for my release.

"Mrs. Jackson," Dr. Marshall said.

"Dr. Jackson," I said.

"Pardon me, Dr. Jackson. I'm discharging you since your test results were good, and the baby is fine, but I want you to go home and rest," he said. "You two gave us all quite a scare.

"Not bed rest, I hope?" That was the last thing I wanted to hear. There was so much I had to do.

"No, not bed rest, but no more stress. So watch what you're eating, relax for a couple of days and I'll see you and the little one back here next week," Dr. Marshall said.

"Thanks." I was glad to have my walking papers.

I called Matt at the house and told him to drive my car over to pick me up. When he arrived at the hospital, I was already sitting in the first floor lobby with my overnight bag in my hand. He took it from me and we walked to the three-story parking lot.

"Thanks for coming to pick me up from the hospital." I tugged on his leather jacket. "I didn't want to call Phil, not with everything that's been going on between us. Things just aren't the same, and I didn't feel like pretending today."

"I understand. Hey, you had us all scared."

"Sorry. When Dr. Marshall said I could be discharged today, I was ecstatic."

Thank goodness my car was parked in the middle of the first row. I was still a little sore from all the poking and prodding from those wretched needles and tests. Still feeling awkward, I slipped into the passenger's seat of my car. Matt hopped into the driver's seat.

"So what was the problem?" Matt looked over the steering wheel and started the car.

"My blood pressure was very high, so they wanted to keep me under observation for a while."

"How do you feel?"

"I feel guilty," I said.

"Guilty?" Matt stopped the car at the red light and glanced over at me.

"Yes, all over again. When I thought I was going to lose my baby, I could imagine how Mama felt burying her child and how Raquel must have felt when we took her baby from her arms and from her life." For the first time, I felt truly humbled.

"What do you mean?"

"I mean, I never stopped to really consider Raquel's loss—always Mama's, but never Raquel's, until I was faced with the possibility of a miscarriage."

"Never thought about it that way." Matt rolled his gum around in his mouth as he listened.

"I know."

"I always thought we were doing what was right." Matt turned to face me.

"So did I. But now I don't know anymore." I started grieving all over again. Tears began to drip from my eyes and I didn't even care. I didn't care about mascara or about vulnerability. I just let them roll onto my cheeks and out of control.

"So what now?" Matt took a pack of tissues from his jacket pocket and handed it to me.

"Now I've got to tell Mama I understand and I've got to apologize to Raquel. I never even told her I was sorry." I took a few of the tissues, as suddenly my heart was filled with shame. *Oh Lord, what have I done?* "I've got to go to see Mama now."

"Don't you want to go home first?"

"No. I've got to get this over with. You'll be going back to California soon, and I don't want to do this by myself."

We were on our way to see Mama. We had put off telling her that we told Makaeli for as long as possible. We stalled for days, but neither of us had heard from Makaeli. We had to tell Mama that Makaeli knew.

Matt drove under the speed limit through the ice-covered streets until we pulled up and parked at Saint Ann's. Matt opened the door for me and I clumsily climbed out.

Our destiny was to break Mama's heart—again. The only difference was I knew God would mend it.

Chapter Thirty-five
Makaeli

Knowing that I had to return to the U.S., I showered, pinned up my hair then slipped into a pair of my best flared jeans. *Versace, the competition.* I tossed three outfits into my Italian leather bag and ran out to catch a flight. It was Thursday morning when I left, bound for a destiny I didn't dare consider.

This time, I took my Bible with me and read it on the train. Deep inside, I knew this was all spiritual warfare. I knew Satan was trying to seal my fate once and for all, but this time, I was prepared to fight.

I bought a sandwich and dialed Antonio's cell phone number from the airport.

"I'm here at the airport, for all it's worth," I said.

"You should've let me go with you," Antonio replied.

"It's okay. I just kind of wanted to be alone."

"I'm proud of you for being so brave."

"You shouldn't be." I leaned against the wall and pushed the strands of hair from my forehead.

"Why not?"

"I'm still very angry," I said.

"So what? No one said you wouldn't be angry."

"So what's the point then?"

"You're taking charge of your fears."

"I wouldn't say that."

"I'd say that. It'll all work out; I promise."

"Sadly, it's not your promises that count right now. It's their promises I have a problem with."

"Go, and don't worry. You'll be home soon."

"Not soon enough for me."

"All of this mess will be behind you," Antonio said.

"Why are you so good to me?"

"Why shouldn't I be?"

"I haven't made things easy for you." I started walking toward the gate.

"God has been good to me. I've got to share the love." Antonio sounded like he was smiling.

"Oh, is that so?"

"One thing I learned while growing up in Little Italy in the Bronx was about the love of God."

"I can see that."

"No, really. I'm no saint or anything."

"I didn't say you were." I imagined his smile.

"There is a lot of religious stuff I didn't catch and a lot of other stuff about God I need to learn, but the stuff about His love, thanks to my mom, I did get."

"I'm glad you got it."

"Me too."

"I've got to go now."

"Come home to me soon," Antonio said.

"I hope I can. Bye."

"Take care of yourself." Antonio hung up the phone and I was cut off from my support system. I kept his voice in my memory for a few minutes just so that I wouldn't feel alone.

I walked quickly through the airport, once again carrying my one overnight bag and purse in my hands. I tried to plan what I would say to everyone when I arrived, but my thoughts kept getting jumbled in my head. There was too much to remember and too much I still didn't know.

By the time I boarded the plane, I noticed a young woman already sitting in the window seat. As I sat down, she turned to face me. She had pale white skin, long blond micro braids and almost blinding blue eyes. She wore a red, green and black cap and a green denim pantsuit with a big black outline of Africa on the back. The contrast was captivating, and I wondered who or what she was.

"Hello, I'm Enricka," she said with an accent I didn't recognize.

"Hi, I'm Makaeli." I sat down next to her.

"I was in Italy on assignment."

"Oh," I said.

"I'm studying photography."

"Oh, you're a student? That's nice."

"I'm from South Africa, born in Capetown, raised in Johannesburg. What about you?"

"I'm originally from New Jersey, but I live here now."

"Really, what do you do?" she inquired.

I crossed my legs and tried to look very professional. "I'm in the fashion business."

"Fashion?"

"Yes."

"What part exactly?"

"I'm a designer." I tried not to sound boastful, but I was proud of what I did for a living.

"Oh, a designer. Now, that's exciting."

"Well, it has its ups and its downs like everything, I guess."

"What's your name?"

"Makaeli Hunt."

"Makaeli Hunt of Designs by Makaeli?"

"Yes. You've heard of me?"

"Of course. All through Milan. I travel a lot."

"I see." It was hard to hide my enthusiasm because my smile was so big.

"It's so good to meet you."

"Same here," I said.

"Wow, what a lucky break for me." She rubbed her hands together.

"I guess you could say that." I laughed at her honesty.

"I've been in the United States for about three years now. I'm studying at New York University."

"That's a great school. What brought you away from South Africa?"

"A sense of adventure. I always liked traveling abroad, having new experiences, learning about new cultures."

"You sound a lot like me."

"My father is a diplomat, so we used to travel a lot, but now that my parents are divorced—you know."

"I understand."

"My dad is still in South Africa. My mom lives in Harlem."

"Harlem?" My bottom lip dropped open.

"Yeah, sweet Harlem. Can't you see my black pride?" She turned her back to me so that I could see her jacket.

"I saw your jacket." I didn't know what else to say.

"But you didn't know I was black, did you?"

"Well—no, I didn't. I was curious, though."

"About what I was. Never let the skin tone fool ya. You should know what I'm talking about, don't ya?"

"I do, but you're so pale that I—and the blonde."

"My mom is blacker than your shoes, love, but it just happens that way sometimes. My dad is white, you know?"

"Mine too, and I thought he had strong genes."

"Not as strong as my dad's, apparently." She smiled, revealing perfectly milk-white teeth.

"Do people always mistake you for being one hundred percent Caucasian?" I wondered.

"Yep, but when I get the opportunity to open my mouth, I make sure they know I'm black underneath it all."

"That's for sure. Don't people ever give you trouble?"

"Sometimes, but I don't let it bother me. I know who I am—a strong black woman, and no amount of pigment can change that." Her bangle bracelets tinkled as she moved her hands.

"I've never met anyone like you."

"Really?"

"It's funny how I've struggled all my life with being mixed and trying to blend in." I felt a little foolish when I said this.

"So blend in, but be you. That's what I do." She shrugged.

"My question always was how do you blend in when your features keep making you stand out?"

"It's not my features that determine who I am," Enrika said.

"That's true, but people don't believe that."

"It's not other people's opinions, either. I'm just me." She snapped her fingers in the air.

"I guess it took me a while to accept that. That's one of the reasons I moved away to Europe. I felt stigmatized and written off as worthless to my black community, and yet not exactly embraced by the white community either."

"My mom taught me to just be me a long time ago, back when the little dark girls would pull my hair and try to poke the blue out of my eyes."

"That's so mean."

"She taught me not to look at myself as different in a bad way, but as special in a good way."

"I guess you're more committed than most of us, because you don't have to be."

"But I 'choose' to be what I am—black."

"I feel you, my sister." I gave her a high five and we continued to talk.

Our conversation was life altering. Surprisingly, I felt comfortable enough to open up to her. She was the poster child for African pride, and yet she looked whiter than some of the whitest people I knew. We chatted and I gave her my business card during the flight because I was always looking for new talent.

"Now, don't forget to give me a call when you graduate next year," I said.

"No doubt. I definitely will," she assured me.

"Good."

"Wait 'til I tell my friends I rode the plane with Makaeli Hunt. They're gonna freak out."

"You take care now." I smiled at her enthusiasm.

"You too."

Back on U.S. soil, I had mixed emotions. I had to see Lisa first because of her condition, yet I needed to begin at the beginning. I had to see Mama.

Before exiting the airport, I stopped by the water fountain and hydrated myself as much as possible because I knew that after a visit with Mama, I'd be hot.

As I was about to walk away, I noticed a little wet-faced girl sitting on the floor beside it. Her skin was a smooth mahogany and her eyes, like her hair, were a shiny onyx color. She wore her hair in two long ponytails. Her tears shone like fine crystal as they dripped down her face.

I didn't see anyone else around, so I decided to investigate in case she was lost.

"Hi." I knelt down beside her.

"Hi," she said through the tears.

"Are you lost?"

"No. I'm waiting for my dad. He's in the bathroom."

I looked up and surely enough, there was the restroom behind us. I almost left, but she looked so sad. There was something familiar about those deep onyx eyes.

"What's wrong?"

"Nothing," she said.

"Why are you crying?"

"It's my grandma."

"Is she sick?"

"No."

"Then why are you crying?"

"Because she beats me."

"She beats you?" I squatted down beside her so that I would be on her eye level.

"Yeah. Every day."

"Well, you know little girls must behave themselves and—" I immediately started in with the speech Lisa and Phil used to give me.

"Not that kind of beating," she corrected me. "I mean she beats me 'til I bleed sometimes, and they told her she couldn't keep me anymore."

"Oh." Instantly, my own memories appeared in my mind, making my compassion for the child endless.

"Where is your mom?"

"She's dead."

"I'm sorry to hear that. Maybe—"

"It's okay. My dad came to get me and now I'm going to live in New York."

"So you'll be okay then?" I was glad to hear there was a plan.

"Yeah, but I had to leave Chicago and all my friends."
Her eyes were full of tears.

"You'll make new ones, I'm sure." I stood up and dusted
myself off.

"I guess so, but I'm still going to miss my grandma."

"I know you are. She probably just has a lot on her
mind. Anyway, it was nice talking to you." As I turned to
say goodbye, she grabbed my hand.

I felt years of energy resonate through my body.

"Miss?"

"Yes?"

"Will you pray for me?"

"Pray? You want me to pray for you?" Now, that caught
my attention. What could this little girl possibly know
about prayer?

"My mom taught me how," she said. "And she taught
me it was important."

"But why did you ask me to pray for you?"

"God just told me you're the perfect one to pray for
me."

"I wouldn't say that I'm perfect for anything, sweetheart." I couldn't believe this was actually happening. It
was as if it were a dream.

"God never lies."

"All right then." I swallowed hard. "I promise I'll pray
for you. What's your name?"

"Brittany. What's yours?"

"Ms. Hunt."

"Thank you, Ms. Hunt," she said as she wiped her little
eyes with her sleeve.

"You're welcome, Brittany. Everything will be fine."

"Will you pray for my grandma too?"

"I will," I said.

"Bye."

"Goodbye, Brittany." I walked away, but I kept looking back to make sure it was real. What was God trying to say?

I saw her father come out of the restroom carrying two suitcases, and I was sure she would be all right. But I had promised to pray for her, so I found an isolated place to sit down and I bowed my head.

"Dear Lord, I come to you in the mighty name of Jesus. I don't know why that little girl said what she said or why she feels the way she feels about me, but I made her a promise and I intend to keep it.

"Please help her with her struggle to heal and with her struggle to forgive. I know her pain, and I don't want her to suffer like I did. Please help her to get to know you better, sooner. Please help her to be okay. Only you know what it takes.

"And please, Lord, help her grandmother with whatever she is struggling with and help her to get to know you, to stop hurting people and to heal also. I thank you. In the matchless name of Jesus, amen."

It was remarkable how satisfied I felt after that prayer. Intercession. That was something Mrs. Pearl used to always talk about. In fact, it was something she lived. Although I clearly felt a strong connection to the little girl, it didn't make sense that God would use someone like me.

Once I was finally outside the airport, I hailed a cab with the intention of going straight to Saint Ann's. Yet, after the cab started moving, I thought about Lisa and her baby, so I told the driver to stop at Mercy Hospital first. I stopped at the front desk to ask for the maternity ward, but forgot to ask which room Lisa was in.

When I finally reached it, I found out she had already been discharged. As I was leaving, I mistakenly turned down the wrong corridor and ran into the nursery. Parents and grandparents were lined up with their noses pressed against the glass, waving and making funny faces. Instantly, I was drawn to the glass. I managed to squeeze in eventually, but an older woman poked me in the ribs and shoved me along as the excitement and anticipation grew.

The babies were in their little beds, wrapped in blankets from head to toe and wearing little head-hugging hats. Their wrinkled faces and tiny limbs inspired awe in me. Some of their mouths were open wide while crying, and others had their eyes closed tightly while sleeping. Nothing seemed to interrupt their flow. Although I didn't really understand this baby stalking, when the crowd dispersed slightly, I was able to get a better view.

Suddenly, I couldn't stop myself from imagining what my babies would look like if I ever decided to marry Antonio. I thought they'd have his silky, dark hair and dark eyes. I hoped they'd look Italian and that there would be no trace of blackness in them. Not that I was against blackness, but the blackness was against me. I knew that unless they had a deep enough coloring, they'd have to endure the same pain that I had endured, hiding. I knew that if they couldn't be black enough, they wouldn't be accepted, and that it would be better to not look black at all. *I'm so glad God judges the heart.*

I found a seat nearby and put my face in my hands. My heart felt like it would stop.

"Do you have a baby here?" A Hispanic lady sat down next to me.

"No. I just got a little sidetracked, that's all." I looked up into her hazel eyes.

"Oh. I'm here to see my nephew. But my husband keeps pressuring me to have a baby. Especially now that his sister has one. I'm not ready, though."

"I don't know much about that, but I do know about

pressure." I was trying to be nice, but I just wanted a moment alone.

"I keep telling my husband I'm not ready because I keep pushing everyone away. You can't call yourself a mother, pushing everything and everyone away. You can't call yourself a mother if you're not together, right?"

"You've got that right." I had enough of her pseudo-analytical philosophies. "I've got to catch my cab. Nice talking to you." I waved and walked toward the elevator.

"Same here," she said.

When the elevator doors opened, I heard a familiar voice behind me.

"Makaeli?"

It was Phil.

"You came back." He walked over to me and pulled me away from the elevator.

"I didn't want to, but I had to." I faked a smile.

"How long have you been here?"

"I just flew in and I stopped here first."

"Lisa was already discharged earlier today," Phil said.

"I know, but the baby?"

"The baby is gone."

"Gone? Oh no."

"No, I mean they're fine, but they're both gone. They just gave us a scare, that's all. I spoke with her doctor."

"Good, so she went home?"

"Actually, I don't know where she went. I got here too late." Phil sighed.

"Too late?"

"I just found out that she was discharged."

"She didn't call you?"

"No. We haven't been communicating lately." Phil avoided my eyes.

"I know the feeling." I did know the feeling, and it wasn't good.

"Will you sit down with me for a minute?" He took a seat in one of the soft beige vinyl chairs.

I sat next to him. "Okay, but just for a minute. I've really got a lot to do today."

"I won't be long. It's just that I haven't had a chance to sit down and talk to you since you came."

"And since my life fell apart?" I said.

"Yes, and I'm sorry. I should have made more time. I tried to stay out of it, to let Lisa and Matt handle it. I—"

"Oddly enough, I understand."

"Big mistake."

"Yeah, you could say that." I wanted to understand him.

"I want you to know that I wanted Lisa to tell you everything a long time ago. In fact, I think that's one of the reasons things started falling apart between us—the arguments, the secrets."

"It's okay. You don't have to explain," I said.

"I've got to explain." Phil dropped his head as he spoke, and I could hear the sadness in his voice.

"No, you don't understand. Yesterday I probably wouldn't have even sat down with you. I didn't want to hear anything anyone had to say, but God has been working on me, working on my heart." I attempted a smile.

"And?"

"And I'm back because I've decided to forgive."

"You've decided?"

"Yes. I don't know exactly how yet, but I will." I nodded my head to confirm my intentions.

"That's a relief." Phil let out a loud sigh.

"Can I ask you something?"

"Sure."

"How can someone abandon a baby who is innocent and completely dependent on them for sustenance?" A tear ran down my cheek.

"I don't know," Phil said.

"How can they survive if their families let them down?"
I wiped my face, but I couldn't erase the scar on my soul.

"Babies are fascinating creatures." Phil pushed his glasses farther up on his nose and looked me straight in the eyes.

"I know that."

"What can I say? They survive. But you're speaking of your mother and—"

"Raquel." I thought of both my mothers in their brokenness.

"I don't have all the answers," Phil said.

"But you're a father of three. Matt has one on the way. You and Lisa have another one on the way. And Raquel had me. Now, that's the clincher; that this horrible woman once held me in her arms, knew I was hers and yet she gave me away, forever."

"Well . . ." Phil shifted his eyes away from me for a moment, obviously trying to gain his composure.

"How could she just give me away?"

"I'm sorry."

"It's not your fault. This happened long before you were even a part of our family." My voice wavered.

"No one ever meant to hurt you."

"Forget about the fact that Raquel beat me for years, and add to it the fact that she must have watched Mama stroke my head and dry my tears. I was all she had, but she wouldn't even tell me I was hers."

I caught the next tear that made its way down my cheek and I kept the others from escaping. Then I remembered about God and how He made me independent, adaptable, and resilient, even as a child.

"We're imperfect and we're learning as we go along. I knew you weren't okay. I knew that since the first day you left."

"How did you know?"

"One clue was when you refused to ever come home."

"I'm sorry, but it was just too painful." I stood up and started walking toward the elevator again.

"I knew you were upset and I begged Lisa to tell you about Raquel. It was just—complicated." He followed me into the elevator and we went down to the ground floor.

"Don't worry. I don't blame you. I'm okay now."

"Are you sure?"

"I'm sure, and I've got to go. I've got a cab waiting outside."

"Why didn't you tell me?"

"Don't worry about it," I said.

"Will I get to see you before you leave?"

"Probably," I said.

"I hope I will."

"Take care of yourself."

"You too." He hugged me quickly and watched me as I walked through the lobby doors.

Within minutes, I was back in the cab and on my way to Mama's. It was already dark.

Snowflakes began to fall softly on the windshield. From my window, I watched them fly effortlessly through the atmosphere, covering everything ugly and distorted with a fluffy white glitz. It reminded me of how Jesus redeemed us and covered our sins forever.

Before long we arrived at Saint Ann's. After I signed in at the security desk, I began walking toward the double doors. I heard Mama's voice screaming down the hall. This time I wore my sneakers, so I quickly ran down the corridor.

An orderly wheeled her into the elevator while a nurse held her down, until they spotted me.

"Mama," I said.

"You're Mrs. Hunt's daughter, aren't you?" The nurse wore latex gloves and carried what appeared to be a hypodermic syringe.

The orderly had a straitjacket over his shoulder. When he saw me, he pushed Mama out of the elevator.

"Yes, I am. What are you people doing to my mother?"

"We were trying to subdue her because she insists on leaving. She keeps saying her daughter is sick." The nurse shook her head.

"Well, I do have a sister who is in critical condition," I said.

"She is also rambling on about her daughter being dead, so you talk to her. That should help," the nurse said.

"Mama, it's me, Makaeli," I informed her.

"Makaeli, I thought you were gone again." Mama was barefoot and kicking her feet. "I'm happy to see you."

"I'm happy to see you too." I bent to hug her and then pushed her over to the couches where it was quiet.

"Have you seen Raquel? They told me she was out of the coma, but I didn't believe them," Mama said.

"Yes, I was there when she came out of the coma."

"When did you get back? I thought you were in Rome somewhere."

"Not Rome, Mama. I live in a nice little villa in Venice and commute to Milan to work."

"I used to travel a lot with my first husband, Douglass. He was in the military and we used to travel all the time." She rubbed her hands together. "He was a good man."

"I know," I said.

"I miss that feeling of being loved." Mama closed her eyes, and when she opened them again, her eyelids were moist.

"I love you." I said it in my usual low voice, hoping that saying the words would make it more real.

"Not that kind of love, but being young and in love." Mama smiled and made her voice sound sweeter.

"Romantic love?" I didn't know why she was telling me this.

"Right. That was a lifetime ago, but I still remember it like it was yesterday."

"Really? Tell me about it." I reached out my hand to touch her face. Her skin was cold and dry.

"When I married Oliver, I thought I would experience that kind of love again, but I never did. I guess I settled." Mama squinted her eyes and I noticed the dark circles around them.

"Settled?"

"Never mind."

"No, please tell me," I said.

"He didn't want to be a father. He just wanted me. I was beautiful then." Mama patted down her hair.

"You're beautiful now."

"No, bondage has taken that away from me. I lost a little piece of myself every day until there was nothing left."

"Jesus can free you from bondage, Mama. Let me pray with you." I took her hands.

"No, not now." Mama pulled her hands away from mine.

"You've never talked to me like this before."

"I'm sorry. It must have slipped my mind. I used to be sharp as a whip. Believe it."

"I believe it." I was being pulled into her story when in walked Lisa and Matt.

"What are you doing here? I didn't know you were back." Lisa tried to touch me, but I moved away.

"For better or worse, I'm back," I told her.

"You know we were worried," Matt said.

"I figured." I turned to face Lisa. "Phil told me you were in the hospital and I stopped by, but . . ."

"I was released today. I'm fine," Lisa said. "Mama, we've got something to tell you."

"What is it, girl?" Mama curled up her lips.

"Mama, we told Makaeli about the baby, about Raquel, everything," Lisa said.

"Everything," Matt said.

"You stupid, stupid children." Fury rose in Mama's eyes. "You should've let me tell her. I'm her mother."

"We're sorry, Mama. Raquel was slipping away fast and we didn't know what else to do but tell her." Lisa's eyes danced in desperation.

"Somebody should've asked me first. That's the problem with you two; you're always afraid of something, always hurrying something. Slow down. Time doesn't control me anymore." Mama shook her fists and gritted her teeth.

I wasn't sure if she was still able to talk rationally or if she had disappeared into herself again.

"We had to tell her." Matt pushed his hands deep into his pockets.

"No, you didn't, but you wanted redemption," Mama said.

"What?" Lisa squinted her eyes underneath her reading glasses.

"Redemption. You two were seeking it. For a long time, I searched for it too. But I had to let my burdens go, stop blaming myself." Mama rolled her eyes up into her head and began to drool. Mama hummed softly. She looked away from all of us. Matt and Lisa kneeled next to her.

"Right, you're right," Matt said.

I missed Mama when she disappeared so abruptly.

"You two ruined everything. Mama and I were having the best conversation we've ever had, talking like human beings, like mother and daughter." I folded my arms tightly as the tears came.

"We love you, Mama." Matt kissed her on the forehead as Mama rocked back and forth. Within minutes, Mama crumpled herself up in her wheelchair and her body fell limp.

So close, yet so far.

Lisa turned to me. "I know you don't trust us anymore, but—"

"Trust you? You betrayed me," I said.

"We tried to protect you. I went to jail to protect you," Matt said.

"Oh, how noble, Matt. Should we applaud now?" I clapped my hands together twice.

"Don't be so bitter," Lisa said.

"Don't tell me about bitterness. I lived with it my whole life," I said.

"We've talked about this at the hospital, at home and on the phone. We were wrong, but we tried to do right. We can't change that." Lisa wiped the tears from her face.

"Maybe you shouldn't have switched babies and played God."

"That's fair," Lisa said.

"Maybe Mama would have learned to mourn. Maybe Raquel would have learned to be a mother. Maybe Matt wouldn't have gone to jail. I don't know. Maybe," I said.

"Maybe fairytales come true too. Be real. We did all we knew to do. Right or wrong, we did what we had to do," Lisa reasoned.

"But I still deserved to know." I couldn't stop my eyes from filling up with tears.

Then Lisa knelt down and I let her put her arms around me. I let her put her face close to mine and our tears mingled. I could feel her breath on my neck.

"I'm sorry. Please forgive me." Lisa stood up.

Ashea Goldson

"We're sorry, okay?" Matt leaned back on the couch and closed his eyes as if exhaustion finally overtook him. He looked like an outcast among us. Thankfully, he never acted like being the only male bothered him. He took the responsibility of being protector very seriously.

I looked down at his scuffed Adidas sneakers and smiled. Poor sweet, misguided Matt. He reached for my hand and I gave in. I was just as tired as he was. I put my head on his shoulder, closed my eyes and ran my fingers through his thick, wavy hair. He probably would have rescued us all if he could. It was all water under the bridge, and the bridge had collapsed.

Chapter Thirty-six

Lisa

Since Matt and Makaeli appeared to be asleep on the couch, I decided to find Mama's doctor. Typically, he was in his office on the second floor. Now that I was finally free, I had to try to free Mama.

I prayed a short prayer before I went in.

It was a huge room with modern leather chairs, a black melamine desk and walls filled with degrees and certifications. There was a photograph of a middle-aged woman and a boy on his desk.

"Dr. Myles, how has my mother been doing?" I sat in one of the black chairs across from his desk.

"In terms of what, Mrs. Jackson?" Dr. Myles began writing in a tablet on his desk.

"Dr. Jackson."

"Dr. Jackson."

"In terms of her psychological profile," I said.

"Mmmm. Her progress?" He leaned back in his chair.

"Yes."

"Very little, if any."

"I know that. Can you be more specific as to why?"

"We've tried antidepressants, tranquilizers to decrease her feelings of anxiety, cognitive therapy to teach her effective ways of managing thoughts or situations reminding her of her trauma, stress management training and other forms of psychotherapy."

"And the results?"

"We've been unable to connect with her in any real way. She'll talk for a few minutes and then she'll regress into an unresponsive state. That has been the pattern."

"So what's the plan, doctor?"

"I'm afraid we're just waiting for your mother to respond to either the medication or the psychotherapy."

"Waiting? Is that what you think we're paying you all for, waiting?"

"Dr. Jackson, I'm sorry, but we're doing all we can for your mother."

"Well, I don't believe that." I stood up.

"I beg your pardon."

"You might beg, but I won't."

"Don't worry, Mrs. Hunt is well taken care of and very comfortable." His condescending tone made my blood pressure rise.

"Don't tell me about comfort when she has been sitting in this tomb all these years listening to your promises," I said.

"I never made any promises." Dr. Myles took off his glasses and looked into my eyes.

"No, you haven't yet, but your institution has and so have all the doctors she has ever had. It has been like a revolving door."

"Dr. Jackson, please—"

"Comfortable? Her home is comfortable." I looked around the room. "This is temporary."

"I'm sorry you're upset."

"Upset is not an accurate description of what I am. Disappointed might begin to cover it."

"Why the dissatisfaction all of a sudden?"

"My Heavenly Father has just opened my eyes to some things and I know I don't have to accept the devil's nonsense anymore." I looked him in the eyes. "Now, what are you going to do about my mother?"

"I'll have my assistant reevaluate your mother's situation on Monday and I'll let you know my findings."

"Your assistant?"

"I'll do it personally, Dr. Jackson."

"Thank you, Dr. Myles. I'd appreciate that."

I felt confident as I walked out of his office and down the hall, but this time I wasn't confident in my own abilities. I had the Lord on my side.

Back in the visiting area, Matt and Makaeli were still peacefully resting, so with the weight of the day's events, I plopped down into the chair and decided to rest too. I leaned back, but before I closed my tired eyes, I heard Mama's shriek on the inside of my brain.

Chapter Thirty-seven

Makaeli

Still sitting next to Matt with my head on his shoulder, I began to have a depression-deep dream. I was tumbling and fighting. I saw my life clearly, the choices behind me and those that were ahead. It was funny how life had all these windows and doors and how it was up to me to decide which ones to open and which ones to close. Sometimes I needed a little sunshine or air, so a window was sufficient, but at other times I needed to go through to the other side, so only a door would do. Windows and doors. It was spiritual warfare, and suddenly I knew how to win. I took God's hand and walked through the door to the other side. Salvation, repentance, and wisdom waited for me there.

I woke up to the sound of Mama's squealing voice, yet I rededicated myself to God from my seat.

"Lord, I'm sorry I betrayed you like others have betrayed me. But I repent and I thank you for taking me back and for loving me even while I was gone." And everything in me was calm.

Mama yelled again. "No, I'm not all right. They put my baby in the ground."

"Mrs. Hunt, please calm down. Your children are alive and sitting right over there, ma'am." The nurse pointed to us.

I stretched then yawned and sat up straight. Matthew opened his eyes and I saw that they were red. Lisa sat up in her lounge chair. Her eyes were red too.

"Alive? You call that slouching mess over there alive?" Mama said. "I beg to differ."

We looked around at each other and all burst out in laughter. I hadn't laughed so hard in years.

Mama was still fussing with the nurse and an attendant. They tried to calm her, but Mama seemed to have her mind made up. What a scene. I wondered if reliving that awful event had pushed her to this point, if remembering her grief had been too much. I hoped this wasn't the beginning of the end of her life.

Suddenly, Mama stopped resisting. Lisa asked Mama what was wrong, as if she was trying to figure out what was going on in her head. But Mama didn't answer her; instead, she talked to me.

"Lovechild," Mama said.

"Yes?" I stared into Mama's dark brown eyes.

"You were a special baby. I named you Lovechild while I was carrying you—or at least the other one of you. She was gone, but you were sent to replace her. You were my special lovechild, and I've always loved you."

"But, Mama, I never knew." My teardrops tasted salty in my mouth.

"I'm sorry I wasn't well enough back then to stay with you, but it wasn't because I didn't love you. I lost two husbands and a child within a few years of each other. One loved me for who I was, and the other one hated me for who I was—a mother. When I saw you in that nursery, I had no doubts filling out the forms for your birth certificate. I knew for sure you were mine. At the time, I could still feel her in my empty womb. You were my last chance."

"Last chance?"

"Last chance for happiness, last chance for a lovechild. I made my choice. I chose to be a mother, and the rest was buried forever."

"Okay, I understand now." I sat on the floor next to her wheelchair. I stroked her wavy hair and looked deeply into her dark oval eyes. They were shaped just like mine, just like Raquel's, and I was proud to carry them. I held her limp hand and rocked with her until she began to hum again. *Always in and out.*

I was grateful, though, for the time we had. I grabbed hands with Lisa and Matt and prayed.

"Dear Lord, I thank you for this family, imperfect as we are. I thank you for bringing us together again and for keeping us safe all this time we were apart. We ask that you continue to humble us and show us your way. In the mighty name of Jesus, amen." I kissed Mama on the cheek and was satisfied. "I'm a new creature in Christ Jesus."

Tomorrow it would be time to see the sister-mama.

Chapter Thirty-eight
Lisa

I could hardly believe my eyes and ears. I watched Matt and Makaeli speed away in a taxi. Once I reached my car in the parking lot, I took a minute to calm down and to call Phil.

Thank goodness for cell phones. Phil picked up right away.

"Phil, it's the most amazing thing. Makaeli isn't angry anymore. She prayed for everyone. She went to run a few errands, but she's going to stay with us tonight."

"No hotel room?"

"Nope, and tomorrow morning we're going back to see Raquel."

"Well, I guess we'll have a full house. What brought on this change?"

"Only the Lord knows, literally." I could hardly believe it myself. What had come over that girl? I guessed it was the same thing that had come over me.

"Time for the big confrontation?"

"I don't think so. For the first time, I believe everything will work out fine. It's in God's hands."

"God's hands? You're not getting religious on me, are you?"

"I am, and that's just what I need to be."

"What are you saying?"

"I'm saying God saved me and I need to know Him for myself. He has delivered me out of a pit and I'm grateful."

"I guess you've got it all figured out then."

My first instinct was to snap, but I paused and then said, "I don't, but I'm working on it."

"Maybe we both need to know Him," Phil said.

"Oh, we do. I'm coming home."

When I reached the house, Phil met me at the door. He took my hand and led me to the living room, where we sat on the sofa. Even though this was Phil's favorite spot, we broke the daily routine by not turning on the television or the stereo. In fact, the only sounds we heard were the sounds of our own voices, each one softly indulging the other.

"Where did we go wrong?" I faced him.

"I don't know, Lisa." Phil turned his body toward me, something he hadn't done in a long time.

"I don't know either, but I want us to start over. I want this marriage to work."

"So do I," he said.

"But you've been so angry; I thought you wanted out of here." I stopped the tear with my hand. I had no time for self-pity.

"I've never wanted out. I just wanted some—"

"Respect?"

"Maybe," Phil said.

"I'm sorry if I disrespected you in any way. It was never my intention to. I just have always been—"

"I know. Self-sufficient. I have no problem with that."

"But I crowded you out and I didn't mean to. I was so

busy fixing and covering and protecting that I just didn't let you take your place."

"It wasn't all on you. I wasn't around much to take my place."

"Let's try harder," I said.

"We will." Phil put his hands on top of mine.

We talked about everything that went on between us for the past three years until we came to some middle ground. And although I knew everything was not resolved, I was relieved that we were at least talking.

When Matt and Makaeli came home, we enjoyed a delightful Salisbury steak dinner with mashed potatoes and green beans. Then one by one, as the late hours came, we all separated. Since Makaeli insisted on sleeping in Mama's bedroom, I didn't question her. I simply replaced the dull bed dressing with fresh linens and pillows.

Then after everyone had gone to bed, Phil helped me to load the dishwasher and clean up the kitchen, occasionally letting the tips of his wet fingers touch mine and engaging me in the detailed medical stories that originally attracted me to him. It was the best night I had in a long time.

At the end of our kitchen cleanup, I climbed the lonely stairs to my room and he followed closely behind me. I felt his breath on my neck as I was about to say goodnight. When I opened the door to my bedroom, expecting him to turn into the guest room, he held the door open for me to go in. Then his footsteps were almost on my heels. I turned to face him and was surprised how close to me he was. He brushed his fingers across my swollen face and over my unglossed lips. His eyes caught mine, and before I knew what happened, we were together again, as man and wife.

Chapter Thirty-nine

Makaeli

Like I said in the beginning, destiny took me by surprise one afternoon and made some things happen in seven days I didn't think were possible even in a lifetime. It was Friday, exactly one week from the time I received that original phone call from Lisa. Since then, my life had changed completely.

Matt and I left Saint Ann's arm in arm, laughing like there were no years between us. We took the path train to New York, shopped at Lord and Taylor and Saks Fifth Avenue before returning home for dinner.

When Lisa came to the door, I handed her a small gift bag.

"Lisa, this is for you. The whole time I was here, I never gave you anything."

"Honey, you've given me everything. You didn't have to do this," Lisa said.

"But I wanted to," I told her.

Lisa pulled the box out of the bag and took out a pair of emerald earrings. "Girl, these are beautiful."

"I never knew she was rolling in dough like that. I would

have asked her to hook a brother up. You know she could have broke me off with a little something, something." Matt laughed at his own ignorance.

Lisa and I laughed too.

"I hope you like it. I would've gone for rubies myself, but I remembered that you like green, like Mama."

"Thank you. They're very special." Lisa put her arms around me, and when she let go, she looked into my gray eyes, brushed the brownish-blond hair out of my pale face and didn't frown.

After dinner, when it was finally time for bed, I asked to sleep in Mama's room and Lisa accommodated me. I didn't explain and Lisa didn't dare ask. I just wanted to feel close to Mama again, the way I felt today for the very first time in my life. I wanted to breathe in her presence, even if it was a false presence. So I slept amongst her things and dreamed peaceful dreams about her.

The next morning, it was time to see Raquel. We all woke up early, grabbed a couple of bagels with strawberry cream cheese and drove to Newark Medical Center.

Inside, the walls were as white as the sterile physicians' coats. They reminded me of the white lab rats we slowly tortured for the sake of beauty, but there was no beauty here. I shuddered at the sight of those stark white, lifeless walls. Lisa, being a doctor, was used to it, but I wasn't.

Raquel was staring in the direction of the door as if she were expecting us. Matt and Lisa had already decided to stay at the back of the room, to give us some time to talk first. Hesitantly, I tiptoed over to her side. She watched my every move with those same oval eyes. I opened my mouth, but my brain couldn't register any coherent thing to say.

"Hi, Makaeli." Raquel closed her eyes briefly and took a deep breath.

"Hi." I nodded and then sat down on the chair closest to the bed.

"I didn't know you were back in town. Thought you had run off again." Raquel braced herself in the bed.

"I thought I had to run, but now I know better," I said. "I know someone better. I'm not running anymore." *Those days are gone forever, amen.*

"That's good; 'cause running will kill you. Running away, I mean. I feel like I've been running almost my whole life. Running and fighting," Raquel said. "I used to fight stuff that wasn't even there. That's what the pipe did for me."

"Drugs are very dangerous." I was careful not to say too much at once.

"Not as dangerous as my own mind," Raquel said.

"What do you mean?" I scooted my chair closer to her.

"Drugs didn't destroy me. I destroyed me when I stopped believing in me." Raquel pointed her bony finger toward her chest.

I squirmed in my seat. It was very awkward at first. As Raquel spoke, scenes of our violent past flashed through my mind. Images of the devil incarnate brushed against my consciousness. I was awake and yet I was dreaming, falling. *Maybe this is how Mama feels.*

Then suddenly I was rescued by the mighty hand of God. I drew strength from a place I wouldn't have expected it to be. I began praising God, and I grew with the Spirit within me.

I finally was able to look at Raquel eye to eye.

We talked very generally, and then I agreed to come back to see her again later. I didn't want to push it too far, too fast. After all, we had a lot of issues to resolve.

When I got home this time, the air was different. I was different. The demons didn't accost me like they usually did. I had power over them. They were trembling beneath my feet because of the spirit flowing out of me.

I walked through the house from the front to the back, stopping to pray in each room. Consecrating them. No more evil forces operating in this house or in my life. It was over.

Later, Phil's parents brought Johnathan home, and I was able to see how much my nephew had grown.

"Hi, Aunt Makaeli," Johnathan said.

"Boy, you had better come on over here and give this aunt a hug." I grabbed him and threw my arms around him.

"So you're in high school now?"

"Yes, I am."

"Good for you. I'm sure you're keeping those grades up because I know your mother." I pointed to Lisa.

"Oh, don't start with me, girl." Lisa balled up a piece of aluminum foil and threw it at me.

Johnathan smiled, and after watching Lisa and me go back and forth for a few minutes, he seemed to loosen up. After catching up on Jonathan's teenage escapades, it was time for dinner.

Then we went into the dining room, where Lisa set the barbecued chicken and rice pilaf on the table. We sat down and Lisa blessed the food.

Matt squinted his eyes up at the way we were acting, but Lisa and I didn't care. We enjoyed each other's company, and we knew who to praise for it. Matt, Johnathan and Phil eventually excused themselves from the table to watch a basketball game on television.

"What are your plans?" Lisa reached over to get the gravy bowl.

"I'm going to take Designs by Makaeli to the next level—to the Golden Triangle in Milan."

"And what exactly would that take?"

"Phenomenal sales, publicity out of this world, a big

cash reserve and boatloads of prayer." I put my hands together as if I were going to pray.

"Well, amen to that," Lisa hollered.

"Amen, indeed," I said.

"You deserve it."

"What about you?" I put my hand on hers.

"Oh, I don't know. I guess I'll finish carrying this baby for starters." Lisa withdrew her hand and rubbed her belly.

"Now, there is an original idea." I laughed.

"Yeah, you think?"

"But really now, what do you want?" I wanted to connect with her.

"I want Phil back. I want us to be a real family again. I know God is working that out right now," Lisa said.

"And your medical career?" I looked directly at her.

"It'll be on the back burner for a little while longer. After this baby is born, I might just give something else a try. I've never been completely satisfied with the area of medicine I chose to specialize in," Lisa said.

"Really? Neonatal sounds very interesting to me."

"It is. I think I chose it for the wrong reasons, though. I think I wanted to save all the babies because of the one I couldn't save." Lisa looked down at her hands. "I have to take time away to see what I'm really supposed to do with the rest of my life."

Matt walked in with his dinner plate to get another piece of chicken.

"What about you, Matt? Are you excited about your little package coming?" I turned to Matt.

"Yes, I am, and I'm expecting a lot of help from you two aunts." Matt held his palm out and wiggled his fingers as if he were expecting something.

"We'll start with the christening." A genuine smile spread across Lisa's face as she nodded her head peacefully.

"I'll make her a beautiful white dress," I offered.

"Her? You've already made up your mind that the baby is a girl." Matt turned his cap to the side.

"Well, why not?" I hit him with my napkin.

"Because he might be a boy," Matt said.

"Then I'll design him a handsome white suit. Dresses are more fun, though." I giggled.

"Not for my son, they're not." Matt showed all of his pearly white teeth.

"Very funny," Lisa joined in.

"Always the comedian," I said.

We laughed with one another like we never laughed before, without a wall of secrets and without a sea of lies. We approached each other with dignity and kindness, and it was evident to me that where the two of us, Lisa and I, were gathered in His name, God was in the midst. And the mood only sweetened as the hours went by.

Finally, it was bedtime, and as everyone went to their own rooms, I decided I wouldn't sleep in Mama's room tonight. I went upstairs to my old room at the end of the hallway, a room I had not seen for ten years. Lisa was practically on my heels. I didn't know what the big deal was.

Hesitantly, I pushed the door open to reveal a beautifully painted mural of the New York City skyline, complete with skyscrapers, bridges, and the seaport.

"Lisa, what have you done?"

"I had it done three years ago when Phil and I had our big anniversary banquet," Lisa said.

"You thought I was coming home?"

"I invited you, and I was hoping you might," Lisa said.

"I'm sorry I couldn't come." My tears started and wouldn't stop.

"I understand."

"I wasn't brave enough. I was hoping one day I would be more like you," I said.

"You've been brave all your life. You're very much like me."

"I'm so glad we have God to lean on now instead of just hoping," I said.

"Me too." Lisa took my hand.

"It's breathtaking. Thank you for thinking of me." I traced the outline of the mural with my fingertips

"I've been thinking of you since the day you were born. I just didn't know how to appreciate you for the beautiful person you are."

We hugged good night and Lisa went to join her husband. After a quick shower and sincere prayer, I fell safely asleep under fresh sheets in the room of my dreams.

The next morning, Phil woke me up with breakfast in bed.

"You guys are spoiling me," I said.

"Are you kidding? We've got a lot of catching up to do."

"So have I. It's just good to be home." I smiled, and the weight of a lifetime became as distant as Italy was from New Jersey.

When we went back to see Raquel, it was easier this time. Matt and Lisa waited outside the room while I went inside. As soon as I sat down at her bedside, she broke down.

"I'm going to tell you what I know you came to hear." Raquel dried her eyes.

"There is no hurry for you to tell me anything. I'm just—"

"I'm going to tell you about how you came to be." Raquel shifted herself under the covers. "I loved a boy from high school, the only one I've ever loved. Of course, you know by now that he was white. It never mattered to me, but it mattered a lot to some." She coughed and spat into a plastic bag beside her.

"What was his name?" My father actually had an identity.

"His name was Todd McPherson. We dated secretly, but
when his parents found out about us, they broke us up."

"That's very sad," I said.

"It is sad. He was out of my life long before you were
born. He never even knew there was a you."

"What kind of guy was he?"

"I don't know, kind of sweet, I guess—at least to me,
anyway. He was a loner, never mixed much with the crowds.
Used to have his own band, though, he and some boys
from the neighborhood."

"What happened to him?"

"The last time I saw him was in June, right before camp.
I wasn't showing enough or anything, so no one would
have noticed."

"But you—loved him?"

"I did, as much as I knew about love then." Raquel
stared at the window.

"So why didn't you tell him?"

"I don't know. Before you were born, I tried to contact
him, but Todd and his family had moved."

"To where?"

"There was no forwarding address. I guess his relationship with me freaked his parents out and they moved. I
don't know where," Raquel said.

"So you gave up on him?"

"What else could I do? You were Mama's baby then,
spoiled rotten and—"

"You didn't regret it?"

"Giving you up? I didn't know what to do. I felt powerless over my own life, like everything was out of my control, you know?"

"I've felt that way too," I said.

"You wouldn't have had a chance growing up with me as your mother." Raquel turned her eyes away from me.

"How did you know that?"

"When I looked into your eyes that night, I knew. So I closed my eyes, my mouth, and my heart and I let you go." She wiped her eyes again. "I had to let you go."

"To Mama?" It was painful, but I had to know.

"Maybe I should have kept you, but I don't think I even knew how," Raquel said. "I think I started to hate you because you loved Mama."

"But I didn't know. I had no choice," I said.

"I was selfish and jealous. I wanted to hate someone." Raquel hit her fists against the side of the bed. "I hated you 'cause I hated myself."

"And the beatings?" I thought my heart would stop the moment the question rolled off my tongue.

"I started filling myself up with cocaine and heroin to kill the pain I was feeling. Daddy was gone, then Todd, then Mama's baby, then Matt, then Mama. I wanted to go too. I wanted to die," Raquel said.

"I was here. I was yours. I wanted to love you. I wanted someone to love me." My tears seemed to have a mind of their own.

"But you weren't mine. No one was mine." Raquel dropped her hands to her sides.

I could see that it was a struggle for her to continue, but I didn't stop her.

"I'm here now."

"I guess I'm glad you're here. All these years I thought you were a mistake, but now I know you had to be born." Raquel's hand crossed the bed rail and touched mine.

I had empathy for this sickly woman who had lost so much. She was obviously a lost soul in darkness who needed light. I wanted to witness to her and be that light.

"Raquel, you were in a bad position. I can't blame you anymore. I can't hate you anymore."

"You don't sound like the Makaeli I know."

"I'm not the same. I have love on the inside of me."

"Love?" Raquel's eyes looked like they were about to pop out of their sockets.

"Yes, God's love. He has been there for me all along, but I wouldn't surrender," I said. "Now I believe I'm a lovechild, and not because of my middle name."

"I don't know anything about what you're talking about," Raquel said.

"I know, but I've got a lot of good news to tell you."

"Good news?"

"I turned my back on God once, thought and did a lot of terrible things, but you know what? He still took me back when I was ready. He loved me all the time, and that's real love."

"I don't know about real love."

"I never understood it either until now. But that's real love. God's love is real," I said.

"I don't trust anybody right now, least of all God."

"That's okay for now, but—"

"This was no accident, this stuff I put into my system."

"You mean the cocaine?"

"I mean the overdose. It wasn't the first time either. I tried to kill myself by slitting my wrists the night you were born."

"What happened?"

"I cut myself but never reached the vein. I just ended up bleeding and then Lisa and Matt came in. When I delivered you, I was rescued. Nobody paid any attention to the marks on my arm after that day. I don't know why I didn't try again." Raquel lifted her bony arm to show me the location of the scar.

"God's grace and mercy kept you alive, just like He has been keeping me." There was a fire on the inside of me now.

"I smoked and shot up and did everything I could think of. I was in a living hell. Then you came here the other day with your simple words and made me rethink my whole life. You made me realize I have to care about myself." Raquel rubbed her tangled hair.

"Me?"

"Yeah, you. I ain't trying to be no mama and I ain't making no promise, but I've got a lot of making up to do." Raquel's voice sounded weak and scratchy.

"We all do," I agreed.

"Forgive me. This is my last chance at rehab."

"I already have. Jesus forgave me, and He can do it for you too." It was easy to let things go when Jesus was your advocate.

"I don't think He could forgive somebody like me." Raquel pulled her sheets up over her shoulders.

"He can and He will. All you have to do is confess that He died for your sins and trust Him to do the rest." *Holy Spirit, guide me in what to say.*

"It all sounds so easy."

"It is. Once I stopped running, it was easy. Now I'm free."

"Maybe I'm not ready to be totally free."

"Not yet. But the Lord will be here when you're ready. So will I." I remembered Antonio. "Excuse me, but I have to make a very important call."

I ran from the room, past Matt and Lisa, with tears still dripping from my eyes.

Chapter Forty

Lisa

We watched Makaeli run from Raquel's room and then we went in.

She tilted her head back and let out a sigh that made me tremble inside.

"We're not giving up on you. We're going to get you the best help this time." I imagined the new facility, the new treatments, but I couldn't imagine Raquel being well. There was so far to go, and as a doctor, I was shaky about her prognosis.

"That's good, 'cause I almost gave up on myself," Raquel said.

"Why did you do it?" Matt rubbed his mustache with his fingers.

"Do what?" Raquel raised her eyebrows.

"Get involved with that white boy when you knew it went against everything we stood for as a family, when you saw what Mama went through with Oliver and all," Matt said.

"I didn't mean to. It just happened. I gambled and I lost. I lost everything," Raquel said.

"We believe Makaeli is involved in an interracial relationship also," I said.

"As long as she's happy," Raquel stated.

"What?" I wasn't expecting this kind of response from her.

"Todd wasn't my problem. He was good to me. It was his parents that had the problem," Raquel said.

"But—" Matt said.

"Every white man is not Oliver Hunt. If her man can love her for who she is, then so be it." Raquel frowned up her thin face.

"You're right." I dropped my head.

"I wanted her to find happiness with a brother, but whatever," Matt said.

"Why does it have to be a brother? That doesn't guarantee anything. I've been with enough black men, and nothing personal, bro, but I ain't braggin' with no success stories."

"But it ain't fair to label all black men, especially since the men you've been with have been . . ." Matt said.

"Have been what? Crack heads? Go ahead and say it. That might be true, but it also ain't fair for you to label all the white ones."

"We still remember how Oliver treated us like little nigger trash." Lisa sucked her teeth to illustrate her disgust.

"Those days are over. You've got Phil. Matt has Carmen. Makaeli has the right to have someone too; whoever she wants, black, white or whatever." Raquel's voice transcended the physical and was bordering on the spiritual. *Was this my hide-the-silverware, good-for-nothing sister Raquel talking?*

"But I went to jail because of white men," Matt said.

"No, you went to jail because of one white man, not all," Raquel said.

"Did you have therapy when you were in your coma?" Matt asked.

"It's funny you say that, 'cause when I woke up, I felt like I did." Raquel smiled, and the weight of all her years seemed to fall off instantly.

"You're right. God loves everybody, even me." I looked up at the clock. "I wonder where Makaeli ran off to. We've got to find her. I've got to tell her it's okay, that she doesn't have to hide or pretend anymore."

"What has gotten into you?" Matt looked at me with one eyebrow raised.

"Jesus has gotten into me. I've been wrong about so many things. I've got to find her and apologize," I said. "I also owe you an apology, Matt."

"For what?"

"I ran into an old friend of yours in the neighborhood the other day."

"Oh, who?" Matt looked puzzled.

"Darrius," I said.

"Okay, so?"

"So he asked about you and I didn't tell him you were here. I also didn't tell you I saw him," I said.

"Why not?"

"I don't know. I was ashamed. I didn't want to relive all that jail stuff, and I'm sorry," I said.

"It's no big deal."

"But it is a big deal. Remember when I told you I'd never change?"

"Yeah."

"I was wrong. I've got to change. Not all at once, but I'm going to change."

"Good for you," Matt said.

Chapter Forty-one

Makaeli

I left Raquel's room, ran down the hall, went into the restroom and closed myself into one of the stalls. Thank goodness the restroom was empty. My hands trembled as I dialed Antonio's number. First I tried him at home, but the answering machine came on. Then I realized he was probably working at the studio, so I tried his cell. He answered on the first ring.

"*Ciao,*" he said.

"Hi," I said.

"It's good to hear your voice."

"Yours too. I know you're probably busy—"

"I'm never too busy for you."

"I don't want to disturb you, but I have something very important to say."

"So say it," Antonio said.

"I love you." My whisper was one of relief.

"You what?"

"I love you. I'm sorry I've been holding out on you, but I do." *Long overdue.*

"Wait a minute; slow down."

"I do, I really do love you." I smiled and hoped he could sense it through the phone.

"That's great news because I love you too." He laughed.

"Yes, it's great news for me too. I've been fighting for so long, and now I don't have to fight anymore."

"What changed your mind?" Antonio sounded excited.

"You probably won't believe this, but it's as if God Almighty Himself stepped down from His throne to rescue me, personally, with His grace. I'm new, Tony, really new."

"I knew you'd come around one day."

"You knew?"

"You're not the only one who talks to God, you know."

"I didn't know." I opened the stall and came out.

"So you're coming home then?"

"Yes, I'm coming home to make a home with you, if you'll still have me."

"Are you kidding? I've waited for a long time to hear you say that."

"I love you, Antonio." I could hardly believe I was saying it.

"So what exactly are you saying?"

"I'm saying that I'll marry you. And that I love you. I do," I said.

"I love you too, future Mrs. Antonio Benzini."

"I've got to go now. I'm in the middle of some unfinished business, but I'll call you later."

"Promise?"

"I promise." I clicked off my cell phone and pushed it into my purse.

I giggled because the joy had seeped in. All the years of animosity were over. No more running from Raquel or from my feelings. I could relax and accept happiness and love, knowing they were my destiny. *What an awesome thought.*

When I went back to Raquel's room, Matt and Lisa were already standing there.

"Makaeli, there was a man who you were talking to at the hospital when you were here before, a white man, and—"

"Yes, he and I are in a relationship. His name is Antonio Benzini. He's Italian-American, originally from the Bronx, and he lives in Italy now."

"I see," Lisa said.

"Do you live together?" Matt wasted no time in getting into my business.

"No. He has a very strict religious background," I said. "But he does live in Venice, not that far away from me."

"Is he Catholic?" Lisa was very serious, as usual.

"Not exactly. I mean, his extended family is, but his mom converted. She's Pentecostal now and still lives in the Bronx. So I guess you could say he's non- denominational now."

"Do you two work together?" Lisa looked me straight in the eyes and I felt like I was on trial.

"Sometimes. He's a photographer, so we're working on a fashion show together right now, but he has his own studio." I didn't know how to bring it out, but I had to. "He has asked me to marry him."

"Do you love him?" Lisa's eyes began twitching.

"Yes, very much," I said.

"Then marry him," she said.

"Wait, you're telling me to marry him?" I couldn't believe my ears.

"I've been wrong about the whole color thing and I'm sorry. Just be happy," Lisa said.

"Yeah, be happy," Matt concurred.

I looked at their smiling faces and couldn't believe Lisa and Matt gave me their blessings. *Now I know God is at work.* When I looked over at Raquel, she was nodding in agreement, and I wondered if this was really my family or if this was some kind of cruel joke.

Then I put my head next to Raquel's on the pillow and counted my blessings a thousand times. Tomorrow I was going to see Mrs. Pearl before my flight. I would go back to Italy, not just as a designer, but as a born again future bride. I was going to marry Antonio and we were going to serve God together. *Be ye not unequally yoked together with unbelievers.* We were going to have Italian/African-American babies and train them up in the way they should go, no matter what they looked like. I was probably going to join that non-denominational church Antonio and I had visited. I was going to make many changes where I went wrong. Tomorrow.

But today, I was just a grateful daughter, sister and servant. I was grateful for family, for forgiveness, but most of all, I was grateful for God's love that, despite my sins, made me His "lovechild."

Chapter Forty-two

Lisa

The very next day, the snow was gone and all that was left was sunshine peering through the trees. I rolled over in the bed to face my husband's glistening body. As he leaned toward me, I was able to study his face. Smiling, I traced the lines in his forehead and the dark circles under his eyes. The years had taken their toll on both of us. Then he reached for his glasses and examined my soon-to-be-round stomach. He didn't seem to mind the stretch marks from the other children, and I secretly hoped he wouldn't mind the new ones I'd surely have.

"You know I love you. I just want us to have a real family home," Phil said.

"I'm sorry I always tried to control everything. I was totally out of order and therefore, out of the will of God." I admitted to the impossible.

"In a sense, you did have to control everything because I wasn't around enough to control anything."

"I used to feel so guilty about switching the babies, regretting it and sometimes not regretting it. But God has forgiven me, and I'm His for the rest of my life."

"What's done is done. No doubt about that. Now it's time for our future."

"I like the sound of that."

"You're my future." Phil sounded like the old Phil I knew.

"A week ago I didn't think we had one, not together anyway," I said.

"Let's move out of this house." Phil took me by the hands as if he were pleading with me.

"Move out of this house?"

"Yes, as soon as we can," Phil said.

"Why?"

"I'm tired of living here, Lisa. We've been here too long, taking care of everyone except ourselves." Phil threw his hands up in the air.

"But what about—?" The words were out and there was no turning back.

"If your mother gets well, the house will still be here. It's already paid off, so all we have to do is maintain it."

"What about Raquel?" As if his suggestion were incomprehensible, I stood up and stumbled toward my dresser.

"Well, she can't be trusted here on her own, but she can get her own little apartment. Maybe even a room at first."

"I guess that sounds feasible."

"Raquel can start a new life out on her own and we can start ours—over."

"In a house of our own?" I looked in the mirror and began to brush my hair.

"Yes."

"That sounds like a good idea."

"We can have a new home and we'll get new furniture. We'll just let go of the past." Phil walked over to me at the dresser and pulled me back down to the bed.

"It sounds a little scary, but I guess I can manage."

"I have confidence in your decorating skills. You'll make our new house into a home."

"No. I'll decorate, but I won't take credit for that. God will do the homemaking. I'm just going to follow His lead."

"Whatever you say. I'll start looking for a realtor immediately," Phil said.

"So soon?"

"I want our new baby to come home to our new house."

"Fair enough, doctor." *Mmmm. Submission is easier than I thought.*

He kissed me like he did when we were first married, when romance was fresh and stress was low. He kissed me like I was the only one in the world worthy of kissing, and I melted in his arms. *Thank you, Lord, for forgiveness and for restoration.*

. He had never had the opportunity to even k...
...existed, so I wanted to correct that wrong. I dream...
...oducing myself to him as his long-lost daughter an...
...into his grateful, strong arms. I dreamed of us de...
...ng a good relationship and of him walking me down...
...le at my wedding.

...od. How are the wedding plans coming along?"
...l set for the first of next month in Venice, with or...
...t my father to walk me down the aisle." I twisted my...
...ement ring around on my finger.
...w, only a couple of weeks to go."
...ope you and Phil can come."
... you kidding? We wouldn't miss it." Lisa sounded...
...for me.
...od, then Phil can give me away."
...sure he'll be honored."
...ven't heard from Raquel yet. I offered to buy her...
...icket. Do you know if she's coming?"
...was a little surprised that she was invited at all, but...
...ou're sending her a plane ticket, I think she'll...

...pe so."
...really proud of you for inviting her."
... you kidding? I wouldn't have it any other way."
...*mom, and I'm her lovechild.*

Epilogue
Makaeli

Before I wiped the sleep from my eyes, I remembered that today was Lisa's birthday. I smiled at the thought of my family and the unexpected reunion we had six months ago.

I turned over under my striped sheets and sat straight up in my canopy bed.

It was Sunday, and church was the most pressing thing on my agenda. Antonio and I were going to meet for Sunday morning worship service at our church.

I showered and put on a bright pink linen suit dress with matching pumps. As I took my bracelet and three-carat diamond engagement ring out of my velvet jewelry box, I remembered the note hidden in its secret compartment. I lifted the main tray and noticed that the note was torn and the ink was smudged. I ripped it to shreds, balled the pieces of it up in my hands and threw them into the trash. The past was the past. My future in the Lord was much brighter.

I reached for my cordless and connected through speed dial. Lisa answered the phone.

"Happy Birthday. It's Makaeli."

"Like I wouldn't recognize your voice." Lisa was calm. "How are you?"

"Very busy, but just fine." I sprayed myself on the neck with perfume.

"That's good to hear," Lisa said.

"How are Phil and the boys?"

"They're good."

"What about Mama?"

"She's really doing much better now that she is working with Dr. Rheinhart. He's a specialist in psychiatric medicine."

"So you didn't have to transfer her?"

"No, but I had to fight at first."

"I don't know how you do it." I still admired her.

"God gave me the strength, once again, to do what I had to do."

"God bless you."

"She's doing so much better now. Prayer does change things." Lisa let out a cackle that made her sound like an old church mother.

"Yes, it does. Mrs. Pearl told me that Pastor Brown and the hospital ministry have been going by to see Mama regularly."

"Oh yes, she has been an angel."

"I'm so glad Mama is finally making progress. God is good." I took my cross pendant out from the jewelry box and placed it around my neck.

"I know that's right. You know Raquel came with me to Bible study last Wednesday night."

"Now, that's a true miracle right there. Six months ago she was against even visiting church, and seven months ago she was against everything and everyone."

"Sure was. Just a month ago she accused me of losing

---

my mind, and I told her I lost it Christ."

"I hear that."

"She said she'll go again soon,"

She didn't sound at all like th nipulative Lisa. *Old things are pa things are become new.*

"Good for you. Anyway, how ha

"Phil and I are working things for the practice on hold until th old, and we've bought a new hou

"Congratulations. What kind?

"Thanks. It's a two-story cold where we are now. We wanted Mama's house in case . . ."

"That's great news. Before you here." I fell back on my bed and my pillow.

"First of all, I'm big as a barre took some getting used to the id

"I'll bet."

"But I'm finally okay with it. A

"Have you heard from Matt?"

"Not recently, but he did se beautiful daughter."

"I know. I got some too. I se made dresses." I was smiling insi

"Are you still searching for yo

"I've got someone on the ca yet. I'm not worried about it, th

It was the week after I left th me, that desperate longing to k had thought about all that Ra and I hoped that he was really

Epilogue
Makaeli

Before I wiped the sleep from my eyes, I remembered that today was Lisa's birthday. I smiled at the thought of my family and the unexpected reunion we had six months ago.

I turned over under my striped sheets and sat straight up in my canopy bed.

It was Sunday, and church was the most pressing thing on my agenda. Antonio and I were going to meet for Sunday morning worship service at our church.

I showered and put on a bright pink linen suit dress with matching pumps. As I took my bracelet and three-carat diamond engagement ring out of my velvet jewelry box, I remembered the note hidden in its secret compartment. I lifted the main tray and noticed that the note was torn and the ink was smudged. I ripped it to shreds, balled the pieces of it up in my hands and threw them into the trash. The past was the past. My future in the Lord was much brighter.

I reached for my cordless and connected through speed dial. Lisa answered the phone.

"Happy Birthday. It's Makaeli."

"Like I wouldn't recognize your voice." Lisa was calm. "How are you?"

"Very busy, but just fine." I sprayed myself on the neck with perfume.

"That's good to hear," Lisa said.

"How are Phil and the boys?"

"They're good."

"What about Mama?"

"She's really doing much better now that she is working with Dr. Rheinhart. He's a specialist in psychiatric medicine."

"So you didn't have to transfer her?"

"No, but I had to fight at first."

"I don't know how you do it." I still admired her.

"God gave me the strength, once again, to do what I had to do."

"God bless you."

"She's doing so much better now. Prayer does change things." Lisa let out a cackle that made her sound like an old church mother.

"Yes, it does. Mrs. Pearl told me that Pastor Brown and the hospital ministry have been going by to see Mama regularly."

"Oh yes, she has been an angel."

"I'm so glad Mama is finally making progress. God is good." I took my cross pendant out from the jewelry box and placed it around my neck.

"I know that's right. You know Raquel came with me to Bible study last Wednesday night."

"Now, that's a true miracle right there. Six months ago she was against even visiting church, and seven months ago she was against everything and everyone."

"Sure was. Just a month ago she accused me of losing

my mind, and I told her I lost it and found the mind of Christ."

"I hear that."

"She said she'll go again soon," Lisa said.

She didn't sound at all like the old domineering, manipulative Lisa. *Old things are passed away and behold all things are become new.*

"Good for you. Anyway, how have you been doing?"

"Phil and I are working things out. We've put the plans for the practice on hold until the baby is at least a year old, and we've bought a new house."

"Congratulations. What kind? Where?"

"Thanks. It's a two-story colonial, not that far from where we are now. We wanted to be kind of close to Mama's house in case . . ."

"That's great news. Before you know it, that baby will be here." I fell back on my bed and propped my elbows on my pillow.

"First of all, I'm big as a barrel. Secondly, at my age, it took some getting used to the idea."

"I'll bet."

"But I'm finally okay with it. Apparently, it's God's will."

"Have you heard from Matt?"

"Not recently, but he did send some pictures of his beautiful daughter."

"I know. I got some too. I sent her a box of custom-made dresses." I was smiling inside and out.

"Are you still searching for your biological father?"

"I've got someone on the case, but there are no leads yet. I'm not worried about it, though."

It was the week after I left the United States that it hit me, that desperate longing to know my biological father. I had thought about all that Raquel had shared with me, and I hoped that he was really as decent as she made him sound. He had never had the opportunity to even know that I existed, so I wanted to correct that wrong. I dreamed of introducing myself to him as his long-lost daughter and falling into his grateful, strong arms. I dreamed of us developing a good relationship and of him walking me down the aisle at my wedding.

"Good. How are the wedding plans coming along?"

"Still set for the first of next month in Venice, with or without my father to walk me down the aisle." I twisted my engagement ring around on my finger.

"Wow, only a couple of weeks to go."

"I hope you and Phil can come."

"Are you kidding? We wouldn't miss it." Lisa sounded happy for me.

"Good, then Phil can give me away."

"I'm sure he'll be honored."

"I haven't heard from Raquel yet. I offered to buy her plane ticket. Do you know if she's coming?"

"She was a little surprised that she was invited at all, but since you're sending her a plane ticket, I think she'll come."

"I hope so."

"I'm really proud of you for inviting her."

"Are you kidding? I wouldn't have it any other way." *She's my mom, and I'm her lovechild.*

Readers' Guide Questions

1) Makaeli is a very complex character. What are you able to learn about her from the very first scene? How do you think Makaeli's problems with her racial identity help to mold her life? How did her coming to terms with it change her life?

2) Do you think that Makaeli's decision to leave her family and past behind in the U.S. was a good one? Why or why not? Would you have handled that situation differently?

3) Despite her lack of success in her personal life, to what do you attribute Makaeli's success in her business?

4) What do you think about Makaeli's attitude toward her family? Is her bitterness toward Raquel justified? Why or why not?

5) What do you think pushed Mama over the edge? Do you believe she will ever be capable of leaving the mental institution? Why or why not?

6) At what point can you see that Lisa's heart started turning toward God?

7) What decisions and/or actions could have been more successful if Lisa had already had a relationship with God from the beginning?

8) Why, in your opinion, was Phillip so hostile toward his wife, Lisa? What do you think Lisa could or should have done to rectify the situation sooner?

9) Throughout the turmoil in the story, why doesn't Makaeli surrender totally to the Lord?

10) What, in your opinion, is Makaeli afraid of? What is Lisa afraid of?

11) Why does Makaeli struggle with forgiveness after so many years? What does God say about it?

12) How did Mrs. Pearl end up saving Makaeli's life?

13) Why does Makaeli finally change her mind and decide to marry Antonio?

14) Do you think Raquel will ever change? Why or why not?

15) Why do you think Lisa and Matt kept the secret all those years?

16) Why do you think Matt left home without ever telling Makaeli goodbye? How do you think this affected her?

17) What are some of the lessons Makaeli learned during this life-altering visit?

18) What does the scene with the little girl at the airport teach Makaeli about her spirituality?

19) Phillip was a successful surgeon. Why do you think he never insisted that he, Lisa, and their children move out of Mama's house?

20) Can you see a pattern with how God intervened in both Makaeli's and Lisa's lives?

Urban Christian His Glory Book Club!

Established January 2007, *UC His Glory Book Club* is another way by which to introduce to the literary world Urban Book's much-anticipated new imprint, **Urban Christian** and its authors. We are an online book club supporting Urban Christian authors by purchasing, reading and providing written reviews of the authors' books that are read. *UC His Glory* welcomes both men and women of the literary world who have a passion for reading Christian-based fiction.

UC His Glory is the brainchild of Joylynn Jossel, Author and Executive Editor of Urban Christian and Kendra Norman-Bellamy, Author and Director of Talent & Operations for Urban Christian. The book club will provide support, positive feedback, encouragement and a forum whereby members can openly discuss and review the literary works of Urban Christian authors. In the future, we anticipate broadening our spectrum of services to include online author chats, author spotlights, interviews with your favorite Urban Christian author(s), special online groups for *UC Book Club* members, ability to post reviews on the website and amazon.com, membership ID cards, *UC His Glory* Yahoo Group and much more.

Even though there will be no membership fees attached to becoming a member of *UC His Glory Book Club*, we do expect our members to be active, committed, and to follow the guidelines of the Book Club.

UC His Glory **members pledge to:**

- Follow the guidelines of *UC His Glory Book Club*.
- Provide input, opinions, and reviews that build up, rather than tear down.
- Commit to purchasing, reading, and discussing featured book(s) of the month.
- Agree not to miss more than three consecutive online monthly meetings.
- Respect the Christian beliefs of *UC His Glory Book Club*.
- Believe that Jesus is the Christ, Son of the Living God

We look forward to the online fellowship.

Many Blessings to You!

Shelia E Lipsey
President
UC His Glory Book Club

**Visit the official Urban Christian Book Club website at *w w w.uchisglorybookclub.net*